CHAIN
PIECING
a Mystery

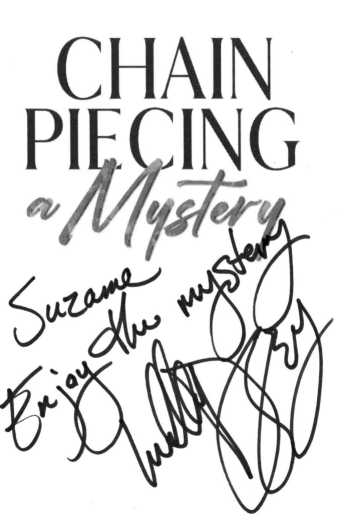

Suzanne

Enjoy the mystery

More from the
Missouri Star Mystery Series

Chain Piecing a Mystery
A Body in Redwork

Serial novellas published in
Missouri Star Quilt Co.- BLOCK magazine

Mystery in the Old Quilt
Bound in Secrets and Lies
The Stolen Stitches

Hillary Doan Sperry

CHAIN PIECING

a Mystery

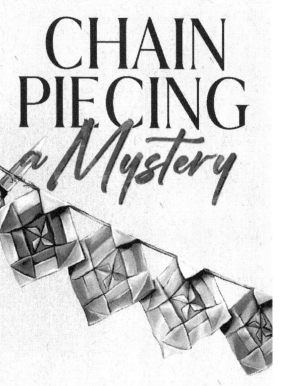

Copper Crow Publishing
coppercrow.com

Published by Copper Crow Publishing
Bella Vista, AR

Printed by.
First printing: July 2021

ISBN: 978-1-7345366-3-8(paperback) |ISBN: 978-1-7345366-4-5(ebook)

Dedicated to my daughter, Ally.

For being a champion
of books, words, and your mother.
For creating stories and dreams
out of mere ideas.

You're more than what I created.
I love you.

1

The groan echoed into Jenny's heart, a sound that curled her toes. Particularly when it came from the man she loved while sitting in a sterile doctor's office.

She slid her hand along Ron's arm and he quieted with a grateful look at Jenny.

"Of all the days, right?" Ron ran a hand over his carefully trimmed white beard, exhaustion filling his clear blue eyes. He stood a good six inches taller than Jenny but sitting next to him evened them out. He was the perfect mix of aged and handsome.

"Don't worry about it. I'm sure Dr. Butler will have us in and out quickly." She leaned over to rest her head on his shoulder. "Besides, Birthday Bash happens every year."

Ron leaned back, eyes closed, in silent agreement.

It was strange how time stood still in a doctor's office. The quiet hum of fluorescent lights and the gentle lull of footsteps in the hall created a kind of barrier that held the world at bay. While outside, the town of Hamilton was preparing for a party.

It was the weekend of the Missouri Star Quilt Company's annual Birthday Bash as it collided with the town's fall festival. It happened every year and by tomorrow morning Main Street would be lined with craft booths and food trucks. As the original host of the Missouri Star's quilting tutorials Jenny played a big part in the weekend's events and she would be booked from dawn till dusk . . . and sometimes longer.

It was one of her busiest weekends, but it was also her favorite party. Quilters traveled from all over the world to shop and participate in the celebration. And what better way to celebrate than with friends, fried foods, and all the crafting she could handle?

Someone paused outside their door, just before it swung open. A handsome man with a wide smile entered the room. "Good morning," he said, holding out his hand in greeting. "I'm Dr. Butler, you must be the Doans."

Jenny stood to shake his hand, taking in his could-have-been-a-television-doctor looks and shot a glance at Ron. Dr. Butler was not their regular doctor. Ron had happened to get sick during the only month in twenty plus years that Dr. Carmichael had taken a vacation.

Strands of ash sprinkled their way through Dr. Butler's dark blond hair, with more than a sprinkling of hair product to keep it all in place. It gave him a distinguished look and Jenny suddenly understood why her assistant, Cherry, had been so anxious to get them scheduled there.

"I'm seeing Ron today, correct?" Dr. Butler

removed his glasses, making eye contact with Ron. "How are you doing?"

Direct, handsome, and professional. Yes. Of course, Cherry was interested.

"Could be better." Ron grumbled.

Dr. Butler moved through the motions of an initial exam and called in a nurse to do a throat culture. It was only a few minutes wait before he returned with another smile and the results.

"It's a pretty simple infection. We'll get you some antibiotics and you should be ready to rejoin society in about a week."

Ron frowned, "A week? Am I contagious or is that till I'm completely better? I don't want to miss the events this weekend. Jenny and I always attend together."

"Oh, right, this weekend is a pretty big deal for Hamilton isn't it?"

"And Missouri Star," Jenny nodded. "There's a hypnotists show this evening that I'm helping with."

Dr. Butler laughed. "The hypnosis show? I heard about that. What's he calling it again? The Greatest Show You'll Never Remember?" The doctor's laughter calmed when the Doans didn't join him. The Missouri Star was hosting it and they were very excited.

Dr. Butler cleared his throat. "That's when you should be fully better, but you do need to lie low for a bit. You'll still be contagious for several days after you start your antibiotics."

"Is that all we can do? That's basically the whole weekend." Ron's frown tugged at Jenny's heart strings and she turned back to Dr. Butler.

"These things take time," The doctor said, tapping his pencil on his knee. "While I can't keep Ron in bed all weekend, it does take awhile to clear an infection."

Jenny watched Ron's face fall. It would be her first Birthday Bash without Ron by her side. Jenny wasn't looking forward to that either.

The doctor held the door for them excusing the couple to the lobby. Jenny wandered the waiting room while Ron stood at the counter waiting for the doctor's receptionist, Nancy, to complete the appointment charge.

One of the bookshelves was filled with old medical journals and antique operating tools. Jenny loved antiques and it seemed Dr. Butler did too. Though she collected vintage irons and sewing machines, while Dr. Butler collected giant, old syringes with fat needles that could easily be used to inject a Thanksgiving turkey.

As disturbing as some of them were, they were also beautiful. The handles were bright silver, with gold and brass accents, stamped in curling patterns.

She picked up a wooden drill with a spiraling bit almost as thin as the syringe. If nothing else, it made the room interesting, and made her more grateful for modern medicine.

"Dr. Butler?" Nancy, jumped from her seat, a smile appearing on her bright red lips.

Jenny fumbled the antique drill, almost dropping it on a brass microscope. Nancy's surprise had startled Jenny and Dr. Butler hurried over taking the vintage tool from her and replacing it on the appropriate shelf.

"I'm sorry," Jenny said. "These are very intriguing."

"I'm glad you like them," Dr. Butler said. "For me, they're more than intriguing, they're inspiring. Most of these tools have been in my family for years."

Jenny's eyes widened looking at the drill. "I hope some of them were carpenters."

She said it without thinking and thankfully Dr. Butler laughed, "They're pretty primitive but that's why they're inspiring. Even with limited resources they persisted in trying to help people."

Dr. Butler looked back at Ron. His brow furrowing. "You know, I may have an option for Ron. I have been working with a fast-acting antibiotic in my research program."

Jenny shook her head, "I don't think we're looking for clinical trials."

"No, no," Dr. Butler held up his hand. "It's not like that. We've been using this to soothe symptoms of patients in a chronic health environment when the experimental drugs aren't working. It helps fatigue, and minor cold like symptoms along with fighting bacterium." He turned a particularly vicious looking syringe over revealing a floral stamp in the brass plunger. It surprised her and she looked back at Ron. She could use with a surprise like that.

Dr. Butler let out a breath and turned to her, as if resolved. "I can't promise anything, but it could help contain the infection so Ron could feel up to being out and about this weekend."

The hope felt like a lifeline and Jenny looked to Ron. "Did you hear that? What do you think?"

He'd come closer when the doctor started talking. "If it gets me better, why not?"

He sniffled and Jenny squeezed his hand. "We'll try it. I'm not sure I'll make it through this weekend without him."

"Well, I'd hate to lose both of you." Dr. Butler chuckled at his own joke and gestured to the lobby chairs.

The doctor made some notes. "Why don't you have a seat in the lobby and I'll get you some samples before you leave."

Jenny watched as Dr. Butler disappeared through a door behind the reception desk. "I can't believe he's making this happen."

Ron sniffed and wrapped his arm around Jenny. "Do you have the insurance card? I can't find mine."

Jenny looked up surprised. "Insurance?" She laughed "I was just thinking Dr. Butler was being quite the hero. We might be getting our festival weekend back."

Cherry really needed to meet him.

"He really is a hero." Nancy sighed, eyelashes fluttering.

Jenny raised an eyebrow at the oblivious woman. *Back off Nancy,* she thought. *I've got plans for that doctor.* She needed to get Cherry over here quick if she was going to have a shot at getting to know the doctor before some other Nancy made that impossible. It's possible Dr. Gregory Butler was the most eligible bachelor in county, probably the state.

"Here's that insurance card." Jenny pulled the card from her wallet and held it out to the smitten receptionist without response. "Nancy? How's Harry doing?"

Nancy sobered slightly. Bringing up Nancy's boyfriend might not be the most subtle hint, but it would hopefully be effective. "I'm not sure. I haven't seen him recently. He's been a little preoccupied."

He's been preoccupied . . . or you have? She bent her head, digging into her purse to keep herself from saying something she'd regret.

Nancy fell into her seat, not doing anything for several blinks of long gauzy eyelashes. "Harry told me he was going to get us a place and then he couldn't even get a loan. I'm not interested in someone who can't be responsible for himself. Dr. Butler, he knows how to take care of people."

"Harry's a great guy." Jenny insisted. "He's been working for Missouri Star for over a year. I'm surprised he couldn't get a loan."

Jenny glanced at the door where the doctor had disappeared. "Doctors aren't the only ones who do alright. You should come to the big show tonight. I'm sure he'll be there."

Nancy glanced up after finally starting to enter their information at her computer. "Oh! I'm so excited about Eddie's show." She tapped a few things on the computer and something started printing. "But Dr. Butler isn't going to be there. I asked him to come but he said he's busy."

"That's not who I meant."

Jenny gave Nancy an appraising look. *Very clever.* The show was the perfect place to take a date. Or meet one, if Jenny could get both Cherry and the doctor there.

"Not who you—Oh, Harry . . ." Nancy forced a smile. "Right." Nancy watched Jenny for a moment then turned away retrieving Ron's paperwork from the printer. She handed it to Jenny. "You know I went to school with Eddie. It's pretty amazing how well he's done. He even gave up being a doctor. From what I heard. He's doing very well, not being a doctor. People find their passions all over don't they. Now he's the Great Eduardo."

Nancy looked up from under her lashes. Jenny caught the message. *Touché.* "He's doing very well."

Nancy grinned. "I wouldn't be surprised if he signs his grocery receipts as 'the Great Eduardo'. Now that he's famous."

Jenny laughed. "Surely not."

Nancy giggled. "I was only a freshman when he was a senior, but he's always had a lot of, well, let's call it . . . confidence."

Dr. Butler came back into the lobby with a handful of bottles setting them out on the counter in front of Jenny. "Mix a teaspoon of this with a glass of water once a day and keep me updated if things get worse." The doctor gripped Ron's shoulder. "Get some rest. We'll take care of you."

"It's a shame you're too busy to come to the big

show tonight." Jenny shot Nancy a smile and turned back to Dr. Butler. "I understand the Great Eduardo puts on quite a performance. He's always had a flair for the dramatic."

Dr. Butler raised his eyebrows. "I'm sure Eddie is very entertaining, but I know better than to let anyone tell me not to believe my own mind. I've been through medical hypnosis courses, and no one is really successful at it."

"Oh, no, Dr. Butler. I tried it in college," Nancy announced. "I helped my roommate get over a bad breakup, like that." She snapped of her manicured fingers as if it proved her story. "It worked."

Dr. Butler didn't look impressed. "I'm not stopping you, but I won't be there. See, I'm a real doctor."

So, he won't be meeting Cherry at the show.

Jenny wasn't sure it was the right thing, but she was going to find a way.

2

"I need a peach pie. Please." Cherry's Southern twang rolled across the park like a Texan heat wave in the middle of the cool Missouri fall.

"I hate to burst your bubble but there are no peach pies here." Jenny whispered to her assistant and friend.

Cherry let a half grin pull up one side of her mouth. "Trust me."

The owner of the pie booth tipped his hat and disappeared under the table of non-descript white packages. Each bag hid a pair of Amish hand pies.

In Jenny's opinion the sugary delights were one of Hamilton's hidden treasures. She scanned labels like blackberry, apple, lemon, even chocolate. None bore the classic peach flavor. She hadn't seen it there in weeks. "Are you sure he still makes peach?"

Cherry's jaw dropped. "Of course, he makes peach. You can't sell pie and not have peach. He sells out quick as a lightning bug blink. So, he saves me some."

Cherry shot Jenny a triumphant look as the man in suspenders and straw hat reappeared with the coveted peach pies in hand.

Cherry paid him and winked turning his cheeks rosy despite the chilly breeze. The two women turned to the park as Cherry pulled one of her pies from the bag.

"Did you want one?" She offered, taking her first bite of sugary goodness.

"No," Jenny answered too quickly based on Cherry's raised eyebrow. "It's too early for pie. Just tell me what's next on our schedule."

She realized too late that she'd made a critical error. Cherry's mouth hung open in horror, her pie frozen halfway to a bite.

She recovered quickly, handing Jenny the second pie. "I think my mama just rolled over in her grave. Jenny Doan, you take that back. This is a fruit-based pastry. It's a complete Southern breakfast."

Jenny handed the pie back when Cherry paused. "I won't stop you. It's just not normal for me. I need protein."

Cherry shook her head, adjusting the pie in her hand. "Fine," she said. "don't eat, but we're meeting Misty for a social media Live event."

Jenny turned to where Misty was set up as someone dashed past in a blur of gingery orange.

Cherry stumbled forward, dropping her phone and crunching the remaining pie between her fingers. The overwhelming smell of peaches exploded, along with a surprising amount of filling, as Cherry cried out.

Chain Piecing a Mystery

"Cherry!" Jenny lunged after her at the same time trying not to lose the man who'd flown by.

In deep orange slacks and bushy sideburns, he was easy to track but would be harder to catch. He pressed his way through the park knocking people out of the way without apology.

"Oh, it's definitely peach," Cherry said, shaking filling from her hands and pulling Jenny's attention back, "not cherry."

It took Jenny a moment to let go of her sense of justice before she could process and laugh at Cherry's humor.

Cherry nodded in appreciation. "Thank you. Now, do you have a napkin? This is a mess."

"Sorry, I don't," Jenny said, still tracking the guy who'd hit her. She didn't understand why someone would do that and not stop to at least apologize or acknowledge it had happened.

"It's fine. But if I can't find a truck load of napkins, I'm going to have to go change." Cherry shrugged.

"What do you mean?" Jenny asked, stifling her grin. "The peaches match your blouse perfectly." Cherry's shirt was painted in pie and if Jenny didn't think about who'd done it, she found the whole problem a lot funnier.

Cherry looked at her pale orange blouse and gave a snarky grin. "That's not what I was going for."

Jenny finally let herself laugh as she retrieved Cherry's phone. The chaos of the park caught her eye. The inconsiderate man had left a path of destruction in his wake. He stood at the back corner of the theater, his hand supporting him against the brick wall. Maybe she could go talk to him. Show him what he'd done.

Squinting to make out his face, she fought with her mind trying to decide if she could trust her eyes.

"Harry?" She muttered looking closely. His thick sideburns and lanky figure were so familiar, but Harry was a good kid. Why would he act so carelessly?

He glanced back and Jenny flinched. It was true. Harry Bolding, Nancy's boyfriend or ex-boyfriend, had just rampaged his way through the park. He worked with her son Al. Jenny should have recognized him sooner.

Cherry waved a sticky hand in front of Jenny. "Hey there," she said trying to get Jenny's attention. "I'm going to go clean up. The guy at the pie stand has got to have something I can use."

"Let me help." Jenny chastised herself for getting distracted again. She should be helping Cherry.

"Aunt Jenny!"

Jenny spun toward the voice. It wasn't her normal title at quilt functions and Jenny quickly spotted her niece jogging toward her, blonde ponytail bouncing as she skirted people and vendors.

"Lissa!" Jenny grabbed the young woman up in a hug. "I haven't seen you for days. Who let you out of the cutting booth?"

Lissa's youthful laugh did a lot to center Jenny again. "I escaped that a week ago! I've been working with Al and Harry in the finance department."

Chain Piecing a Mystery

"Oh, are you guys headed somewhere? Harry went that way." Jenny pointed but he was gone.

Lissa pulled back, shaking her head. "No way. He ran off to take care of something. I came to have fun!" Then she caught sight of Cherry. "What happened?"

"Oh, this?" Cherry asked, extending her arm to fully display her pie disaster. "Nothing. I just got a little too personal with my pie."

Jenny blushed. "Sorry. I can help in a second."

"Don't you dare," Cherry said, already walking away. "You two have fun. I'll be right back."

Jenny reveled in the gratitude Cherry always seemed to produce in her and turned back to Lissa. "So, how are things going?"

It was all Jenny had to say to get Lissa talking excitedly about everything she'd been doing for the last month.

Lissa had called Jenny over the summer, after graduating with a business and marketing degree, and arranged an internship with the quilt company.

Behind her Jenny could hear a group of women collecting and knew she'd better get moving if she wanted to finish her conversation with Lissa.

She shot Cherry a text and the two of them started walking toward the booths near the road.

Detouring around large groups of people, Jenny absently steered them around the park while Lissa talked. After several questions Jenny happily shared how lucky they were to be in the business of quilting. Then with a quick movement, Lissa pulled them to a stop.

They'd walked further from the group of people than Jenny realized. An argument drifting from the street behind the theater.

"That's not what we agreed to." An unfamiliar voice complained.

They'd reached the end of the park, stopping almost exactly where Harry had stood earlier. They were alone. Except they weren't.

"We should go," Jenny whispered, gesturing back to the festival.

"Wait," Lissa said. "Harry's back there. And I think he's talking to Benji."

"Look, if you want the whole fee, you'll have to do two shows. I need two shows." Harry's voice confirmed Lissa's statement . . . and he was mad.

"Well, you can't have them. We have somewhere to be."

"Who's Benji?" Jenny asked.

"The Great Eduardo's assistant." Lissa whispered. "He's the one who negotiated the shows for the Bash."

Harry was talking again, and Lissa quieted. "Eddie already said you're available. Do the shows, get the money. It's that simple."

"Well, he's wrong. If you wanted two nights, you should have booked two nights. Our next show is big enough I should have canceled this one altogether. Maybe I will."

"They can't do that," Lissa said. She leaned closer, her brow furrowed, as if she needed to make sense of it.

"Maybe you guys need to talk." Harry's tone had

turned into a snarl and a shiver ran through Jenny's skin. This wasn't the man she was used to joking around with.

The other guy, Benji according to Lissa, snapped at Harry. "I don't need to talk to anyone, Eddie should be checking with me."

"I don't care who's in charge with you guys," Harry said. "If you want your money you've got to do what I say."

"Or what?" Benji laughed. Harry didn't sound like he was in the mood to take that well.

"Or I'll ruin you." Harry's voice had lost some of its confidence.

Benji laughed harder. "I don't have to do anything. I'll pack up right now. How will it look if big, tough Harry loses the whole show?"

"Are you threatening me?" Harry asked. "You're not going anywhere. I'll make sure of it."

Jenny leaned in as Lissa pulled back. "Let's go." She hissed. Jenny shook her head and stepped closer as Benji's laugh turned cold.

There was a thump and a gasp and then more silence. Before Benji's voice drifted back, quieter and more menacing than before. "You have no idea what I'm capable of."

The silence that followed seemed to tie a noose around Harry's neck and Jenny reached up, half convinced a rope had circled her own throat, cutting off her breathing.

Eddie wasn't done. "You want Eduardo to stay? Sure, we'll stay. We'll do your shows. But I want double the original fee."

"We can't, we can't do that." The pitch of Harry's voice had risen, nursing a delicate waver at the end.

"I think you can." Benji's voice was icy. "Double the fee, or we walk ..." A metallic clang rang out from the distance followed by a crash that jolted both Lissa and Jenny.

Footsteps pounded into the distance and Jenny's lungs found room to function again. She reached out to steady herself against the rough brick wall.

"I don't think we were supposed to hear all of that," Lissa said.

Jenny held her finger to her lips. The alley was quiet but if someone was still there ... Jenny didn't want to think about how easily Benji's threats had turned to actions.

Jenny peaked around the corner of the theater and slowly stepped out into the open.

Both men must have left because the alley was empty. A box of construction debris lay next to the dumpster. *The crash,* Jenny thought, taking in the arc of metal and plastic contents scattered across the alley.

"Harry?" Jenny called out. "Is everything all right?"

"Why are you calling him?" Lissa hissed from behind her.

"Why not?" Jenny asked. "If he can hear us, he knows we're here. If he can't it doesn't matter. Might as well not look suspicious."

"Harry?" Jenny called out again, her voice echoing against the old brick.

A dumpster sat at the corner of the building.

Smears of red swiped across the side of the metal container. Jenny put a careful hand out and touched the bright red marks. Her finger came back bloody. It was fresh.

"Do you think it's Harry's?" Lissa asked. Then, without waiting for an answer, her worries poured out. "It was an accident, right? I mean, it's just a show. He told us he'd scheduled two but I guess not. But who really cares? Why would he hurt Harry?"

"We don't know that Harry's hurt," Jenny said patiently. She hoped the blood wasn't Harry's. She hoped Harry hadn't hurt anyone else either.

"Maybe we should go look for him." Lissa was still focused on the blood.

Jenny cleaned her finger off as best she could, wiping it against the corner of the dumpster, and pulled her niece away. "That's a good idea, do you have his phone number? Let's go."

Lissa pulled out of Jenny's grip. "We have to go this way. If Harry's hurt we need to help him."

Jenny looked at the space between the buildings where Lissa pointed.

Tucked on the wrong side of the block, the theater had a rarely used road on one side and an alley on the other. A narrow pass through connected them at the back of the building.

If someone was going to disappear, this was a great place to do it.

3

"There he is," Lissa said pointing down the sidewalk where they'd emerged from the alley.

"Where?" Jenny asked.

A string of quilt shops stretched out along both sides of the road, their bright colors mingled with festival booths, and tourists, and Jenny couldn't see Harry anywhere.

It took her a moment longer, but a flash of deep ginger orange caught her eye triggering the memory of Harry's voice.

Do the shows, get the money. It's that simple . . . or I'll ruin you.

That conversation couldn't have gone as planned. Harry wasn't a violent person, though his words made her question that.

Are you threatening me?

Jenny shut the replay in her brain off and started toward Harry. She didn't want to go over it again. It didn't take long to get close enough to see him clearly. He was talking to someone in front of the batik fabric store, having what looked like a private conversation.

"He looks fine to me." Lissa muttered, sounding almost disappointed. "Why was he even there? Al signed the contracts with Eddie weeks ago."

"Al signed them? Not Harry?" Jenny paused against the wall of the notion's shop, scrutinizing Lissa.

"Yeah," Lissa glanced toward the man in question. "Harry's not in charge of scheduling any of this. He's handling the numbers and financials but that's it. Except, —" She paused remembering something. "Harry told us Eddie wanted a second show. Do you think Harry lied?"

"It looks like he must of."

Harry's words kept running through Jenny's mind. She couldn't seem to shut it off.

I need two shows . . . Do the shows, get the money. It's that simple.

Jenny took a few more steps down the sidewalk, ready to walk right past Harry and the woman he had cornered there until she got a better look at the woman. She was terrified.

Jenny grabbed Lissa and pulled them both into one of the recessed shop entries. "That's Elsie Emerson. From the bank."

Harry had one hand against the brick, leaning toward Elsie, his other hand resting on the opposite side of her head, effectively caging her in place.

"What's he doing?" Lissa asked leaning around Jenny's shoulder.

"Nothing good," Jenny whispered.

Chain Piecing a Mystery

Harry's lip curled up in a snarl when Elsie shook her head. Without the anger, and the age difference, it could have looked like a romantic interlude, but that wasn't a friendly exchange.

Jenny pressed herself to the wall trying not to look as worried as she felt.

"It's Jenny." "I see her too."

The sound of her name pulled Jenny out of her questions. Music played and people were laughing. Why did she always end up finding trouble?

She'd begun to feel invisible. Her name being passed among the whispers reminded her otherwise. And they'd been gone for a while. Cherry was not going to be happy.

"Should I say hello?" someone asked while another hissed loudly, "I just watched her video."

Jenny held a finger up to Lissa and stepped out of her not so hidden, hiding place. "Good morning!" Jenny said. "How's everyone enjoying the party?"

Her voice was naturally loud, and Harry turned.

The quilter's excitement helped the commotion, as they introduced themselves around the circle.

"Would you guys like a picture?" Jenny asked and in seconds several phones and cameras were produced. *Perfect.* "Let's go this way. The flowers by the batik shop will be a great background."

The group moved as a whole, the sidewalk clearing ahead of them. Jenny's heart thumped as they approached Elsie and Harry. Then Jenny made her move. "Elsie! Come with me. Will you? You've got to tell the group about your last quilt."

Elsie was not a quilter and Jenny knew it but no

one seemed to care.

Elsie nodded leaning out from under Harry's arm. Harry shifted stopping her and glared at Jenny, then back to Elsie. He watched her for several seconds. Then with a smack, Harry hit the wall beside Elsie's head and walked away.

A red smear marked the spot Harry had hit. As he stretched his palm Jenny's mouth went dry. The slice through his palm was bloody and festering. It looked like it hurt.

Good.

The blood in the alley must have been his.

"Wow." Someone said, and another laughed uncomfortably.

"Let's take that picture," Lissa said. The group resumed their mission forming up near the railing. "Smile, Jenny," Lissa said and clicked the camera.

As soon as the quilters had moved away Jenny turned to Elsie. "Is everything all right?" Her adrenalin made it hard to keep her voice down. "Did Harry hurt you?"

Elsie pinched the bridge of her nose. "No. I was just saying hello. He's always so nice. He's been in so much lately I thought I'd be friendly. But this time—I don't know—I—I have to go." She cut off, her skin paling deeper than before. "I'm sorry. I have to take care of something."

Elsie apologized again and hurried away toward the bank.

"Umm, Aunt Jenny?" Lissa said looking off in the distance. Then Jenny saw it too, or rather, saw her. "I think Cherry's upset."

Chain Piecing a Mystery

Down among the food trucks Cherry had the pie man by his shirt collar, waving her hand around like she was telling a terrible story. The others in the park were giving Cherry a wide berth.

"He must have finally run out of peach pies," Jenny muttered.

"Cherry!" Lissa called and started toward her.

As soon as Cherry's fiery gaze snapped on them Jenny wished Lissa had stayed quiet. Cherry's strawberry blonde hair whipped behind her in a breeze like pale flames.

Her expression changed quickly, wild eyes of worry and determination softening, just enough to be steely. She patted the pie man's collar down and turned back to Jenny, nostrils flared.

"This way," Cherry said when they reached each other. "Where have you been? I left you right there. And you missed the Live with Misty filming, and . . . heaven's sake, Jenny. I said I'd be right back."

Jenny groaned. "How late am I?"

"It's been almost half an hour. Misty finished filming five minutes ago." Cherry raised her eyebrow, at her but her voice had already started to soften. She could never stay mad "I was so worried about you. I thought I'd lost you. And with Ron being sick and you weren't answering your phone. I thought something had happened. And now I'll never get peach pies from the pie man again."

"He does seem a little scared of you." Jenny laughed apologetically. "I'm sorry. We got distracted with a . . . situation."

"She saved a friend," Lissa said, trying to be helpful.

"She's exaggerating," Jenny started.

Cherry cut her off. "It wouldn't surprise me." She paused at a booth with towers of sunglasses and handmade accessories. Cherry pulled a pair of red cat-eyed sunglasses with turquoise tinted lenses. "How do I look?"

Jenny slipped on a pair of boxy cobalt blue sunglasses and turned to Cherry, posing dramatically. "As good as me? Can we wear them to the trunk show?"

Cherry coughed and grinned. "I will if you will."

"You guys are too much." Lissa muttered. "Do you need any help with the show? I'd love to see you work your magic."

"Oh, you think I'm magic?" Jenny wiggled her eyebrows at Lissa behind her sunglasses. "You must have me mistaken for 'the Great Eduardo'. No magic here. I want credit for every stitch of my quilts."

Lissa giggled. "Hypnotism isn't magic either. You should talk to Eddie. Hypnotism is science, sort of. Everything they do is real, just a little fantastical." Lissa bowed dramatically, flourishing her hand with the dip of her head.

The way Lissa was talking made Jenny think of the doctor's frustrations that people would ever believe someone could hypnotize for real. She just wanted to have a good time.

The theater, where the show would be, still boasted a large sign near the door. In bright neon, it proclaimed that "astounding feats" and "unbelievable displays" would occur during the show that night.

Lissa continued, "I guess you can call it magic when someone is so charismatic. At least, he was at dinner the other night."

"Charming?" Cherry questioned, looking at the man's promotional images.

"Entertaining," Lissa corrected with a grin. "He's cute, too."

"Ooo," Cherry grinned. "Maybe I should stop by his trailer before the show."

Lissa laughed, pulling her gaze away from whatever or whoever she'd seen. "No use, he's married."

"Well darn. I thought I'd found a way to stop Jenny from setting me up with every eligible bachelor in town." Cherry squeezed Jenny's arm as if to soften the blow. She'd never mentioned that before.

"I don't know what you're talking about. I don't set people up." She tried not to think about her plans for Cherry and Dr. Butler. She'd just wanted them to meet each other.

"You don't?" Cherry raised an eyebrow at Jenny. "What about Chad from shipping?"

Jenny almost denied it until she remembered how things had gone down. "I only suggested to him that you both liked the same kind of movies! It was a connection, not a set up."

"Right. And Luke from the construction crew?"

"Okay, that one's true. But he's so handsome! You two would be adorable."

"He's handsome . . ." She looked at Lissa with a knowing glance. "And dumb as a bag of rocks."

Lissa let out a full laugh.

"And Louis?"

"Come on," Jenny defended, a hot blush spread across her cheeks. She hadn't realized she'd arranged so many dates. "He's funny."

"And Todd? Oh wait," Cherry held up a finger and slowly turned, aiming it right at Jenny, "Robbie."

"The security guard?" Lissa asked.

Cherry nodded, solemnly leading them across the street. "Pretty much if he's male, single, and in the neighborhood, she'll give him my number."

Lissa was rolling with laughter and Jenny's blush flamed to atomic levels. "Oh, my goodness, I had no idea."

"Don't feel bad, Aunt Jenny," Lissa said, catching her breath. "You can't help seeing the good in everyone."

Jenny blushed as red as the candy apples in the booth they'd passed. "I'm going in the next door we pass, and I don't care if I'm scheduled there or not, I'm staying for the next hour."

"Perfect. Eduardo is waiting for you inside." Cherry pushed open the glass door of the theater.

Jenny pulled back shocked that they'd made it

back to the theater. "What are we doing here?"

The usually friendly theater had become ominous after hearing Benji's fiery argument with Harry. But she was meeting Eddie, not Benji.

"Eddie invited you to be part of the show tonight. Remember. Is there a problem?"

"Of course not," Jenny said going inside.

A small group of people were in the lobby with Eddie front and center. "Welcome Jenny. It's great to meet you. This is our team. We've got several stagehands, and this is my lovely assistant, Krista. She'll be helping you on stage and this is my right-hand man."

A young man with thick muscles wrapping his arms and shoulders turned to meet her. His blond hair was tinged in platinum and swept up off his forehead in a gravity defying wave.

The young man smiled and held out his hand. "Mrs. Doan, it's good to meet you. I'm Benji."

4

Eddie clapped Benji on the shoulder and beckoned Jenny to follow him. "Alright, now that you've met everyone let's get you up on stage."

"Is Benji coming?" Jenny asked, eyeing Eddie's assistant. She hadn't expected a smile and handshake after hearing him arguing with Harry.

"No," Eddie said looking between her and Benji. "Did you want him to help?"

Benji was talking to Tommy Webb. Jenny knew his mother Brooke, though she hadn't seen her since her husband had passed away.

"No, it's fine." She tried not to look to relieved.

Eddie led her down the hall and around the corner to the backstage area. He flipped several switches, filling the stage with light. "Our pre-show rehearsal didn't go particularly well."

"I didn't expect a rehearsal anyway," Jenny said. "I thought hypnosis was real."

"It is real." Eddie laughed light-heartedly. "Our pre-show is usually more of a prop check than anything. We never really know what's going to happen. That's the nature of using live volunteers, right?" Eddie lounged in a bucket chair, watching her.

"I completely understand. At my trunk shows I think I'm the wild card though." Jenny could feel herself relaxing. "We get everything set on one show, and halfway through I start telling new stories and Ron is scrambling to find the right quilts. But when you know a show and each other as well as we do, it just works."

"Well, that's good to hear." Eddie leaned forward resting his elbows on his knees. "I'm glad you're willing to come on stage. Hypnosis makes people nervous sometimes."

Jenny looked around the stage and held up her hands to the room. "You don't need to worry about me. Aside from my sewing machine, the stage is my happy place. I've been a theater girl since the first time I saw one. Just tell me what we're doing."

"I like you, Jenny. I think we're gonna get along fine." Eddie jumped out of his chair and went to the back corner of the stage.

Charming, Jenny thought. That was the word. Eddie was very charming. It was easy to understand how he'd done so well in entertainment.

Eddie returned with a long, thick rope, striped in neon colors. "This is our tightrope."

It was as thick as her fist and flatter than it was round. It was so heavy she nearly dropped it when Eddie passed it to her. "Aren't tight ropes usually a lot thinner than this?"

She really didn't know, but from dozens of feet in the air, she'd always imagined them to be bobbin thread thin.

Eddie nodded. "You are not wrong. But I don't like people to get hurt on this show. It's just entertainment. Anyway, we'll stretch this across the floor, and my wife will help you demonstrate how simple it is to balance and walk on. Would you like to practice?"

"I won't be hypnotized?" The relief Jenny felt was like changing from a felted wool quilt to an open weave cotton sheet. She could breathe and hadn't even known there was something stopping her.

Eddie turned his lips down in a quick mouth shrug. "Not unless you want to." He walked the end of the rope to the side of the stage. It was long, spanning almost the full length. "Oh, and you should take your shoes off. It'll be easier."

Jenny did so, climbing onto the rope with Eddie holding her hand. He let go and she instantly slipped off the rope. "Sorry," she said, gripping his hand. "This is harder than it looks."

The rope had enough curve that her feet seemed to slip on their own from one side to the other. When she stepped off the far end of the "tightrope", Jenny's grin was wide.

"You are going to be perfect!" Eddie announced, giving her a short round of applause.

Jenny took her bow. She was pretty proud of her simple feat. Not to mention that it was fun. "Do I get to tell people that I've walked a tightrope now?"

"Let's wait till after the show," Eddie said, already coiling the large rope into a pile. "I like to keep a little mystery."

Jenny felt a whole lot better about this gig and Eddie in general. He led them off stage and Eddie paused at one of the dressing rooms.

"Krista?" He called through the door, knocking. He looked at Jenny. "She's the one who'll be walking you across the tightrope. I thought I'd introduce you."

"Thank you. That's very nice." Jenny looked over his shoulder as he pushed the door open.

"Krista?" The room was empty, aside from a clothing rack full of skimpy, sparkly scraps of fabric.

Following Eddie into the room Jenny looked at several of the outfits. The fabrics were definitely beautiful, but she held up one that looked to be a glittery skirt attached to the bodice by a string. She stuck her arm through the dress and turned to Eddie. "You know we have a lot of fabric in this town. I can fix these holes."

He snorted a laugh and Jenny put the dress back, grateful he wasn't easily offended. On the counter was a pair of glasses. She picked them up and Eddie took them back. "Yeah, she doesn't like to wear them. She's a little vain."

"And she's the one who'll be helping me across the tightrope?" Jenny asked with eyebrows raised.

Eddie grinned. "You'll be fine. She squints."

That didn't make Jenny feel better.

"Eddie?" Krista's voice came from the hall.

"What are you doing in there?"

"Waiting for you." He swept her out of the doorway, into his arms, all the way into a deep kiss.

After several seconds Jenny cleared her throat. hoping to remind the couple that she was still in the room. "How are you liking Hamilton?"

Jenny tried not to take it personally when Krista laughed. "There's not much to see."

Eddie grinned, keeping Krista pulled close, he played with a strand of her platinum hair. "I may have told her too many times that I'd never be back here. Now, she's holding it against us."

"Well, I hope you get a chance to enjoy some of it. Thanks for your help, Eddie." Jenny backed her way out of the room. *The Greatest Show You'll Never Remember* had given her one memory she'd rather forget.

A light flashed and Jenny released her hold on the woman beside her.

"Thank you, Jenny! I love your tutorials," she gushed and disappeared into the growing crowd.

Jenny knew the old theater wouldn't hold the whole town but from the looks of the crowd it seemed like they'd all tried to come anyway. It didn't excuse his behavior, but it was no wonder Harry wanted Eddie to do another show

Another woman held out a camera and Jenny posed beside her. The woman wore a pantsuit with a black beaded blouse and an enamel MSQC pin.

Jenny had begun to feel underdressed. It didn't help that Cherry stood beside her, manning the cameras, in a fitted purple dress that made everyone look underdressed. Jenny turned to greet another fan, before thoughts of introducing Cherry to Dr. Butler could resurface.

A woman squealed behind Jenny and she turned to greet her. "Hi! It's great—oh!"

A flash of shimmering silver flew by, almost knocking Jenny over.

Cherry was quick to lean in and steady her. "Well, that was interesting."

The woman pushed herself to the front of the crowd. Her glittered dress shedding sparkles from her elbows to her toes.

Jenny couldn't help feeling grateful that it wasn't her she'd been after.

"Oh! It's Eddie!" The woman was nearly in tears. "It's him. I've been waiting all day!" Her hands fluttered as her emotions bubbled onto the man Jenny hadn't realized was Eddie Paris.

"I think the Great Eduardo has been spotted," Jenny whispered. "I wonder why he's not backstage?"

"I heard he likes to walk through the crowd before it starts incognito. It supposedly gives him a feel for the crowd," Cherry said it as if the idea were mystical.

In a dark coat and sunglasses, he was simultaneously trying to escape and quiet the overcome fan.

And from the reaction of the crowd, she wasn't the only one who'd realized Eddie's identity. As more people began to approach him Benji stepped forward. He deftly held back the glittered femme fatale and ushered the star to the back entrance of the building.

"Why don't we go in," Cherry said corralling moving them toward the doors "It looks like it's almost time to get started."

Inside, red fabric chairs lined the theater floor as it sloped downward until it met the stage. Flanked by red velvet drapes, a gaudy display of neon striped apparatuses, buckets, and ropes were set up across the back of the stage.

Based on the conversations of people already seated they were as intrigued as Jenny. It was all interesting but the only thing that really looked like it belonged to a hypnotist was the massive wheel at center stage.

Easily eight feet across, its swirling red and white lines spiraled from the center of the disk. Jenny couldn't focus on it for long without getting dizzy. It looked like it could hypnotize the entire audience.

"Front or back?" Cherry asked.

"Back," Jenny said decisively. She wanted to see the crowd's reaction to the show.

Lissa came in next taking the seat next to Jenny followed by Officer Wilkins. His casual clothes showed he was off duty, and he slid into the row ahead of them.

"Nice to see you, Officer Wilkins," Jenny said, leaning forward and patting the officer's shoulder.

"I hope things haven't been too exciting for you."

"So far, so good. It's nice to see you, Jenny. Cherry, you look great."

Cherry grabbed Jenny's shoulder when the officer turned to face forward in his seat, , "What is he doing here?"

Jenny raised an eyebrow at her. "I imagine he's here for the show."

Cherry tried discreetly to lean and get a better look at him. She smiled and lifted her eyebrows at Jenny. "He cleans up nice."

Jenny chuckled, looking at the officer. Cherry's interest in him waned high and low. Tonight, was a good night it seemed.

"Jenny!" Nancy Adams from Dr. Butler's office had slipped into their row, towing Dr. Butler himself behind her.

"You came!" Jenny said excitedly, "Dr. Butler, this is—" She hesitated, remembering Cherry's accusation. Officer Wilkins looked up from the other row and she stumbled over the love triangle formulating before her eyes. At the same time, Nancy was here with the doctor.

Jenny had inadvertently made a love square, if that were possible.

She'd always been angle-ly challenged. Just watch her try and lay out a quilt.

Cherry leaned forward, her golden-red hair sweeping across her shoulders in long waves. "I'm Cherry, Jenny's assistant. It's nice to meet you, Dr. Butler."

"Call me Greg." He flashed a smile and Nancy

wrapped her arm around his possessively.

Cherry politely pretended not to notice. "It's nice to meet you, Greg." She said and then gave Jenny a discreet wink. "I knew getting you an appointment there would be a good thing."

Someone bumped the back of Jenny's head as the shifted their way down the row of chairs behind them. "Excuse me. Sorry. I'll just . . . Excuse me."

Jenny turned to excuse the gentleman working his way down the row and found herself confronted with Harry for the third time that day.

5

Harry's smile looked perfectly normal. He nodded to Jenny as if she hadn't just heard him threaten and blackmail Eddie's team that morning and finished working his way down the row.

His movements had a kind of nervous edge to them. He'd settled himself in the corner near the entrance, nodding at people as they poured past him, shooting regular glances to the stage and tapping on the door frame.

Cherry followed Jenny's line of sight and watched Harry briefly giving Jenny a questioning look.

"Does he look anxious to you?" Jenny asked.

"A little," Cherry said turning away. "He's probably worried about things going well."

"What do you mean?" Jenny asked, "It looks like things are going great."

With a shrug, Cherry settled into her chosen seat and glanced back at the man as he shot a glance down to the stage. "I called him about your trunk show tomorrow. He moved the location from here to the retreat center and was asking about having you do some extra events. Apparently, Eddie is costing more than they planned."

Jenny mulled that over. It put a new light on the argument from that morning. Maybe she'd mention it to Al. Even if it was justified Harry's tactics wouldn't reflect well on the company or himself.

Dr. Butler directed his attention back to Jenny. "How's Ron doing?"

"He's fine." She nodded at him. He'd fallen asleep almost as soon as they'd gotten him home and he'd only been up for a few hours of the time she'd managed to be home before the show that night. "He stayed home to rest on your recommendation."

Cherry patted Jenny's hand and looked knowingly at Dr. Butler. "Jenny was singing your praises this morning. We're all grateful you're trying to help Ron."

He chuckled and sat back in his seat. "When doctors go on vacation you realize very quickly how much you need them."

"We're glad you're here," Cherry added before the lights dimmed for the first time.

Jenny's matchmaker instincts were tying themselves in knots. The eligible bachelors were no longer the problem Cherry was. She'd be good with anyone. Darn her and her sweetness.

As the lights lowered, Lissa reached across the doctor to squeeze Nancy's hand. "It's nice to see your headaches getting better."

Nancy sputtered a giggle and shot Dr. Butler a look. She smiled, "It is. Getting better . . . I mean. I think I'm getting a solid grip on how to handle him—it! —the headache."

"Excuse me?" Dr. Butler looked confused, though it was clear to Jenny that Lissa and Nancy had been talking, and apparently about him.

A spotlight lit the stage as the curtains closed, hiding the display of props. Benji walked into the light his white-blonde hair reflecting the light almost as sharply as his shiny silver leggings. Polite applause spattered across the room. This was not Eduardo.

As he spoke, Jenny leaned over to Lissa. "How do you know Nancy?"

"Remember that stomachache I had when I first got here? Mom made me go to the doctor, which was silly, because it was just a stomachache. I wasn't gonna go but mom scheduled an appointment for me with Dr. Butler.

"I got there early, and Nancy and I talked." She glanced down at Nancy and the doctor and grinned. "A lot. She's super sweet. And she really likes the doctor."

Jenny looked at the two of them as well. Nancy and the doctor might be a good pair, if Dr. Butler ever relaxed.

On stage, Eddie appeared as Benji set a group of silver rings spinning.

"Settle in, my friends," Benji announced dramatically, stepping back and letting Eddie take center stage. "As the Great Eduardo opens your mind to a world of new possibilities."

"Thank you Benji. Now, are you ready?" Eddie asked clapping his hands together the center of the spinning silver rings lit in flames. "With more fun, more surprises—"

The glitter of fire pulled an appropriate "Ooh," from the crowd. Jenny gasped and applauded along with the rest.

Then a crack from the back of the room cut him off, the spotlight going black. Followed immediately by the loud ringing of a fire alarm. The dark room filled with squealing, metallic rattle, like a room full of vintage telephones.

Jenny's hands flew to cover her ears as the sound reverberated between the walls of the theater. The guests who'd filled in around them vacated their seats along with others running to the exits.

Cherry perched on her seat scanning the room, while Dr. Butler was already moving toward the exit, one hand on Nancy's shoulder. Lissa stood forcing Cherry and Jenny forward with her. In the aisle, people surged forward, forcing themselves toward the doors and out of the building.

Between the squealing peals of the alarm someone behind them screamed. Jenny turned and saw a figure in the darkness lit by the glow of the still spinning circular flames. They looked stuck in the middle of a row of chairs. Shadows and dark figures passed around them. She reached for Cherry. "Go, I'll be right back." It was more miming than talking with the alarm going off but she pointed enough that Cherry got the jist.

"No." Cherry mouthed, shaking her head.

Officer Wilkins was leading them out and Jenny gave Cherry a push to follow, then turned around.

She maneuvered her way past the crowd of people and slipped into the row where Jenny found Nora Mullins tugging at a man in his chair.

It looked like her husband, Frank. He held his head like it would explode and Jenny leaned in trying to get his attention.

"We have to go," Jenny said.

Frank stared at her, then closed his eyes. When he opened them, he looked up at his wife.

Even in the darkness you could see her tears reflecting the firelight.

Jenny pulled again and he followed, getting up painfully slow, holding his head and inching down the row of seats. As they reached the aisle Jenny ran into Officer Wilkins.

She let go of Frank, and he dropped low keeping his fists gripped over his ears. Jenny moved out of the way so the officer could step in. He slipped his arm under Franks, lifting his upper body and helping him forward.

Nora grabbed Jenny's hands, tears streaming down her face. They walked to the exit and Nora followed Officer Wilkins to the outer door.

She turned to go, noticing a fire alarm in the corner. Right where Harry had been sitting. The lever was pulled.

Do the shows, get the money. It's that simple . . . or I'll ruin you.

Squinting against the sound and darkness Jenny scanned the theater. The fire wasn't much light but from the stage to the seats, everything looked still.

Harry was nowhere to be seen but a scissor point had settled in her chest. What if this whole thing had been Harry's messed up form of revenge.

The evening had transitioned from dusk to full night. People huddled together in groups, spilled from the theater parking lot into the grassy area of Penney Park next door.

Jenny still hadn't seen Harry, but the crowd was large enough that she wasn't sure who was there and who had left.

The alarm was quieter outside the building, but it was short-lived relief as seconds later the local volunteer fire department arrived, sirens whirring. The firemen rushed into the building. Her son Josh jumped from the truck and detoured to her side when he saw her.

"Is everyone all right?" Josh had only recently started volunteering with the fire department, but it fit him well and Jenny gave her youngest son a quick hug.

"I'm so glad you're here. I think everyone's alright. It wasn't much of a fire."

"Well, it's an old building." His brow furrowed and he pulled his helmet down. "We'll make sure there's nothing else."

Chain Piecing a Mystery

"Hey Josh," Jenny followed him all the way to the theater doors. "I think someone may have pulled the alarm. So, uh, keep an eye out for Harry, alright? And be careful."

"Harry?" he asked skeptically, accepting it when she nodded. He squeezed her hand and pushed through the door, following the last of the crew inside.

At the second set of doors Benji burst through, silver leggings flashing. "Have you seen Eddie?"

Josh replied and Benji got frustrated. "The Great Eduardo? Eddie Paris."

Josh looked back seeing her there and pulled the man inside letting the door shut.

Eddie was missing too . . . Jenny looked back at the crowd. No one that looked like cast and crew were out here. She had thought everyone was out but she now realized she'd only had access to audience members.

She worked her way through the crowd, casually roving the smaller groups of friends and acquaintances. The Mullins had gone home along with several other families. But no one had seen Harry or Eddie.

Ending up where she started Nancy and Dr. Butler stood speaking quietly. Lissa rubbed her neck like she had a headache and talked with Cherry. Wilkins stood beside them with Cherry wearing his coat.

"Have you guys seen Harry?" Jenny asked casually.

"No." Lissa shot her a heavy glance. "He's not here?"

Cherry pulled Wilkins coat tighter around her. "I haven't seen him either. Are you worried about him?"

Jenny smiled, not wanting to rouse suspicion. "I haven't seen him since the show started."

Officer Wilkins watched Jenny closer than the others. "What did he do?"

"Nothing." She'd responded too quickly, and Officer Wilkins raised an eyebrow. Jenny bit her lip. "Nothing that I know of. He had an argument with Eddie's assistant this morning but really, that's all."

"His assistant? Benji or Krista?" Wilkins watched her with an eye that said he'd learned to pay attention to what she said. Though it didn't seem he always believed her.

"Benji," Lissa cut in. "The blond guy with the silver legs."

Jenny looked back to the building. If both Harry and Eddie were missing she needed to talk to Benji.

Jenny started to the door and Cherry grabbed her arm. "What are you doing?"

Jenny smiled at Officer Wilkins and Lissa. "We'll just be a minute."

She took Cherry to the side. "I'm looking for Benji."

"Why are you looking for Benji? We just saw him."

"I'm hoping he knows where Harry is." *Mostly.*

"You're running into trouble," Cherry said pointedly. "Don't go inside. It's not safe. The firemen are still checking things."

Jenny paused. "Cherry. I'm not going far."

"Not inside."

"What if I only talk to the fireman? He's right inside the door?"

"Open the door. He'll be able to hear you."

"What if Josh is walking by? Being in the lobby is no different than leaning in the door."

"Fine. The lobby. But only to find Harry and I want to be able to see outside."

"Fine," Jenny said.

"Fine." Cherry nodded.

They looked at each other among alarm bells and confusion. But it felt like silence.

Cherry spoke first. "You're going to do whatever you want, aren't you?"

Jenny grinned, "Probably."

Cherry pursed her lips and pointed at the doors. "Be careful."

Jenny turned to the doors as they burst open. Benji came through, breathing hard. Followed by a very grumpy Harry.

"How did you—?" Jenny looked back at Cherry. "Oh, well played, Cherry. Well, played."

Cherry looked at the two men and burst out laughing. "I guess you don't need to go in after all."

The laughter was short lived.

Clapping his hands Harry stepped in front of Benji and Benji turned back suspiciously.

"Hey, everyone. Bad luck, huh?" He was almost yelling to be heard over the alarm. "Looks like we'll all be going home."

Benji stared, fists clenched as Harry spoke. His neck tensing till the muscles stood out in tight chords of tension. In a quick move Benji leapt in front of Harry with his hands out.

"Don't leave, please don't leave!" He was smiling but it was so tight and his face so red it came across like a snarl. "The show is tonight. We may not be here tomorrow. So, if you want to see the Great Eduardo, you've gotta stick around." He laughed, throwing his arms wide. It felt like he was trying to find his stage persona behind his anger. "We're not canceling till the fire department tells us to."

"But the fire—" Harry growled trying to step in front of Benji.

"Was contained." Benji grabbed Harry's collar and spun him away from the crowd, fist cocked and eyes wide. "I told you to leave us alone."

6

Wilkins quickly stepped in, avoiding a rogue punch from Benji. He clocked the man back and grabbed Harry by the collar setting his other hand against Benji's shoulder.

The officer had effectively taken control of the situation. Till Harry let loose a punch that cleaned Benji's eye.

The universal intake of breath pulled Harry back harder than Officer Wilkins had been able to.

"That's enough," Wilkins yelled as the alarm shut off. He looked between the men and lowered his voice. "Let's keep this civil."

"Now that's attractive," Cherry whispered, her eye keenly centered on the man keeping the troublemakers in check.

Nancy made a disappointed sound and Jenny turned to see her and Dr. Butler in conversation.

"I'm sorry. But this isn't going to end in time. I've got to go." Dr. Butler worked himself out of Nancy's grip, but it made little difference. She left with him at the same time.

Others followed before finally, Eddie strode through the double doors into the courtyard.

The crowd got quiet, the two men straining at either side of Officer Wilkins stepped back, people whispering Eddie's name.

"Excuse me," Eddie said coming up to the standoff. "I need to talk with my assistant."

The glittering woman who'd gone after Eddie earlier called out. "Eddie! Eduardo! Don't let them cancel. This is your show! You're amazing."

Eddie smiled at her. "Thank you for your confidence. We'll do whatever the officials say." He turned to his assistant. "Benji?"

Benji stepped out of Wilkins grasp and patted Harry's shoulder with a grin before following Eddie to the side of the building.

Wilkins and Harry also moved away. Having a private conversation on the other side of the crowd.

Following Eddie to the side of the theater, the woman in silver called out her support for the young entertainer several more times. Eddie gave her polite nods here and there, but she didn't let up. It wasn't until Krista joined them that Jenny did a double take. She bore a striking resemblance to Eddie's wife.

The woman in silver had dark hair while Krista was blonde, but in her short, sparkling dress she could have pulled off being a duplicate of his lovely assistant.

The only exception was the long swath of dark hair that hung low over the right side of her face.

She brushed it back briefly, revealing a scar spidering over her eye and cheekbone.

Jenny watched her fawn over Eddie a bit longer. This was a dangerous level of fandom.

Leaning over to Cherry Jenny whispered. "Did you know Eddie had super fans?"

She giggled and nodded toward the woman who'd been following Eddie all night. "You won't believe it. They call themselves Parisians. Because, you know, Eddie Paris. Benji warned me about them. I guess they get a little excitable."

Jenny grinned, "I've noticed. Though I think I'd rather meet a Parisian in Paris."

People were starting to chatter again.

"So, is it okay to go in?" someone asked.

"I'm going home," another announced.

Cherry leaned close to Jenny. "I'm not sure I blame them. That was quite the argument."

"No kidding," Jenny said. It wasn't often she was at a loss for words but after watching the two men argue, it was all she could manage.

Wilkins walked up as the fire chief and Eddie had a few words near the entrance of the building.

"Where's Harry?" Jenny asked, looking around. The crowd was steadily thinning now, conversations about the event and safety happening all throughout.

"I sent him home." Wilkins folded his arms and watched the corner of the street where Harry stood waiting to cross.

Eddie shook hands with the fire chief and stepped forward.

"Ladies and gentlemen," Eddie said, taking a breath. "We need to apologize for what you just witnessed. There was a disagreement about the nature of the show and potentially a little posturing."

He glanced at Benji who stepped forward beside him. "Sorry folks, I got a little carried away."

Eddie patted Benji's shoulder and turned to the crowd conspiratorially. "I heard the other guy made a comment about Benji's pants. I've tried to get him something classier, maybe black, but what are you gonna do?"

The crowd laughed and Benji looked down at his skintight silver pants in shock. The self-deprecating humor was the perfect antidote, and the crowd began to relax.

Eddie made a wide gesture to the fire chief, projecting his voice even louder than before. "Ladies and gentlemen, as anticipated, the firemen have cleared the building! It has been deemed an alarm malfunction. So, if you'll follow me, I have a show for you!"

Colored lights reflected off the walls as the audience gasped. Eddie walked across the stage pulling successive cords that released everything from ribbons, to birds, to a cloud of pink and orange smoke.

"It's time for you to forget the world and settle in

for more fun, more surprises —" Here Eduardo took a long pause looking up at the ceiling, as if waiting for the alarm.

Lissa made a sound beside her while the crowd laughed. Eddie wiped his brow in mock relief. "And the best magic you'll never remember."

Applause spread quickly across the crowd. In the midst of the clapping, Lissa held her stomach and groaned. "Aunt Jenny, I don't feel so good."

"Is everything alright?" Jenny asked.

Lissa shook her head and stood, working her way down the row. Alternately holding her forehead and pressing the sides of her head.

Jenny followed, catching up to Lissa in the lobby as she fished the keys from her purse.

"Go back inside," Lissa said. Her smile looked painful. "I don't want you to miss out on the fun. I'm fine. I'm gonna go home."

"Okay, but put those keys away. I'm driving you." Jenny insisted turning back to get her purse.

"No." Lissa stopped her, keeping her smile in place. "No, thank you, Aunt Jenny. I need to rest. And take some painkillers."

Lissa kept one hand at her temple as she left, and Jenny watched until her car drove away. She smoothed over the threads of her sweater. She frowned. Why when she needed something to fiddle and worry, she couldn't find a single stray thread.

A crash sounded behind her, and Jenny's hands flew to her ears. Removing them almost as soon as she realized the alarm hadn't gone off.

Through the doorway, applause accompanied

Krista in a sparkly flapper dress as she walked across the stage toward Eddie.

No one in the theater had noticed the sound.

It was probably nothing. No one was rushing to fix it. It was fine.

A moan came from the hallway.

"Hello?" Jenny called, unsure if she wanted a response.

She leaned into the darkness beyond the lobby and it's faux-painted marble pillars.

The sound came again, and Jenny felt along the wall for the light switch. She couldn't do much in the dark, but the faux painting hid the lighting hardware a little too well sometimes.

"Hello?" she called again.

No one spoke or moaned or made a reply of any kind. Or maybe the blackness had swallowed it.

Then a scuffing sound came from further down the hall and Jenny took a breath, moving forward.

A shiver ran down her spine, goosebumps rising on her skin. The darkness itself loomed at her, keeping secrets she wasn't sure she wanted to know.

"Where are you?" she whispered into the room, almost pleading.

Something crunched on the floor and Jenny jumped. A large piece of glass shattered beneath her foot.

She pulled out her phone turning on the flashlight since the overhead lights seemed out of the question. The tiny spot of light brought a sense of control back. A shattered lamp base hung from a cord plugged into the concession counter.

That must have been the crash but who had done it and why wouldn't they answer?

Something hit the wall where the hallway turned a corner to the dressing rooms. Jenny spun toward the sound. The flashlight beam disappeared quickly in the extensive space.

A thump echoed as who or whatever it was landed on the ground.

Squinting into the darkness Jenny moved slowly down the hall. The ding of a phone notification rang and a light flashed on briefly, illuminating a portion of someone lying on the ground several yards in front of her.

They moaned again, rolling over. As the phone's notification screen went dark Jenny's instincts kicked in. She followed her light down the hall, hurrying until she saw the figure again.

She knelt beside them unable to identify who it was. Their arms curled over their head, holding it together like Frank had been.

Lissa had complained of a headache too. Jenny shoved those thoughts away. She wasn't having this same issue. Hers was a normal headache.

"Are you okay?" Jenny asked, putting a hand on the person's arm. They jerked away and Jenny pulled back.

"Sorry," she whispered. She cleared her throat and tried to speak normally, venturing a louder tone. "What happened?"

Suddenly, the overhead lights glared on and footsteps sounded at the end of the hall.

The figure was a young man. HE cried out at the

sudden light, rolling toward the wall. Based on his entirely black ensemble, he was probably a crew member.

"Make it stop," he groaned.

"Hey!" Benji called jogging closer. "What are you doing?"

Jenny's heartrate jumped when she saw him running toward them. "Stay back," she said grabbing hold of the young man protectively. "He's hurt and we don't need some hothead showman scaring him."

Benji paused, looking from the young man to Jenny and back, "Okay. I won't scare him." He gave her a strange look and bent down on one knee. "Tommy? I've been trying to get ahold of you. You alright?"

"I wanna go home," he said through the grimace that seemed to affect his whole body, from his pinched expression to the tightly curled fetal position he'd pulled himself into. He projected pain.

Jenny watched Benji respond to the young man, not sure what to think. "He isn't doing very well, I heard him fall twice."

"Are you hurt?" Benji asked.

"My head," Tommy said through clenched teeth.

Benji leaned down, gripped him under the shoulders, and lifted him up. "Remember there's no insurance if you get hurt on the job."

He didn't sound like he was joking.

Tommy kept his hands pressed to his ears. He had dark hair and a face full of acne. One of his hands slipped down, rubbing at the base of his neck.

Chain Piecing a Mystery

Jenny thought of Lissa again and how she'd done the same thing.

"I can't stay. I'm sorry, Mr. Hicks." Tommy was doing his best to stay upright but he swooned, stumbling back against the wall. He groaned. "I don't feel right. I need to go home. I have to go do . . . something."

"If you leave, you're not getting paid." Benji shot a glance at Jenny after he said it. Probably knowing how cold-hearted it sounded.

She helped the young man stand. "He is in no condition to stay."

Tommy stumbled again, so unsteady that Benji nodded. "You're right." He slipped an arm under Tommy's shoulders. "Do you have a car? Do we need to call you an Uber?"

"I don't think you can get an Uber in Hamilton," Jenny said.

"Call my mom," Tommy mumbled, pausing to pull his phone out.

He turned it on, the screen flashing his last text messages. Benji Hicks' name was at the top of the screen. He'd sent the text that had shown Jenny where Tommy had fallen. A line above that popped out at her as Tommy clicked out of the screen and back in.

— *I'm not picky. I've done a lot of things. If it helps cover meds and food I'll do it.*

"Tommy, do you need a ride?" Jenny asked.
"I'll call my mom," he repeated.

He was still fumbling with the phone screen as Benji walked him to the doors.

"What's her name?" Benji asked.

"Umm, mom." Tommy said squinting at the screen. "No, Brooke Webb. That's her name. But I can't find her. Can you help me?" He held his phone out.

Jenny smiled. "I know your mom. Stay right here," Jenny said. "I'll take you home."

"And the show?" Benji asked, confused.

Jenny paused. She'd forgotten she was supposed to go on stage with Eddie. But Tommy needed help.

She smiled at Benji. "It's okay. Cherry's going to do it."

Jenny pulled to a stop in front of a collapsing, double-wide trailer.

"This is home?" Jenny asked trying not to sound too concerned.

Tommy nodded. "Thanks."

He'd stopped holding his head, and his grimace had relaxed, but as he opened the door Jenny reached out, grabbing his arm.

"Are you sure you're alright?" she asked.

"I don't know," he said. "It's calmed down a little. At least I don't want to flatten my head anymore. Thanks for the ride."

Jenny didn't feel any better. "Are you going to have trouble getting to school?"

Tommy raised an eyebrow. "I took my GED last year. I'll be alright."

"Well, call me if you need anything. And tell your mom I said hello," Jenny offered.

Brooke had been a good friend of Jenny's for a long time. But having not seen her in so long the sentiment held a deeper purpose. It looked like it wasn't only Brooke's son that needed help.

Tommy only frowned. "She doesn't care. But . . . if I see her, I guess. It'll be a surprise." He winced suddenly and his hand flew up rubbing the back of his neck. It almost looked swollen but it was hard to tell with his skin trouble. She didn't say anything and Tommy climbed out of the car. "I've got to go."

As Jenny backed out of the driveway, her headlights reflected off something near the garage. A stack of buckets lay on the ground, one had large neon stripes, exactly like the buckets Eddie had used during his show.

The Webb family's front door shut as Tommy went inside and she finished pulling away.

Driving home in the dark something gnawed at Jenny's mind. Tommy worked with Eddie. Maybe he'd needed to take the bucket home for some reason . . . But maybe not.

She hated to admit it, but in his situation, he may not have asked to take the prop at all. But why steal a bucket? Jenny couldn't help wondering what was really going on.

7

"And you couldn't have warned me?" Cherry shot back.

"I'm sorry." Jenny begged again. "He told me he wasn't going to hypnotize me. So, I assumed he wasn't going to hypnotize you. I really didn't think you would mind."

Cherry scoffed and shot her a grin. "I don't mind. I was just surprised. And he asked if I wanted to participate with the others in the hypnosis, so I guess I can't blame my tightrope exploits entirely on you."

Cherry slowed her pace as she finally let Jenny off the hook. Main Street stretched out in front of them, the end of their four-mile loop. The sun staining the shops and roadside craft booths felt a little too bright for this early in the morning.

When they had first started walking together, it had taken a couple weeks of Cherry near jogging against Jenny's long stride before they could keep the same pace. Today Cherry had been pulling

Jenny along at a good clip while she tried for an explanation of leaving her in the hot seat.

Cherry looked her over as they passed the hardware store and slowed them further. "Alright, time to spill," Cherry said.

"What?" Jenny asked, surprised that Cherry had caught her worries. "There's nothing to spill."

"Uh, huh." Cherry glanced at Jenny, her ponytail flopping from one side to the other as she bobbed along. "You're worrying about someone else's quilt blocks, aren't you?"

"What does that mean? I haven't done any sewing for days." Jenny loved Cherry's abstract thinking but sometimes she didn't make sense.

"It's metaphorical." Cherry nudged her and the two picked up their pace. "Whose problems are you worrying about when I know you've got your own."

"No ones." Jenny quickly shoved thoughts of Lissa and Tommy out of her mind. "Maybe that's the problem. My brain needs more than a metaphorical diversion."

"A giant party isn't enough, huh?" Cherry asked, "Okay, well you've got to start filming tutorials next week. Is there anything you need to do for that? Or you could work on settling next years block of the month. The product team is going crazy since we decided to switch some of the blocks."

"No! Keep your mis-cut quilt blocks on your table. I don't want them!"

"I do not mis-cut—" Cherry pinched her lips and walked a little faster. "Never mind, tell me what you're worrying about? Is Ron alright?"

Jenny frowned. "No. But he's only had a day and a half on the new antibiotic treatment. So, I'm sure it won't be long. But Lissa wasn't feeling well last night either."

Not to mention everyone else that Jenny was trying not to worry about.

"Is that why you left early? We could stop and see her if you want." Cherry's breathing was heavier than before but concern was the main thing Jenny heard in her voice.

"No. She had already gone home when I left. Did you ever meet Brooke Webb?" Jenny didn't know quite what to say but Cherry was listening, and it always helped to talk things out. "Well, her son, Tommy, was working on the stage crew last night, and he wasn't feeling well either. I gave him a ride home."

"Heavens." Cherry looked at Jenny in concern. "Is there something in the water? Everyone's getting sick."

"I don't know. Lissa and he both had headaches. I called Lissa last night, but she didn't pick up." Jenny really shouldn't worry. Everyone got headaches. Even bad ones. She pictured Tommy curled up on the floor. Maybe not like that, but it's still a headache.

"Hopefully a good night's sleep will do the trick," Cherry said.

Jenny took a cleansing breath as they crossed the street near the grocery store. "It usually does. Besides, she said she'd call and let me know how she's feeling today."

She hadn't called yet.

But it was still early.

But not so early there wasn't smoke rising from the metal stacks atop food trucks. Food, crafting, and quilting all promised to be the focus of the day in her small town. Jenny prayed it was true.

"Anyway," Jenny said, ready to let things be. "How was your night with . . . Wilkins?" Jenny turned, but Cherry wasn't there. "Hmm."

She turned around finally stopping when she saw Cherry in the middle of Main Street, on her way to a group of people huddled near a neon painted motorhome. Of course, she was.

It was obviously Eddie's "touring bus". The not so fancy version of a touring bus anyway. Painted in bright neon ripples that matched the Great Eduardo's color scheme, the motorhome had multiple points of chipping and peeling paint. On top of that it looked like someone had keyed it in giant lines around the front of the vehicle.

She followed Cherry's lead crossing the street only hesitating when she recognized the blond swoop of gravity-defying hair. Benji still made her nervous. He'd been an odd mix of helpful and rude with Tommy last night.

"Benji?" Cherry called out as she approached. "What's going on?"

Benji looked when she called him, a disgruntled expression across his face. He didn't bother with any fancy flourishes or airs, just bent over and grabbed a hunk of metal, wires spraying from both sides.

Chain Piecing a Mystery

"This is going on," he said, shaking the object. "Or, not going. Someone pulled a chunk of our trailer out. And I can tell you who it was. But guess what?" He seemed to shout it to the world. "I'm not doing his second show. No matter how long Harry keeps us here!"

"You think Harry did this?" Jenny asked, surprised. He was the likely suspect but how did all this sabotage really help him?

"Yes!" Benji snapped. "No one else would vandalize our tour bus to keep us in this little town."

Jenny could think of one person in a sparkly dress and heels that would very much like to keep Eddie around no matter how small the town.

"And tell him he better pay up," Krista said, stepping forward. She was already dressed in full makeup and a tight bodice. Stomping over to stand by Benji her six-inch heels lifted her a couple inches taller than the assistant, even with the sweeping hair. "We did our job. We weren't the ones who tried to burn the place down."

Jenny's jaw dropped wondering how she'd become the messenger for this mess.

"I don't know anything about that," Cherry said. "But we can get this fixed. Have you talked to anyone yet? Days Auto is out on the north side of town. I bet they'd send someone out to look at it."

While the suggestion appeased Krista, it didn't seem to make Benji any happier. It seemed like he might throw the chunk of motorhome engine at her.

This was the Benji Jenny had expected last night with Tommy.

Jenny grabbed Cherry's arm pulling her out of range. "I'm sorry this happened," she said to Benji. "I'm sure Eddie—" She glanced unsuccessfully around the group of stage crew. "Where is Eddie?"

"He's inside. No one wakes his majesty before nine," Benji fumed. "I can't believe he did this to us."

He squeezed the ruined engine part in his hand as if it were a stress ball. She didn't want to be around to see him get his hands on anything more fragile.

The blonde woman took the greasy metal from him, careful not to let it touch anything but her fingertips. "Benji, honey, it's gonna be okay. Eddie didn't mean to get us stuck here." She turned slightly towards Cherry. "Thanks for telling us about the repair place. We'll try 'em out."

It was clearly a dismissal, so Jenny and Cherry offered a few unreturned farewells and gratefully walked away. Their pace had slowed considerably as they walked toward their homes. Jenny took a deep breath, leaves crunching under her shoes. It was almost peaceful. Things didn't have to be crazy.

When there weren't strangers getting marooned in the middle of town and causing drama, Hamilton, Missouri was the picture of quaint, small-town life. The Sheriff raced past, but Jenny wouldn't even let that ruin her pretty picture. Either Benji had found his culprit or he was off to rescue a cat out of a tree. There really weren't many other options.

"I hope Harry didn't do that." Cherry worried.

Jenny sobered at the thought. "Me too. It's not like him at all."

After the arguments the two men had the day before, Jenny was almost certain he would be the one blamed. Unless Officer Wilkins had also noticed the obsession of the woman at Eddie's show.

The roof of Jenny's home crested above a patch of red berried bushes in the distance. Her neighbor was out, raking leaves.

"I'll see you in an hour, okay?" Cherry said turning toward her place.

Jenny waved and started down the block. A familiar blue car zipped past, stopping Jenny in her tracks. That was Lissa's car.

She turned to watch it pull into what looked like the police station parking lot a couple blocks behind her. Even being familiar with her niece's car Jenny doubted herself until she saw Lissa's blonde hair in the window. Lissa was really in there.

She backtracked quickly, coming up on the car as Lissa finally opened the door. Her pale hair was disheveled, as though she hadn't slept well and hadn't cared to fix it.

"Liss, is everything alright?"

Lissa didn't turn around. It was like she couldn't hear her. She held onto the door frame of the little blue vehicle, gripping it as though she would collapse without the support.

"What is it?" Jenny stepped closer, not sure what was going on. She circled around the girl, trying to get her attention. Lissa's eyes were locked on the police station, her lip caught between her teeth.

"I don't want to be here." She spoke softly, not

making eye contact with Jenny.

"Then let's go." Jenny walked into Lissa's view and her niece's eyes refocused. "Let's go have breakfast."

Lissa leaned back, mumbling, "I have to tell them." She let go of the car and shut the door. A smear of blood gleamed deep red where she'd been holding the door. She walked around Jenny to the door of the police station, repeating herself like it gave her strength. "I have to tell them."

"Let me see your hand," Jenny said.

Lissa paused and held out her hand to Jenny her breath coming in heavy gasps. A gash ran down her palm, like Harry's had been the other day.

"What happened? Did someone hurt you?"

Lissa took her hand back and shook her head. She started toward the station doors again. "I have to tell them."

This didn't sound good. Jenny needed details, and quickly. "Tell them what? About your hand?"

Lissa sucked in a quick breath, holding it as she reached for the door. She looked at Jenny and shook her head again. "I have to tell them that I killed Eduardo. The Great Eduardo is dead."

Jenny didn't say anything, waiting for the joke. Lissa pulled the door open and stepped inside. Leaving Jenny with her jaw open wide.

"Wait, that can't be true," Jenny said. Grabbing the door handle as it closed, she pushed her way through.

Lissa was already standing at the counter when the door shut behind her. Jenny marched across the room, slapped her hands down on the counter, and leaned forward staring down the young officer on the other side of the desk.

"It's not true, Officer . . ." She looked closer at the young man on the other of the desk, going from his face to his name tag when she didn't recognize him. "Gibson." She looked at him sharply, trying to regain her momentum. "He's sleeping. Eddie always sleeps till nine. He's not dead."

"I killed him," Lissa argued.

"Okay," the young red headed officer looked confused. "We have a bit of a situation. Do you mind . . . waiting?"

"This is not a situation," Jenny said ready to clear up whatever he might be confused about.

"That's fine, thank you." Lissa interrupted Jenny, looking relieved.

The officer shook his head and picked up the phone. "Hi. Finnegan? Wilkins is still out, right? Yeah. We've got another one. Okay."

Another one? Jenny barely had time to wonder what he meant before the officer hung up the phone.

"Officer Finnegan is gonna be out to help you in a moment." He smiled awkwardly, his eyebrow twitching as he looked at Lissa. "You can sit . . . If you like."

Lissa gave a polite smile and sat down as the station door opened.

Officer Guy Finnegan opened the door and his jaw dropped. "Jenny? Did you—" He looked to the desk officer probably hoping he wouldn't have to ask and missing Lissa completely.

"No! I didn't do anything. And neither did she," Jenny said, pointing to Lissa.

Guy looked at her niece and visibly relaxed. "Oh, good. I thought I was going to have to bring you back." He strode over to Lissa and gestured for her to stand.

"You're not taking Lissa," Jenny said placing herself between the two of them. "She's hurt and confused."

Officer Finnegan furrowed his brow and turned to Officer Gibson at the desk. "She's confessed to murder, hasn't she?"

Lissa nodded and Jenny threw her hands up. "How do you even know that? What's going on?"

Officer Finnegan seemed to consider her and shrugged. "We've had two other people confess to the same murder today."

"Two other people? Did they kill him?"

"I can't talk about that. It's all the same though. Normal people, mostly good. Swearing they've killed someone, with injuries as evidence." He reached around Jenny taking Lissa by the arm.

"But it's not true. At least, for Lissa, I was just there. Eddie's alive. I think. I didn't see him exactly, but his friends said he was there. Sleeping."

"I hope that's true but until we know better, she has to come with me." He looked behind him. "Gibson. Can you get the door?"

The younger officer dashed over opening the door.

Inside Frank Mullins and Tommy Webb sat against the far wall. The hair stood up on the back of Jenny's neck. "Those are your other criminals?"

Guy gave her a look and Jenny tried to remember exactly what had happened the day before.

"I need to talk to you." Jenny's throat was dry but the connection was like a neon striped sign.

"Not now," he said guiding Lissa from the station lobby. "And don't go making trouble. I'm sure we'll get it sorted out soon enough."

Jenny shook her head. "No. Tommy and Frank were both at Eddie's show last night. And they all left early with headaches."

"That sounds like a problem for a doctor," he said. "Anyway, this is Wilkins case. You can call and tell him anything you know later. It was good to see you though Jenny. Tell Ron I said hi."

"I will. He's not feeling well today."

"Not a headache, I hope. If that's your theory, we could have another person trying to kill Eddie." Guy laughed, cutting it off with a loud "ahem" when Jenny didn't join in.

"Lissa, are you alright?" Jenny asked. Guy's comment about Ron got into her head. She hadn't seen him since she'd left for her walk over an hour ago.

"I'm fine. Thanks." Lissa smiled, quite content with what was happening.

Her brow furrowed. This couldn't be real, but they were shutting the door on her already. "I'll be back, okay. Don't let them get you in trouble."

Guy frowned at her.

"What? She should always watch out for herself."

The door closed between Jenny and Lissa and

went straight to the desk. "Officer Gibson." Jenny leaned in smiling, trying to appeal to his kindness. "Can you have Officer Wilkins call me when he gets here? Preferably before he questions Lissa."

"Why? Did you kill 'the Great Eduardo', too?" His freckles and red hair made him look like a teenager. The young officer smirked, "Cause you can tell me. I've taken multiple confessions already. We've got a nice, padded cell ready for whoever really did it in the back."

Jenny considered humoring him for the briefest of moments. "I have to go. But my niece isn't crazy. And she didn't kill anyone. We're going to figure out what happened."

8

"Ron?" Jenny swung the front door open, taking only a couple steps into the house before stopping.

It was quiet.

"I hope that's a good thing," she mumbled, walking through the empty rooms.

It still felt strange to come into an empty house after so many years of constant children underfoot. Though it was easier to appreciate the quiet when she didn't have a background of worry in her mind.

She climbed the stairs finding Ron in the bedroom. Still sleeping.

Relief made it easy to dote on his discomfort. She kissed his forehead and Ron groggily opened his eyes.

"Good morning, sweetheart." He tried to sit up derailed by a coughing fit. When it settled, he dropped back to his pillows and watched her from there. "Did you get to walk today?"

"I did. Cherry and I went about four miles." She stumbled coming to the next part but managed to relate the mornings events.

When she was done. Ron rolled over and closed his eyes. "That's too bad," he mumbled. "We should have her over for dinner."

Jenny frowned and placed a hand on Ron's forehead. He was burning up and she couldn't leave.

Pulling out a bag of English paper piecing, Jenny sat on the bed next to him. She checked her phone and Ron whined a little rolling away.

"Sorry, hun, I thought I'd work on a few things while you're resting."

He peeked one eye open at her. "Why?"

"Well, you're sick. I don't want to leave you alone."

Ron closed his eyes again and chuckled softly. "I'll be fine. You could bring me cookies later."

Jenny watched him settle into sleep. His breathing quickly softened to a light snore. She only managed to stitch three sides of her project together before Cherry texted.

–Are you coming in today?

Shoot. Jenny had gotten completely lost in her world. She changed her clothes, fixed Ron his antibiotic and wrote him a quick note. With a kiss on his cheek she hurried down to the car.

Another ding from her phone.

–Party on the Patio is in 30min. You've got to be here and packed into a cake before then.

Jenny cringed. Cherry had texted again, and she'd forgotten to reply. She typed out a quick note.

–On my way. I just have one stop first.

Jenny pulled out of the driveway and drove the

few blocks to the police station.

Opening the door, Jenny was prepared to do whatever it took to get her niece back and completely unprepared to see her standing there on her own arguing with Officer Wilkins.

Wilkins rubbed his jaw stopping mid stroke when she came in. "Jenny, we need you." He took several steps back making room for her between him and Lissa. "She won't leave."

"Good. No, wait. What?" Jenny turned to Lissa. "Why don't you want to go? I mean, let's go." The confusion was tripping up her words but the idea that Lissa could go home and wouldn't was maddening.

Lissa grimaced and rubbed her neck with a bandaged hand.

"I'm not leaving," Lissa stated adamantly. "They're supposed to arrest me. That's what's supposed to happen. Aunt Jenny, can you please tell them to arrest me?"

"No." Jenny took Lissa by the elbow and started backing her toward the door. Lissa pulled free and glared at both of them.

Jenny gave her niece a wary glance and turned to Wilkins. "What happened?"

Officer Dunn came through the door and paused facing Jenny. His blond hair and height were a sharp contrast to the dark-haired, shorter Officer Wilkins.

Dunn lifted his sunglasses briefly, looking straight at her. "I knew I smelled trouble." He grinned and sidled up to the counter watching them. "Did you still need me, Wilkins?"

Jenny went on defense incase Officer Dunn wasn't looking as favorably on the case as Wilkins. "Lissa is convinced she killed Eddie but there's no way that's true."

"The Great Eduardo." Lissa corrected. "I stabbed him. I know it's terrible but look." She held her hand out as if they could see through the bandage. "I cut myself when he fought me."

Officer Dunn's eyebrows lifted behind his sunglasses and Wilkins tapped the counter. "See that's one of the things that doesn't make sense. Eddie Paris is in decent shape, and no offense but you're not very big. If he fought back, you wouldn't be able to kill him. Hurt him maybe but killing him is very unlikely."

"Has anyone even bothered to find out if he's really dead?" Jenny asked exasperated with the whole thing. "Where's your evidence?"

Officer Wilkins looked at Jenny and ran a hand through his hair. "It's too early in the morning for this. Dunn? Would you?"

Officer Dunn nodded, stepping into a very formal, and intimidating, parade rest. "In fact, we did investigate the situation. We just got back from Mr. Paris' trailer, and Eddie is fine. He is very much alive. So, unless there's some other crime you've committed besides harassing the good people in our department, you need to go home." He held up his hands, jazzing them beside his face. "Yay! You're not a murderer."

The false cheer in his voice brought on a dangerous glare from Lissa.

"You're free to go. We've released all of you," Officer Wilkins said with a sense of finality. "Jenny, please take her home. I'd recommend getting those injuries checked out."

He motioned to Dunn and they both turned to the door leading into the station.

The door opened and the final piece of the puzzle seemed to fall into place as Eddie Paris entered the room. He presented himself before the glass entry in black skinny jeans, a t-shirt emblazoned with his stage name, and a hoodie.

Very professional, Jenny thought.

"The Great Eduardo," Lissa whispered, subsequently cowering into Jenny's side.

All her insistence of the morning was gone, just like that. She whimpered, as if she were afraid even to see him there. It didn't seem to matter that they'd been told he was alive, seeing him there disheveled and real was a relief, if a bit ghostly.

"What are you doing here?" Officer Wilkins grabbed Eddie by the elbow, walking him to the side of the station lobby.

"You said people were trying to kill me." Eddie complained looking over his shoulder as Wilkins walked him away from Lissa. "Should I be worried?"

"Of course, you should be worried. Three people confessed to killing you." Wilkins glanced directly at Lissa and Jenny could have shaken him.

Eddie followed his gaze and raised his eyebrows in shock, looking her over.

"Is she one of them? She's cute." He sauntered a

couple steps her direction before Wilkins pulled him back.

"You're not dead." Fear filtered Lissa's breathy words.

Eddie grinned flirtatiously. "The Great Eduardo doesn't die." He seemed more amused than worried. "Hey, I didn't know she was one of my murderers. Can we get this on TV? Talk about more fun and more surprises!"

There was a moment of silence, and Lissa rushed at Eddie. Her lips curled back and teeth clenched, she slammed against him, fists pounding against his chest. In her rage the bandaged hand didn't seem to faze her.

"I know what I did," she shouted. "I stabbed you. You deserved it and I stabbed you!"

"Okay, I'm sorry." Eddie raised a questioning eyebrow at the officers. "I'm obviously dead."

She glared at him, but instead of being more riled at the mocking words, it settled her.

Officer Dunn came forward reaching for her shoulder, but Jenny got to her first.

"We're gonna go," Jenny said linking her arm through Lissa's.

"Not so fast," Dunn interjected holding a finger up to Jenny and turning his next question to his partner. "You don't think we need to worry about this? Look how she reacted to him."

Wilkins ran a hand through his hair and made a note on a small yellow notepad. "Not unless he wants to file a restraining order."

Eddie looked at Lissa and narrowed his eyes.

"Who are the others?"

Wilkins looked at Jenny and hesitated. She rolled her eyes and answered for him. "Frank Mullins and Tommy Webb."

"How do you even know that?" Officer Wilkins scanned the room as if she'd installed cameras.

"I have eyes," Jenny said annoyed.

"Mr. Mullins?" Eddie asked.

Officer Wilkins pulled out his notebook suddenly interested. "Do you know him."

"Of course, I know him. I dated his daughter in high school." Eddie fidgeted, shifting his hands from his pockets to crossing his arms and generally looking uncomfortable.

"Did you stay in touch?" Wilkins prodded.

Eddie shook his head. "No, no. It, uh, didn't go well."

Wilkins waited and eventually Eddie shrugged and kept going. "She got pregnant. And Mullins cut us off. I never heard anything else."

"You just decided it was fine? To never see your kid and girlfriend? How old where you?"

"We were eighteen. And no, I didn't want to walk away. But Frank thought I had ruined her life. Any time I tried to see her he would start yelling and threaten me until he took a restraining order out against me. I figured that was my cue."

"Did you love her?" Lissa asked. It was the first thing she'd said that hadn't carried an underlying tone of crazy. They all noticed. Lissa shrunk back under the attention. "I'm asking him. I don't even know the girl."

"Yeah, I loved her," Eddie said.

Lissa frowned but before she could say anything Eddie started up again, this time watching Lissa closely. "I wouldn't have left if I had a choice. She was always more fun, more surprises."

Lissa immediately tensed. "You jerk. I don't know who you are but you're not the Great Eduardo. I killed him. I killed you! I know I did! Stabbed you right in the heart. —"

Dunn had Lissa by the wrists before she could get her fists on Eddie a second time. Which was a good thing since it looked like her hand had started bleeding again.

"Wilkins, I don't know if we can let this one go."

"Actually," Eddie put a hand up. Lissa gnashed her teeth at him, and he pulled back. "I don't think we have to worry about it."

This time the attention of the room swiveled to Eddie. And it almost seemed like he got taller, basking in the attention.

"Did you see the same thing as me? Because that is a little concerning."

"Not really. It was a test. She's been hypnotized."

"Hypnotized?" Officer Wilkins voiced the same shock that Jenny felt.

"Yeah. It's what I do for a living so, maybe I'm biased but she sure acts like she's being triggered. That's how hypnosis works." He paused, maybe hoping someone else would jump in. "I'm not trying to sound self-centered or anything, but it sounds like she's being triggered by my tagline."

"You have a tagline . . ." Wilkins looked at him

like he was from another planet. "Do you have a theme song too?"

"Of course." Eddie returned the look of bizarre incomprehension. "I'm the Great Eduardo," he said, looking between them expectantly. When no one said anything. He clicked his tongue and turned to Lissa. "Watch this. Hey Lissa, are you ready for more fun, more surprises?"

Lissa hadn't really had much chance to calm down but when Eddie said those words, she started flailing in Officer Dunn's grip. "I don't know who you are because I killed the Great Eduardo. Drove a knife right into his chest. Look at him. How can anyone believe this is the Great Eduardo? If it was him, I'd kill him too."

Eddie laughed, "Nope your right. I'm not really the Great Eduardo. My name's Eddie. Nice to meet you."

He held his hand out and Lissa calmed her expression a turmoil of anger and confusion. She kept looking from him to Jenny and even to Officer Wilkins.

"How is that possible?" Jenny asked watching Lissa relax as Eddie played along. "Who would have done that."

"There's something else," Eddie said gesturing for Wilkins to step away. Jenny went with them. "She keeps calling me 'the Great Eduardo'. It's a bit of an amateur technique but it works. You take something in the persons world and use it to fixate them on the object. Well, usually it's an object. We don't usually want people obsessed with a person.

In the real world you would do this to divert someone's attention when they're maybe trying to lose weight or quit smoking. They're having a craving and as soon as they see the object, *boom*! Now the only thing they want is a glass of water or to go read that mental health book."

He shrugged and Jenny's jaw dropped.

"Okay, that makes sense. Are you saying you don't want us to hold her?" Officer Wilkins asked.

"She's not really a threat unless someone triggers her on purpose," Eddie said nonchalantly.

The officers stared at each other as if in silent conversation. Dunn shrugged lifting a single eyebrow.

"I want you to come with me." Wilkins started toward the door.

They all followed, Dunn gave Jenny a look as they approached. And Jenny glared at him. "I'm staying with my niece."

"Why am I not surprised," he said and gestured for Jenny to go through the door ahead of him.

9

"Where's Frank?" Jenny stood in front of a short row of holding cells.

Wilkins glanced up from his place by Tommy's cell. "Nora came and took him home already."

Tommy lounged at the back of the cell, eyeing Jenny. "Is she here for me?" he asked. "I'd like to get going. I'm gonna be late for work."

Like Lissa, he had a bandage on one hand. He had to use the tip of his finger to scratch his ear. The bandage wrapped up his wrist.

"That's quite a cut," Jenny commented softly, hoping it had been well taken care of.

"It's not a cut," Tommy said.

Jenny was speechless for a moment. "What is it?"

"I burned myself."

"How did you do that?" Jenny asked, surprised.

Tommy gave her a look of disbelief. "It's a chemical burn. I drowned the Great Eduardo in a bucket of concentrated chlorine."

"How did you get chemicals like that?"

Tommy frowned, scratching his neck. "I just had it . . . I'm not entirely sure."

"Alright you two. That's not why we're here." Wilkins held the door open but when Tommy didn't come out, he and Eddie went in.

At the sight of Eddie, Tommy sat up.

"Tommy, have you ever met Mr. Paris?"

"I just said so, didn't I?" Tommy scoffed, looking Eddie over. "I worked for him. And I killed him."

Wilkins flinched and glanced at Eddie. "Mr. Paris is here to conduct a little experiment."

"Am I? We don't know his trigger words." Eddie hesitated.

"Do it anyway," Dunn said adjusting his grip on Lissa. "We're not here for a party."

"You know how unlikely it is that they were hypnotized with the same trigger words?" Eddie looked uncertain. "People are so unique. If they're not personal the hypnosis doesn't hold, or you have to drug them to make it stronger. It becomes more brainwashing than hypnosis at that point."

"So, if your catch phrase is Lissa's trigger, she may just really hate you." Dunn's straight-faced insult seemed to get under Eddie's skin.

"Fine," he said turning back to Tommy. "Are you ready for more fun, more surprises."

On cue, both Tommy and Lissa started yelling and it took both police officers to settle them down.

"Okay. So, someone's an amateur," Eddie complained smoothing his disheveled t-shirt.

"Or you want it to look like that," Jenny said. She'd very quickly calculated the known hypnotists in the area. Even at an amateur level, there was only one.

"That's quite an accusation, Mrs. Doan." Eddie shifted, folding his arms.

"If you're right about them being hypnotized, and it looks like you are, there are not many people capable of doing this." Jenny stepped closer to Lissa. If she was going to confront Eddie anywhere this was the place. "Correct me if I'm wrong but we're pretty much looking at him, aren't we?"

Dunn gave a nod of silent agreement while Eddie scoffed. "There's no way I'm the only person around that knows how to do at least some hypnosis. I mean both Benji and Krista have done some. Why aren't they on the list?"

Wilkins pulled out his notepad. "They are now."

"No wait." Eddie held up his hands. "They would never do this to me. We're partners. And why would I hypnotize anyone to kill me."

"But they didn't come to kill you, did they. They just think they did. Maybe you're looking for publicity." Wilkins theory had some weight to it.

"He did ask about getting them on television." Jenny pointed out.

"That's cause she's cute. And who doesn't take advantage of a decent marketing opportunity. I mean, it's free publicity." Eddie sounded sincere, but if it wasn't him that left his team.

And Nancy . . . She'd bragged about her skills from years past, but it seemed unlikely that hypnotizing a roommate in college was enough.

"Look, I was supposed to be headed out of town

but since we're currently stranded, there might be a way I can help them. If you want me to."

Jenny watched Lissa struggling against Officer Dunn and gave Eddie a hard look. "What do you mean?"

Eddie's eyes lit up, "We can do what I'm calling medical reversion hypnosis. It's my own process I've been developing. I use it to send you back in your mind. It could be used to find and undo the old hypnosis. I'd love to test it on someone that's not stuck hopping on one foot or clucking like a chicken."

"What does that mean?" Wilkins asked with narrowed eyes.

Eddie took a moment before he answered, stretching his neck and taking a contemplative breath. "In my career I occasionally have some situations that require more undoing than I planned. So, it's not untested, just new."

Wilkins looked less than convinced "You're telling me you want to have one on one time with a group of people that either believe they killed you or plan to kill you?"

"What about the other side?" Jenny asked. "We're going to put these kids, alone with him when he might have been the one to hypnotize them? Whoever did it convinced them to injure themselves and is torturing them with this memory of killing someone. We can't put them alone together."

"That's a good point," Wilkins said and asked. "When did you get into town Mr. Paris?"

"I can't believe you're asking me this. I'm the victim here."

"I don't think so. Lissa, and Frank, and Tommy are the ones suffering. They're the real victims." Jenny cut in earning a glare from Officer Wilkins.

"I've been in that theater. Setting up, rehearsing, figuring out how to *safely* use that old building."

"So, you didn't have any contact with the victims before this morning?"

Eddie shot a glance at Lissa and shifted his jaw as if he was deciding something. "Well Tommy worked with me so he was there. And I saw Frank too. Every time I come back to town, Frank finds me. I swear he has some kind of radar. He just wants to warn me away from Sarah."

"But not Lissa?" Wilkins asked.

Eddie looked away.

"We had dinner Tuesday night." Lissa piped up. "I didn't know he was married and Eddie came by the office looking for copies of the contracts. Al and Harry had already gone home and I told him I was headed to dinner. He decided to join me."

Eddie closed his eyes.

"I see." Wilkins made more notes. "So you had contact with all three victims prior to this morning when all their hypnosis memories were triggered."

Eddie snapped to attention at that. "No. No, we don't know when they were triggered. It could be set to happen and then they wait. Or maybe they got a phone call."

"Or they went to your show and heard you shout the phrase at all three?" Jenny could place each of the three victims at the show and with obvious reactions to Eddie's words.

Eddie's mouth moved to form words and after a moment he simply closed it.

"Yeah." Jenny stared at the arrogant man who'd dropped his eyes to the floor.

"This is a terrible and scary situation but please, let me try and help them. Undoing hypnosis is not something most people think you can do. Let me try. Bring them as a group. Put it on camera, then you can prove I'm not doing anything wrong. Or don't but I'd really like the chance to help them. If you'll let me."

Jenny glared, relaxing when she could see his sincerity. She didn't know who had hypnotized her niece and hadn't completely ruled out Eddie, but it did seem that he honestly wanted to help.

"Hypnosis is my job. So, if you'll allow it, I'll reach out to the hypnosis victims and schedule with them."

"Hold on, if it's medical reversion, shouldn't we have a doctor here?" Wilkins seemed to have hit a nerve.

Eddie's nostrils flared. "You may not know this, but I learned to be a hypnotist while studying to be a doctor. I was in my clinical trials when I decided to pursue entertainment full time."

"But you're not a doctor." Dunn pointed out.

"Thank you, meat head," Eddie said to Officer Dunn. He clenched his jaw, "But yes, it would be beneficial for them to be cleared by a doctor before undergoing any kind of treatment."

"So are you still thinking you'll keep Lissa here? Or can I take her home until all of this happens? Because I'd like to talk to Lissa about this alone."

"That's fine Jenny. I'm sure we'll schedule as soon as we can get a doctor in here." Wilkins took Tommy by the elbow. "Come on. Let's get a hold of your mom. It's time for you to go home too."

"Cherry?" Jenny answered the Bluetooth call and turned the wheel as she pulled onto the main road.

"Good morning!" Cherry's chipper voice rang through the car stereo. "Are you on your way?"

"Of course." *She was on the way. Sort of.* Jenny thought as she turned toward home. The rental place Lissa had booked for the season was only a couple of houses down from Jenny's and it would be quick work to drop her off and make it back for the Party on the Patio.

"Good. Cause there's a giant cake on wheels here waiting for you."

"I'll be there in ten minutes," Jenny said, keeping an eye on Lissa.

"You mean five?" Cherry corrected.

"I'll try. See you in ten-ish minutes." Jenny hung up the phone. They'd left Lissa's car at the station and, judging by the way Lissa stared out the passenger window, it was a good thing she wasn't driving.

Lissa leaned back against the headrest, "Why is this happening, Aunt Jenny? Do you think it's real? Do you think I killed him?"

Jenny's response was immediate. "Of course not, You couldn't. And he's not dead anyway."

"I understand that. It just doesn't make sense. I woke up this morning knowing I had to turn myself in. And now I'm here. I feel like I screwed up. And all I want to do is go back to the station and try to make them understand what happened."

Jenny slowed pulling into the driveway of Lissa's blue and white cottage. After finding her in the station she hadn't taken the time to question anything except Lissa's proclamation that she'd killed Eddie. She wasn't sure she wanted to know anything else. But she had to ask. "What did happen?"

"I don't know. I can see him in my mind. I can feel the knife in my hand, and I'm so angry when I think about it." Lissa paused. "I swear he's hurting you. That's why I killed him. I mean, why I wanted to kill him."

Jenny rubbed Lissa's shoulder her finger hitting a small bump on her neck and Lissa winced.

"Sorry. I've got this spot right there, that's bothering me." She ran her fingers over the irritated red lump. "I'm sure it's nothing. I'm just sore. My hand is worse though." She flinched when she looked at her bandage. Blood had seeped through the palm.

"Why don't you let me help with that."

"Thanks, Aunt Jenny." Lissa pulled open the door

and slid out of the car.

Jenny followed Lissa up the path. Blood trickled along the rocks. A trail of spatters leading from the driveway to the door.

On the porch, Lissa walked right through a line of red, talking the whole time. "You really don't have to do this. I know you have to go soon."

Jenny grabbed her as she reached for the doorknob. "Don't touch that. It's covered in blood."

"What are you talking about?" She gasped as if she was seeing the scene for the first time. "Oh my gosh. Is that from the Great Eduardo?"

Jenny frowned. It was almost frustrating that she couldn't see past the fact that Eddie wasn't dead. "It's yours Lissa. I hope anyway. Because Eddie's fine which mean's this is from your hand or someone else got hurt at your house."

Lissa's face paled and she grabbed the doorknob despite what Jenny had just told her. She shoved it open and stumbled inside. "Oh, no. Oh my gosh."

Blood trailed everywhere, from the bedroom to the door. It wasn't thick but the pristine white walls were speckled with handprints and white towels lay crunched in piles of red like she'd been washing off stage makeup.

"What happened?" Lissa's face had fallen her lips trembling and her eyebrows pinched so tight Jenny hurt for her. "I don't want to remember this. I don't want it in my head. I don't want it to be real." Lissa hiccupped, tears running down her cheeks.

"You must have cut yourself here," Jenny said gently.

"No. It happened in the theater. He was on the stage, and he was going to hurt you and I stabbed him. It was there. Why does my house look like this?"

Her breath was coming in shallow gasps and Jenny grabbed her in a tight bear hug. "It's okay." Jenny rocked her, stroking her hair. "It's going to be okay. Let's get you over to my house. Okay?"

Lissa didn't say anything. She was sucking in air through her tears and all Jenny could do was hold her and hum.

It took at least thirty seconds to calm her and twice that much to get back in the car, locking the door behind them.

She drove her to the end of the block and walked her inside. "I want you to go upstairs and take a nap. Do you understand me?"

Lissa's hand was over her mouth, still crying but she nodded. Jenny held her shoulders and looked her in the eye. Then turned her to the stairs and walked her up herself.

Ron was still in bed, but Jenny didn't have time to worry about that. She showed Lissa to the guest room where she lay on the bed clutching a pillow to her chest letting her breathing calm down.

With a goodbye to Lissa and a silent kiss for Ron Jenny ran back out the door.

10

With a bang, the topper of the five-foot-tall cake flew into the air. Fabric rained down around the crowd. Jenny had made the cake herself several years before, specifically so she could pop out of the top. She still thought it was hilarious but this year as she came out the top someone had figured out how to rig an exploding pod of fabric squares to shoot off like confetti.

The quilters loved it. They clapped and danced, catching fabric while the emcee played the music.

Jenny escaped the cake and Cherry stood to the side watching, giving a lackluster, slow applause.

"Wow, that was great," Cherry monotoned, through a strained smile. "I'm amazed they were able to hold off the celebration for an extra fifteen minutes."

"You say that like someone was holding it all together trying to keep the cake from exploding. Not like they had to wait a few minutes to push a button." Anxiety brought out Jenny's sass and she'd been waiting for a call from Officer Wilkins since she'd arrived. "But I'm sorry I was late."

Cherry shrugged, softening almost immediately. "I understand. I'm glad you were there for Lissa."

Her mind drifted over what she'd shared with Cherry earlier. She hadn't held anything back. Now, Jenny couldn't seem to shake the image of Lissa curled up on her guest bed. "Me too. I'm just waiting on—"

"Well, ladies and gents, that's the whole MSQC crew and aren't we glad Jenny's here!" the emcee said into the mic and the crowd erupted in applause.

Jenny's smile jumped into place automatically when he said her name. She felt a little silly as her emotions jumped from one extreme to the next, but she waved, grateful for the contagious excitement of the quilters. She needed a break from the turmoil of the morning. And a distraction while she waited for Officer Wilkins to call.

The emcee walked a stack of fabric bundles and prizes over, handing them to Jenny and Cherry while Jenny's grandkids drew numbers for guests to walk and dance around the "fabric" cake walk.

"Yes!" he said. "Jenny's here to award the prizes. Now, who's ready to win?"

Al whistled a loud call and the crowd responded with enthusiasm applauding and calling back.

Jenny needed to be excited, she needed to be present. She couldn't get her mind off of Lissa. Grabbing Cherry's arm, Jenny pulled them back a step before she lost her chance. "Has Wilkins called yet?"

Cherry blushed and ducked her head. "Not yet.

He's supposed to be at the burger place for lunch later though. So, I was thinking I'd go in for a milkshake."

That was not the response Jenny'd been expecting. "Oh, right. He drove you home didn't he?" But it was intriguing. "You made plans, then?"

Cherry's blush deepened. "Not exactly. I was thinking I'd bump into him around town . . . And we have to eat, right? So . . ."

"No need to explain. You're right. You definitely need to eat. And I'll want to hear all about it." Jenny chuckled under her breath. "But that's not what I meant. I'm expecting a call, from Wilkins, and I gave him both our numbers, in case I was wrapped up in cake or something. Can you let me know if he calls you?"

"You gave him my number?" Cherry nearly choked on the words.

"Sorry?" Jenny asked it like a question, working to relax her face as cameras clicked and people laughed.

Cherry shook her head and handed Jenny a prize to give out when the music stopped. "No. I was expecting to visit with him a few times and see if I liked . . . well, never mind. It's fine. I'll keep an eye out."

The party carried on around them without a phone call for the next hour. Five minutes before the giveaway event ended Cherry took Jenny's arm and waved to the crowd. "Thanks so much for being here everyone! And good luck winning prizes! Come see us at the Quilt Auction tonight!"

She walked them across the street, past the festival booths, and handed Jenny the phone. "It's him."

Jenny grabbed the phone. "Hello? Officer Wilkins? Is that you?"

"Yes. I'll need Lissa here at three o'clock."

"Wait, today?" Jenny's brain tripped over his words, trying to keep up. "What do you need her for?"

"Isn't that why you called? To find out when the hypnosis reversion session was."

"No, but that is good to know." Jenny would have to check the schedule with Cherry, but it was nice to see the police moving on this so quickly.

"If we can un-train their brains maybe they can remember what happened and who did this. So, what did you need?" Wilkins said abruptly, like he'd been interrupted.

Jenny paused, staring at the neon painted motorhome parked ahead of them, in the lot across from the grocery store. Seeing it brought on a mix of emotions.

"I tried to take Lissa home this morning—"

"What do you mean tried. She didn't go anywhere, did she? She's still here?" Wilkins was suddenly highly engaged in the conversation.

"No, I put her on a plane and flew her home cause she was upset," Jenny said, biting her tongue after the words were out.

"What?" Wilkins voice cracked a screech and Jenny rolled her eyes.

"Wilkins," She chastised him impatiently. "You

know I wouldn't do that. Of course, she's still here. I tried taking her home and it was a mess. There was a lot of blood. I know it's not Eddie's but in case someone else was there or if you needed to see anything. I figured you'd want to take a look before we clean up. I'm just worried about her and I want her to be safe as much as I want to find out what's going on."

"I appreciate that. We'll check it out," Officer Wilkins said in his detective voice.

"Do you really think Eddie's safe?"

Wilkins hesitated. "Look, we don't know what happened. And we all want to find out. Thank you for the call. I'll let you know if we find anything at Lissa's place."

"Thank you." Jenny hung up more nervous than before. Staring up at the bug eyes of Eddie's motorhome she couldn't help wondering how much of Lissa's situation he'd caused.

Handing Cherry's phone back, Jenny sighed. "It will feel really good when all this goes away."

"Eddie's bus?" Cherry asked.

Jenny made a face. "Well, I meant the hypnosis problems but that too."

"So, Eddie and his bus." Cherry grinned and Jenny tried not to smile along with her but failed.

The Birthday Bash celebration was several blocks down the road. They'd come further than she thought, and she dropped onto one of the benches with Cherry. It felt almost quiet at this end of the street.

They were directly across from the neon

motorhome. Its windshield had a line down the center giving the vehicle giant glass bug eyes. The door separating the cab from the living area was open and Jenny found it odd that no one was there.

The broken part lay on the ground near the door with the panel popped off the engine at the back. Apparently, they had yet to fix things.

"Do you really think she's hypnotized," Cherry asked. "That's so wild."

"I don't see another option. She wouldn't be doing this on her own."

"Who would?" Cherry looked back to the festival. "Who goes to bed excited about their future and wakes up ready to confess to a murder they didn't commit? On the other hand, who brainwashes a person to make them think they killed someone else. It's torture for the hypnotized person. Who would do that to Lissa?"

"I don't know. She's not even from here. I don't think she knows anyone well enough to have hurt them. This has to be about Eddie. He was with all three of them yesterday. And he's the only one that could do it."

"I wonder if anyone else on Eddie's crew can hypnotize." Cherry asked.

"They can," Jenny said. "He told Wilkins this morning that both Benji and Krista can do some hypnosis. But he swears they'd never do this to him."

"I agree. It doesn't make any sense. Why try and take him down if he's your bread and butter. There's got to be someone we don't know about."

"We should check in with the Mullins." Jenny hesitated.

"Why? Are you worried about Frank?"

"I am but not the way you think. It sounds like he's been pretty upset with Eddie for a long time. Ever since Eddie dated Frank's daughter. Frank even got a restraining order against Eddie. I don't know why he'd wait so long to do something. The relationship would have happened at least six, maybe eight years ago."

"Why would he do this at all? Frank's a nice old guy." Cherry defended him.

Jenny's gave a sad smile. "People do crazy things for their kids. That was his baby girl. I think she's his only child." Jenny started across the street. "So, he had motive. I wish I knew what changed."

Gravel crunched underfoot as she approached the empty tour bus, Cherry following close behind.

"What are we doing?" Cherry asked.

"I'm not sure but we're here and Eddie's not, so, it's as good a place to start as any." Jenny didn't know if Eddie was a victim or a suspect. But Lissa's home was covered in blood and this showman, at the center of it all, was barely being investigated.

Cherry followed Jenny to the back of the bus where the panel leaned against the bumper. Wires hung in a tangled mess but without Ron the engine meant very little to her.

A shout from inside the motorhome startled her, and Cherry tripped over a large rock and a pink crowbar. She held it up and waved it at Jenny. "You're going to make me break my nose."

Jenny shushed her and took the crowbar away, trying not to laugh. "Quiet, someone's here."

"So," Cherry scrunched her nose and looked back to where the sound had come from. "You don't think they'll be excited for guests?"

"I could go knock and we'll find out." Jenny laughed quietly, aiming the crowbar at Cherry.

Cherry's lips puckered. "With a weapon? Maybe not."

"It's not a weapon," Jenny said, looking at it in mock surprise. Then she noticed something she hadn't seen before. Wiping her finger over the end of the crowbar neon paint chips fell away from the edge of the tool. "Where was this?"

Cherry pointed to one of the back tires.

Holding the edge of the tool to one of the long lines that had been scraped around the bus. Jenny traced it all the way to the back side where the words, "It's not OVER", were scratched in the paint.

It looked like more than the engine had been vandalized. Someone had threatened Eddie, but had it happened before or after the confessions?

The scrape continued around the bus and Jenny slid into the narrow gap between the vehicle and the wall to follow it.

Voices rose inside and Jenny stopped, Cherry bumping into her from behind.

"He is not going to do this to me." Benji's voice rang loudly. Not even attempting to hide his anger

"Is that Benji?" Cherry hissed, only inches behind her.

Chain Piecing a Mystery

Jenny held up her finger, miming the universal be-quiet sign.

"*He* is not doin' this. The engine is dead." This was a woman's voice that Jenny vaguely recognized. Possibly Krista, though she sounded more frustrated than she had that morning. "Eddie didn't rip that part out."

"But you heard him. He's staying to hypno-doctor those people." Anger threaded through Benji's reply. "We are entertainers! He's wasting our time."

Inside, something slammed hard enough to rock the vehicle.

With a sharp intake of breath Jenny flattened herself against the opposite wall. Cherry didn't react as quickly and in the tight space the movement of the bus caught her shoulder.

Lurching to the side, her head knocked against the cement wall and Cherry dropped with a cry.

The voices inside quieted.

11

"This heap isn't going anywhere." Krista sounded completely resigned to the idea that the tour bus was dead. "What do you care if he tries to catch a little media attention while we're stuck here? Make some money on a few saps that don't know any better."

Jenny was barely listening anymore. "Cherry," she hissed, crouching near the young woman. "Cherry!"

She had fallen in a heap, caught between the tour bus and the wall. Jenny leaned awkwardly around her, trying to lift her. "Please? Wake up."

"I want my own show, Krista."

There was a short pause before the woman spoke and Cherry moaned. Jenny sucked in a breath. Trying to keep her waking and quiet at the same time.

"You're a hundred times the performer Eddie is. You'll get your own show . . . soon."

The conversation going on behind the thin wall beside her barely mattered.

"Cherry? Are you hurt?"

Cherry blinked and pulled a hand to her head smacking the side of the bus in the process.

"We'll have our own show," Benji said.

Jenny released a breath. They didn't seem to have noticed the sound of Cherry hitting the wall.

Krista giggled and as Cherry sat up with Jenny's help. She had gravel pressed into her cheek and dirt in her hair but she didn't look injured.

The voices inside had grown quiet. The two women stood.

"Can we go?" Cherry asked softly.

Jenny nodded and the side of the trailer rocked again as platinum blonde curls appeared in the tiny window. Benji's hand was mixed up in her hair and it didn't take much to realize what was happening inside.

Jenny shooed Cherry down the gap. Eddie was obviously not home, and this was not the kind of situation a polite person walked in on. They shimmied out of the nook, finally free as the engine panel clattered to the ground. Cherry's sweater had snagged on the rough metal and the sounds inside the bus stopped.

Jenny picked up the metal panel, it was even more scraped up than the bus. She shoved it into place on the back end of the bus.

"Who's out there?" Benji called.

Jenny's heart stopped. They were too close. The door opened and Cherry jumped. Jenny peeked around the corner to see Benji standing on the step.

She gave a sheepish wave.

Chain Piecing a Mystery

"What's going on, Benji? Is the vandal back?" Krista had a hand on his shoulder sliding toward his chest. Jenny blushed when Benji stepped out of the bus and she saw the woman's thin robe wrapped around barely-there clothing.

She didn't seem concerned at all and followed Benji to check the bus exterior. They stopped when he got to the panel only half wedged into place. "What are you doing?"

How was she going to dodge this one? *With honesty*, she thought.

"Hi," Jenny said stepping forward with her hand held out to shake Benji's hand. "It's good to see you again. I was looking for Eddie?"

"He's not here," Benji said at the same time that Krista said, "He's at the news station."

Benji shot her a grouchy look.

There wasn't a local news station so the answer didn't tell Jenny much but it had annoyed Benji anyway.

"Oh, that's too bad." She took a step back, with Cherry always one step further. "Well, we'll get out of your way then."

The woman flipped her blond hair and cocked a half-smile, as though she knew something Jenny didn't. "Did you want Eddie's signature?"

"No. No, I—"

"Don't say another word. Benji, do you have a napkin or something? I need to sign something for this poor girl." She started patting her hips. Benji didn't move an inch, but apparently, he didn't need to. Krista whipped a pale blue cloth from her pocket and produced a slick black marker from the same space. Jenny hadn't even realized there was a pocket on that robe.

"This should do it," she said happily. "Tell me your name again, sweetie?"

"Oh, um, Jenny." Had she just forgotten her name? "Thanks . . . I really, loved your . . . sparkly outfit and the way you . . . helped . . . last night." Jenny fought for a way to compliment the woman appropriately.

Krista beamed at Jenny and she let out a breath. It must have worked.

"Aren't you precious. Here, this is for you and your friend. To Jenna. — May all the stars be as bright as you! Krista & Eddie." Krista winked at Jenny, who accepted the blue napkin.

"Krista, this is great." She fawned over the markered inscription. Krista had at some point managed to kiss it with her hot pink lipstick. "Wow," "This is amazing. Thank you, Krista."

That brought Krista's smile back. She waved goodbye and grabbed Benji's arm, pulling him back into the tour bus.

Cherry pulled Jenny down the road like they were in a walk-a-thon.

"Goodness you're in a hurry," Jenny complained. She understood she was nervous but Jenny was a good thirty years older than Cherry. "Way to not look suspicious."

"Me?" Cherry sounded surprised and finally let go. "I had to get you away from them before you did something else to get us in trouble."

Jenny chuckled. From Cherry's point of view it made sense. "You're the one who got herself knocked out, while they were having some, er, private time."

"That's just wrong," Cherry said. "And don't make fun. I'll take you with me next time."

"Fine." Jenny agreed. "I'll be good." They walked back toward the festival booths and Jenny took a breath. "Hey, if it's all right with you, I've got to run an errand."

Cherry narrowed her eyes not at all fooled by Jenny's casual demeanor. "Will it make you late for the quilt auction?"

"No, but it will keep me busy until three when Lissa has to meet with Eddie."

Cherry scrolled through her phone checking details or something Jenny hadn't thought of.

"Okay," Cherry said, "but I'm driving." They turned the corner and Cherry pulled out her keys. "So, where are we going?"

"Our boys were friends? I'm so sorry I don't remember you." Rachelle Paris apologized as she welcomed Jenny and Cherry into her home.

It was entirely opposite of the impression Eddie had given. The nineties brick exterior transitioned to a completely pristine interior, with no color at all. It felt a bit like she was caught in a roll of cotton poly batting.

"Don't worry about it." Jenny waved off her concern, taking a seat on the thin white sofa.

"Please, have a seat." Rachelle gestured to the couch where Jenny had already positioned herself.

Choosing to ignore the touch of haughty disdain in her comment. Jenny introduced Cherry.

"Hi, Mrs. Paris." Cherry reached out shaking her hand. "I'm a friend of Jenny's. It's nice to meet you."

"Of course, any friend of Jenny's . . ." She trailed off not sure exactly how to finish.

Cherry sat and Rachelle hovered over them. The awkwardness was palpable, but Jenny refused to let the lack of welcome bother her.

"Would you like some tea?" Rachelle asked retrieving a steaming tea set from the counter. Pouring small cups of tea from a white ceramic kettle.

"Thank you," she said accepting the miniature teacup Rachelle handed her. "I thought I'd stop by, since Eddie's in town, and see if you two were enjoying your time together."

Rachelle Paris gave a tight smile. "I haven't seen Edward yet." She adjusted the picture Jenny had been looking at back to its original position. "I'm not sure I will. He hasn't come to see me in quite some time. I'm not sure he likes it here."

"Not surprised." Cherry muttered.

"Excuse me?" Rachelle asked.

"Not so wise." Cherry smiled stiffly. " . . . Of that young man. Not wise at all. No one should miss time with their mother. It's just sad."

Chain Piecing a Mystery

Jenny silently applauded the rambling rescue Cherry'd preformed after her original comment. Though Rachelle still seemed unsure. Her teapot hovered over a second teacup before finishing and taking a seat on a leggy bucket chair.

There were no family pictures on the walls and Jenny couldn't get over how unlike Eddie the house was.

"He must come back to see you every once in a while," Jenny said sipping her tea.

Rachelle scrunched her lips into a tiny frown. "We don't really talk," she said sitting primly on her chair, she only allowed a moment of silence before continuing. "I'm sure you know how it is. Kids grow up and think they know everything. Then last year, he walks away from medical school . . . who does that? Anyway, I got a little upset. I was going to have a son that was a doctor."

"It's the white coats, isn't it," Cherry said, adjusting a white pillow on the white couch.

"What was that?" Rachelle asked her brows pulled together an angry question in her eye.

"Dreamboats. Those doctors are dreamboats, aren't they?" Cherry's smile was somewhere between plastic and clownish.

Rachelle's upper lip hitched, and she glared at Cherry. "Sure, I wanted him to be a doctor because they're a catch. Oh, and we'd spent almost a hundred thousand dollars on his education. That was a little bit important too."

"A hundred thousand?" Jenny plunked her teacup down snapping the thread of tension and drawing

Rachelle's gaze. "That's a lot of money to throw away."

Rachelle nodded, "And he had good scholarships."

"Is there any way he could go back and finish?"

Her nod slowed and she picked up her teacup, "If he wanted. It hasn't been too long yet but he'll have to reapply for residencies and find a program that won't ask questions about his behavior while on sabbatical."

"He was already in residencies? I thought he only graduated six years ago." The detail stood out to Jenny like a spool of neon thread.

Rachelle's building frustration ebbed and she tipped her head back, looking at the ceiling. "Seven." She had a touch of pride behind the emotion brimming in her voice. "He'd been working on it so long. All through high school he took concurrent courses, graduated early, and fought his way into competitive programs. Then he takes one extra course, hypnosis," she shakes her head and almost spits the word out. "And only because a friend is doing it. After that class he just walked away."

"He must really love hypnosis." Cherry offered more sincerely this time.

Rachelle folded her hands in her lap. "We obviously feel differently about it. Eddie hasn't been home since."

A tiny pleat formed in Jenny's throat, her breath catching in the tight space. "He's here now."

Rachelle's face went cold. "As if that makes a

difference. You are so sweet to walk me through all those memories. Were there any other tragic experiences you'd like to relive with me?"

Jenny could feel the ice in the room.

Cherry reached in front of Jenny and picked up her thimble of tea, finishing it off for her. She was surprised it hadn't frozen.

"I think it's time to go," Cherry said. Clapping her hands against her knees, she pushed herself up to standing. "This has been so nice. I hate to impose on you further. Jenny, are you ready?"

"It is about that time. Rachelle, thank you for being so gracious. Especially with everything going on with Eddie. I'm sure you know about the murder confessions." Jenny shook her head. "I can't imagine how stressed you must feel."

"Murder?" Rachelle asked, the color draining from her face.

Jenny watched her closely. "Yes, three people confessed to murdering your son."

Rachelle dropped her teacup the tiny ceramic piece shattering on the floor. Tea and glass scattering.

It was the reaction she'd been hoping for. Rachelle was shocked. Jenny dialed it back, hurrying over to put a hand on her shoulder. "No, no, he's fine." Jenny reassured. Cherry started picking up pieces of white ceramic and Jenny knelt in front of Rachelle. "They confessed to his murder but he's fine. No one tried to kill Eddie. In fact, he's worried about them. He thinks they've been hypnotized and that he can help them."

Rachelle's breathing was shallow, and she was repeatedly squeezing Jenny's hands as she held them.

"I didn't mean to surprise you like that. I'm sorry." Jenny let the silence hang before broaching her next question. "It's terrible to see Eddie going through this. Especially here where he grew up. You wouldn't know of anyone that would want to hurt him, or was jealous of him, would you?"

Rachelle flinched. "People were always jealous of Edward. He had lots of friends. He dated the prettiest girls. Graduated at the top of his class and went on to medical school. So yeah, people were jealous."

"He mentioned an old girlfriend, the Mullin's daughter."

Rachelle frowned, "I think that's right. They dated for a few months in his senior year. But Edward didn't have time for relationships. Especially with girls who were just trying to get a leg up."

"What does that mean?" Jenny asked.

"Edward's very compassionate by nature. It often lands him in the lap of gold diggers. Very pretty gold diggers."

Jenny recoiled from the words, letting go of Rachelle's hands, she stood.

"We should really go now. I'm so sorry Mrs. Paris," Cherry said, taking Jenny's elbow.

Rachelle walked them to the door and opened it. "Edward was a good boy. He liked to help people. But people rarely like it when someone else's compassion highlights their flaws. The Mullin's thought Edward was too good to be true. And he was.

"When their daughter got herself in a compromised situation, they blamed Edward." Rachelle's gaze fell over Jenny's shoulder, a vacant stare that made her look numb to whatever pain she was reliving. "He tried to destroy Eddie's life. Involving the authorities in things and making decisions that weren't his to make. Eddie spent his last year at home trying to help his girlfriend and save a relationship that never should have happened.

"I lost him that year. If anyone is holding a grudge against my son, it's Frank Mullins. I'll never forgive him for that."

Rachelle closed the door on them, and Jenny looked at Cherry. "How soon is our next event?"

Cherry frowned reading Jenny's mind. "No, Jenny. We don't have time."

12

"Why aren't we putting the top up?" Jenny asked digging through the console of Cherry's lipstick red convertible. Even driving at "town" speeds Jenny's short curls whipped her face mercilessly.

"Because the sun's out and I'm not ready for fall." Cherry wore her new red and turquoise sunglasses with a yellow handkerchief to keep her hair back.

In the vintage styled convertible, with the chrome trim package, she looked like she'd stepped out of a fifties commercial.

After a few more seconds of digging, Cherry reached out. Moving Jenny back against her seat, Cherry shuffled a few things around in the console and retrieved a pair of hot orange sunglasses, handing them to Jenny. She hadn't even looked away from the road.

"Thank you," Jenny said, sliding the frames on.

The flashy bejeweled sunglasses were less about fashion and more about eye protection.

Cherry turned the corner headed toward Jenny's

home. "Are you sure we can't stop at the Mullins'? I only want to ask them a few questions."

"A few questions with you is not a quick visit." Cherry teased.

"Aren't you curious about her and Eddie though?" Jenny watched Cherry's nonresponsive face closely. "If Frank really took a restraining order out on Eddie there may have been more going on than we realize."

"If he did, it was years ago. Do you really think it matters?" Cherry twisted her grip on the steering wheel.

"Rachelle said she'd never forgive them." Jenny pointed out.

"I heard." Cherry sounded annoyed. "We can go, after the trunk show."

Jenny slumped in her chair. She really couldn't miss the trunk show. "How much time do I have?"

"Fifteen minutes."

Jenny pinched her lips closed. It had to be done. She leaned into the seatback letting Cherry drive. The wind scattered her hair freely, clearing her mind. Until the jerk of momentum flung Jenny forward.

"Woah," Cherry said, slowing the car quickly.

Police cars lined the road as they approached Lissa's rental. Wilkins had done more than just come check out her place. He'd brought the entire department to do a run down.

"Stop," Jenny said as Cherry hit the brakes already pulling over behind Lissa.

She was standing on the sidewalk shivering. As

soon as the car stopped moving Jenny jumped out followed by Cherry.

"What is all this?" Jenny asked wrapping her arms around her niece. Only then remembering that she'd told Officer Wilkins that morning to check on the mess in the apartment.

"They needed me to let them in." Lissa's nose was red, and her voice trembled. When she sniffled Jenny couldn't tell if it was from emotion or the chill in the air.

Wilkins walked toward them, his eyes straying to Cherry. In a move of solidarity, Cherry stepped closer to Jenny and Lissa. The officer refocused on the group and reached his hand out to Jenny.

"It's good to see you. I'm going to be honest ladies, I haven't found much here."

Jenny relaxed and Lissa's head dropped to her shoulder.

Wilkins held his hands up. "Unfortunately, that's not necessarily a good thing."

"What does that mean?" Lissa asked. Wilkins took a breath before responding and Lissa turned to Jenny. "What does he mean?"

Jenny patted her shoulder, "It means something that should be there isn't." Wilkins glanced at Lissa's hand and Jenny closed her eyes. The one piece she'd assumed would be easy. "The knife."

"What knife?" Lissa asked.

Wilkins looked behind him as if making sure it hadn't been recovered in his absence. "The knife or tool used to cut your hand. The one you claim was used to murder the Great Eduardo."

"But it has to be there. I had it when I woke up. I could feel it."

"Did you see it?" Jenny asked. "If you only felt it could that be a part of the hypnosis?"

Wilkins pulled his notepad out considering the possibility. "If that's true It could be a good thing it's not here. Maybe this piece falls on whoever hypnotized her." Wilkins looked at Lissa, "You don't have any idea where it is?"

Her trembling turned to shaking and her eyes welled with tears. "I—I don't know. I could feel it in my hand. That's all I know."

Wilkins nodded, "We're about finished here. You can get back inside within the hour."

"Don't worry about us," Jenny said. "We'll be at my house if you need us."

"Ladies," Wilkins nodded at them and paused as he turned giving one more nod, "Cherry."

The Birthday Bash trunk show was a new one. She'd only gone over the different pieces a few times before the event. And normally that's how Jenny worked best. She was a wing it kind of girl.

As Natalie ran back and forth across the stage trying to keep up with Jenny's scattered brain. She couldn't help wondering if this hadn't been the right weekend to introduce a knew show. Through mishaps and laughter Jenny confessed her faux-pas and by the time she and Natalie fell into step the show was over and they were sitting on the patio having lunch.

"That was craziness." Jenny bounced at the table. The energy of a show always left her on pins and needles.

"I thought it went great," Cherry said laying open a large folder with their schedule. "Okay, there's fabric line bingo in twenty minutes and another Live filming event with Misty this afternoon, but neither of them are mandatory . . . yet. I'm pretty sure they're expecting you at the filming."

Natalie laughed, "I know they are. It's Misty's show but you're both MSQC."

"I'll make it to the filming," Jenny promised. Natalie was right but, even considering that, she still had enough time to break away. "Is that everything on my to-do list this afternoon? Are we ready for a field trip?"

Cherry closed her folder and gave Jenny a long stare. "You won't change your mind?"

Jenny shook her head and Cherry pulled out the keys. "Alright, let's go."

"What's this field trip? Did you find a new antique store?" Natalie teased gathering the remains of their lunch basket.

"Your mom's investigating another crime. The involuntary hypnotizing of your cousin."

Narrowing her eyes at Cherry, Jenny tried to be honest without being so alarming. "I'm going to visit the Mullins'. Frank wasn't feeling well at the show yesterday."

Natalie gave them a suspicious smile. "Okay, I

was planning to stop in and see Lissa today anyway. Do you think that will work?" Jenny confirmed and Natalie kissed Jenny on the cheek. "Thanks mom. She'll tell me what's going on. I hope your field trip goes well and doesn't get you in trouble. I'll see you tonight." She waved to them both and disappeared into the building.

Jenny climbed into the car with Cherry and frowned. "Way to out me to my family."

Cherry grinned and pulled out into traffic making her way carefully past the crowds. It was a quick trip to the large Victorian near the old ballpark and Jenny was barely ready when they knocked.

Nora opened the door, rosy-cheeked and in her house apron. "Jenny! I wasn't expecting company. What can I do for you?"

"Hi, Nora," Jenny greeted her, "I wanted to see how Frank's doing."

Nora sucked in a breath and smiled, "Oh, you mean after the show? He's fine. The headache's all gone. He went to work this morning."

"I'm surprised he's feeling up to that already. Lissa's been struggling to keep it together all day," Jenny said.

"Lissa? That's your niece, right?"

"Yes," Jenny confirmed.

Nora opened her mouth to say something else, closing it again with a nervous glance around the porch. "Why don't you come in?"

Nora Mullins' home was a stark contrast to the Paris home where Jenny and Cherry had visited earlier that day. The warm deep colors of natural wood and floral wallpaper welcomed her in. The house was clean, but the shelves were filled with knick-knacks, pictures, and memorabilia.

Nora sat with them at the dining room table by a plate of sliced homemade breads. She picked up a piece for herself offering the tray to Jenny and Cherry.

Breaking the corner from a piece of lemon loaf, Nora let out a deep breath. "What happened with Lissa. Is it the same as Frank?"

Jenny nodded, as their hostess nibbled anxiously at the bread. "She thinks she killed Eddie. I saw Frank at the police station this morning. Is he okay?"

"So, you believe it? That they were hypnotized?" Nora whispered the word as if she was afraid of it and broke another piece of bread off.

Cherry coughed, "Sorry I should go— um, do you mind if I go get some water?"

"Not at all," Nora said barely looking at Cherry. Her eyes on Jenny as if she held a lifeline. "Glasses are next to the sink. Is your niece okay?" Nora asked Jenny. "Frank seems fine, but I can't understand how it happened. We were only at the show for a few minutes. And this morning he woke up on the back porch with rope tangled all over him, his hands raw. I never expected I'd have to pick my husband up from the police station."

"It's okay." Jenny reassured her. "I understand, Lissa's house had blood all over. She cut herself."

"But that's different. She didn't have rope burns?" Nora asked sitting back, her bread shredded to crumbles on the plate in front of her.

"It seems like they're all different," Jenny said. "Tommy has chemical burns."

"Oh." Nora looked shocked. "I saw Tommy when I picked up Frank. I thought he'd gotten himself in trouble. I didn't even check on him."

Nora's distress grabbed hold of Jenny's heart. "I'm trying to figure out what's behind all of this."

"Well, it's Eddie. He's hypnotized our families and is torturing them for past sins."

Jenny hesitated in her response. "I don't know, Lissa didn't even know Eddie. She had dinner with them the night they got to town and that was for work." Jenny looked to the door where Cherry had disappeared. She was still gone. "I heard your family knew Eddie years ago. Is there anything you can tell me about their relationship?"

"There's not much to tell. My daughter, Sarah, and Eddie dated. I always thought they were cute together, but my husband wasn't a fan. He went to some pretty extreme measures keeping them apart after . . . well, after they made some mistakes. But that's all it was. A teenage relationship and a protective dad."

"Sarah got pregnant, didn't she? That's a pretty life changing situation. Is that when Frank started taking extreme measures?"

Nora's eyes widened. "How did you know?"

"I had a conversation with Rachelle Paris this morning. She was worried your husband was the one who'd want to hurt her son."

"Frank would never hurt someone. He was upset.

Sarah had so many plans. She was going to dance in college, she was a ballerina. When she got pregnant Frank was pretty upset. I was too. But then—" Nora took a slow breath as her cheeks flushed and her eyes glistened with emotion. "Then she lost the baby."

"Oh, I'm so sorry." Jenny honestly wasn't sure how Nora felt about it but her instinct was to care. Even if the baby was unwanted, losing a child hurt a piece of your heart in a way that never fully healed.

"It's okay. As her parents we were relieved, for a while. I hurt for her, of course, but I thought she'd get her life back." Nora smiled through tight lips. "She eventually went to college, but she was never the same. She never danced. And when she got married, I thought again that she'd finally be alright. But she and her husband struggled to have kids for three years with no success. They divorced this year. For more reasons than that but it played a part."

"Nora, I'm so sorry." Jenny leaned closer as a tear spilled over her lashes.

Nora put a hand to her forehead trying to regain her control. "It's okay. And it's not Eddie's fault but I don't think Sarah will ever be the same and Frank blames himself. Well, outwardly he blames Eddie. As soon as he heard Eddie was coming to town it's been constant talk about Eddie's mistakes, how Eddie should be feeling the same pain as Sarah. But I know him. He cries at his desk when he thinks no one is looking. I think part of him wishes he'd let them stay together. That maybe then things might have been different. Just don't expect him to ever tell Eddie that."

"I wouldn't." Jenny sympathized. "How does he deal with all of that."

"Not well." Nora gave a weak laugh and pinched some of her breadcrumbs together. "That's why we were at the show. He gave us tickets and I thought Frank should go and try to get some closure."

"Eddie gave you tickets?"

"Yeah," Nora said thoughtfully. "I don't think we would have gone otherwise. They came in the mail."

"Do you still have the package?" Jenny asked. It was as close to a paper trail as she'd seen so far but Nora shook her head.

"No. It was a plain envelope. Not even a return address, which is understandable since it looks like he lives in a bus. I think Frank tried to return them after they got to town. He still had the tickets when he came back and said he'd changed his mind, that he would go."

"Frank went to visit Eddie?"

"Yes. He said he stopped by after work. The theater is right there by the bank you know. I thought it was a good thing. That they were working things out. Then this . . . I never dreamed he'd do something like this."

Jenny wasn't sure if she meant Eddie or Frank, but Cherry reappeared and Jenny thanked Nora for her time.

"Nora?" Cherry asked. "Do you have pool

chemicals stored around here?"

She looked up surprised. "Yes, everything but the chlorine. We usually have a supply of all of it for the pool."

"What happened to the chlorine?" Jenny asked.

Nora pulsed a confused frown on her lips and shook her head. "I don't know. It went missing a few days ago."

13

D r. Butler stood outside the police station talking to a camera crew as Cherry pulled into the parking lot.

Lissa leaned forward from the backseat, her blonde curls in her fist to protect them from the wind while they drove. "Why are there camera men out there?"

"I don't know. Eddie said he wasn't going to have them come." Jenny also heard Krista contradict Eddie but it hadn't meant much until the cameras were right there in front of them. "I'll go find out."

"Go get 'em, Jenny!" Cherry called, lifting herself up on the side of the car door.

Both Dr. Butler and the camera crew turned her direction at Cherry's shout. Jenny chuckled to herself. Cherry did many things naturally well but socially discreet wasn't one of them.

By the time Jenny reached the front doors Dr. Butler had gone inside and the camera crew was talking amongst themselves.

"— one camera and one reporter inside." A man

said like they were checking off a list.

"Then what am I supposed to do?" A guy holding a sound mic asked and the other one shrugged.

Jenny walked right into their circle. "Good afternoon. Who gave you permission to be here today?"

The first of the group looked her over. Dressed in slacks and a button up shirt she was likely the reporter. "We don't need permission to be on public property."

"But I'm pretty sure you do to film private medical interviews." Jenny pointed out.

The three of them looked at each other and then recognition lit the reporter's eyes. "Oh, right, we were just talking with Greg. He was very helpful, but we aren't here for the medical part."

Jenny smiled politely. "The entire thing is medical."

The three exchanged confused glances and a slow shake of their heads. "I thought we were shooting a new hypnosis technique. Is that what you're here for? Are you one of the Great Eduardo's clients?"

"No." Jenny didn't elaborate as Lissa and Cherry joined them. "Did you speak with Eddie or Officer Wilkins?"

"Neither," the reporter said, tapping her fingers thinking. "A lady called us. Her name was . . . Finley, no, Finsta . . ."

"Finkle," the guy with the camera said.

"Finkle?" Cherry repeated the name in question.

"That's right, Krista Finkle." The reporter nodded in agreement.

Krista Finkle. Jenny thought about Rachelle's comment that Eddie's nature attracted gold diggers. Jenny didn't know Krista well but if fame and fortune was her goal, she fit the bill. Probably more than Sarah Mullins did.

"Yeah, she works with Eddie, I guess, and thought this would be an interesting segment for us. Since the technique is so new."

"I'm sure she did." Jenny agreed as Krista appeared on the other side of the parking lot in full sequined costume.

"He's happy to help," Krista said, swiveling so her sequins flashed under the artificial lights.

"You don't think Eddie did this himself, do you?" Lissa whispered. "Just so he could magically undo it all on live TV and save us?"

Behind them Wilkins narrowed his eyes, "I hope not but either way he's our main shot at clearing this up."

"That doesn't bode well." Cherry muttered.

Jenny rolled a miniature spool of thread between her fingers.

The reporter had set Krista up in the police station lobby, shuffling everyone else, anywhere else.

Jenny, Cherry and Lissa watched from the door to the main area of the police station. Where they were waiting for Lissa to see Dr. Butler. He was currently with Tommy, but they'd been told he'd be ready soon. So, Jenny watched the door to Dr. Butler's temporary clinic as closely as she watched Krista's interview.

Eddie was nowhere to be seen.

The door to Dr. Butler's makeshift office opened and Tommy exited, followed by the doctor.

"Are you next?" He said gesturing to Lissa.

Jenny followed Lissa and the doctor into the room. It was all gray and empty. Jenny laughed, "This is worse than a doctor's office."

Dr. Butler looked around. "Well, I hope so. Are you saying my office is boring?"

"Stark might be a better word." Jenny slid her chair closer to Lissa's, taking her hand.

The doctor hesitated, "Did you want to wait outside Jenny? We'll only be a minute."

"Oh," Jenny hadn't considered not being there. "I guess, Lissa did you want me to go?"

Lissa's brow sunk low over wide eyes. "No, please stay. I don't want to be alone."

Jenny relaxed. "I'll stay. I'm right here."

The doctor grabbed a clipboard and replaced a sheet of paper on it. "That's fine. I just wanted to be sure."

"Okay ladies, as you know our intent today is to do a simple health evaluation and give Mr. Paris a clean starting point for his, um, hypnosis therapy." He cleared his throat and Jenny could see his discomfort. "After the checkup we have a simple medication Mr. Paris requested for you."

"What medication?" Jenny asked.

Chain Piecing a Mystery

The doctor glanced up, one eyebrow raised as if surprised he was being questioned. "It's a simple muscle relaxer. Nothing dangerous. We'll do that at the end of the checkup as long as Ms. Fisher passes with a clean bill of health."

He shuffled a few things in his bag and pulled out a rubber mallet and small metal flashlight. "If you don't mind sitting on the table for a moment I'm going to start with your reflexes."

He went through the standard procedure, checking her temperature, balance, and various cognitive responses. Finally, he set the list down and opened a small, insulated tote. "Alright Ms. Fisher, we've only got to give a shot and rebandage your hand and you're one step closer to the camera crew out there."

Lissa smiled wanly. "Maybe we could hang out a little longer."

"I'm impressed," Dr. Butler said as he filled a syringe with the medicine he'd taken from the insulated bag. "I rarely have people ask to stay while I'm prepping a needle for them."

"They don't bother me." Lissa's lips turned up in a half smile.

Dr. Butler pulled her hair back. The red spot Lissa had mentioned earlier was still there. The doctor must have noticed Jenny noticing because he ran a finger over it, stretching the skin around it till it whitened slightly and released it.

"Hmm, that's an interesting spot," he said. "Did you get a bug bite?"

Lissa looked away. "A bug bite, yeah."

Dr. Butler glanced at Jenny as if questioning her. She shrugged and bit her lip. "It looks normal enough, but I saw a similar one on Tommy. That's my only concern. I haven't seen Frank close enough to know."

Dr. Butler nodded. "I'll check Frank when he comes in but I'm guessing it's coincidence. Besides," Dr. Butler cleared his throat. "With Tommy, well, when you have as much acne as that young man it's not so unusual that he's got a bump on his neck."

Jenny chuckled softly, "I suppose so. You're not worried then."

"No," he said wiping the skin down near Lissa's bug bite and giving her the prepared shot. He put his things away and turned back with a handful of gauze and ointment. "It's interesting though that they've all been injured on the same hand. Don't you think?"

Jenny hadn't seen all of the victims close enough to know that. "They all hurt their right hand?"

Dr. Butler paused his brow furrowing briefly before he nodded and took Lissa's injured hand. "Yes. Different injuries but all in the same place."

Unwrapping it slowly he pinched the wound together. The slice that split her palm was at least three inches long and the sight of it turned Jenny's stomach. Healing would be slow for a wound that size.

"We're about done ladies." Dr. Butler looked up. "I'll need to reset some of my things. Would you mind checking to see if Frank is here? I'm on a bit of a timetable. You know, appointments back at the office." He smiled, and with a nod from Lissa, Jenny stepped outside.

Tommy was the only one in the folding chairs by the door. His hand was wrapped in a clean white bandage covering a chemical burn, clear up to his wrist, on the *right hand*.

"Tommy did you know the Mullins?" Jenny asked thinking about their missing chlorine while she scanned the rest of the office.

She could hear Eddie's voice in the lobby and wondered if the camera crew had waylaid Frank.

Tommy gave her a lazy glance. "Sure. I worked for them too. I cleaned their pool."

Jenny paused her search focusing on Tommy. "You didn't ever take chemicals home, did you?"

"No. I don't think so." He looked confused.

Jenny shot him a hard look. "You don't know?"

Dr. Butler opened his door as Tommy tried to explain. Lissa took a seat in one of the empty chairs.

"I thought you were looking for Mr. Mullins," Dr. Butler said looking between her and Tommy.

"Yes," she said flustered. She looked at Tommy hoping she'd get a chance to talk to him longer. "I'll be right back. Frank's probably in the lobby."

Jenny left them in a hurry, opening the lobby door to chaos.

The news crew was packing bags and dismantling lights, people rushed back and forth, they all seemed to be working their way to the door.

Officer Gibson spoke quietly into the phone at the front desk, his hand up as if hiding the conversation.

"—called it in. Yes, sir. Noted. I'll tell the Chief."

"Hurry," the reporter said to her camera man. "I don't want to miss this—"

Even Cherry seemed involved. Gripping Wilkins by the elbow she spoke furiously at him. He pointed to a chair and left.

Jenny elbowed her way across the tiny room to Cherry. "What's going on?"

"How would I know," Cherry huffed dropping into a chair. She shoved a backpack to the side and a cameraman picked it up as he shot out the front door.

Cherry glared at the man. "There was some kind of alert on the police radio. Then I got a phone call from MSQC's management. I told Tyler about it, and he freaked out, telling me to stay here. Of course, everyone else is headed to follow him."

"What did Missouri Star want?" Jenny asked, she pulled her phone out but there were no messages for her.

"There's an emergency meeting. Apparently, there's some kind of internet trouble and they're gonna be changing the schedule. Then they're worried about what happened downtown too. It's all fixing and damage control. Which Wilkins could clear up that last part for me, but I'm not wearing the right uniform for him to tell me. Never mind that I'm being briefed on it in a few minutes."

Jenny grabbed Cherry's arm. "Let's go."

"What do you mean?" Cherry followed Jenny looking behind her as if the hated chair was now her safety net.

She tapped out a message to Lissa and jumped in Cherry's convertible as the last news crew vehicle left.

Cherry slid in. "Are you sure?"

"Yes, drive!" Jenny insisted. "Don't lose them."

"Okay," Cherry said. And peeled out of the parking lot.

Jenny and Cherry slunk low in the seats of the conspicuous red convertible. Neither woman said anything for a moment, ready to duck should Wilkins or Dunn appear.

Then Cherry leaned over. "What are they doing in there?"

The bank sat behind a handful of festival booths, set up to the side of the parking lot entrance. The lights of the police cars parked in the road alternately casting white and red light across the whole scene.

Tourists and booth owners gathered in the street with a few members of the bank staff. An air of anxiety-rattled among the small crowd.

"Something happened," Jenny said watching the camera crew from the police station unload on the sidewalk. The reporter hovered near the front door. "What do you want to bet it has to do with Eddie and a murder confession?"

"I think you'd win that bet," Cherry said softly.

Jenny clicked her seat belt free of its latch and got

out of the car. "I'll be right back. I'm gonna go see what I can find out."

"Jenny," Cherry snapped, leaning after her friend. "Jenny, I do not want to bail you out of jail tonight." Cherry shook a finger at Jenny while she closed the door. "I will. But Jenny, I don't want to!"

"Thanks," Jenny grinned.

"You are a bystander," Cherry hissed. "Remember that. Jenny?" She leaned so far past the door that she looked ready to tumble out of the car.

"I'll be right back." Jenny insisted and plunged into the crowd.

All around her people were asking questions. "What happened?" "Are we shutting down our booths?" "Why are the police here?" There were answers floating around as well, but they felt like rumors, and nothing seemed to reassure anyone. "It's only a precaution." "They're going to reimburse us." "It's a publicity stunt."

The questions didn't stop and neither did Jenny. She wove her way across the street.

"Is Eduardo safe? Stop the killers!" A dark haired woman stood alone, calling constant commentary to the officials around the building. "Did the murderers try again?"

Jenny almost passed her by, but the last question caught her attention. What did she know about murderers. Did she know about the confessions or was it coincidence?

She waved a neon green rope in the air. It looked like one of Eddie's. "Who tried to kill the Great Eduardo!"

When she turned Jenny spotted the scar across her cheekbone. She was the woman who'd led the super fans at Eddie's show the night before. The Parisians.

Her accusations earned her several wary glances from bystanders and caught the attention of one of the police officers. He zeroed in on the woman and started moving toward her. "There are killers on the loose. Protect Eduardo!"

The comments made Jenny sick. Lissa and the others had only come forward that morning. How could anyone know about it already?

Ducking through the crowd Jenny pushed faster, emerging at the front of the bank. Trying to look casual she stepped up onto the sidewalk and moved toward the entrance.

Then Officer Dunn walked out.

Jenny panicked.

She took several hurried steps around the corner of the building, hoping the officer wouldn't notice her. Hiding from her favorite police officers wasn't one of her preferred activities, but desperate times called for desperate measures. While Officer Wilkins hadn't expressly told her to stay away, she knew he wouldn't be fond of her snooping around the crime scene.

She retracted the thought as she circled to the back of the building. This wasn't snooping. She was *observing situations* . . . that were occasionally dangerous.

All the excitement happening at the front of the building had kept the other observers corralled. The back parking lot deserted. She glanced around and walked over to the employee entrance. It was always locked, but Jenny gave the door a quick test pull anyway. No luck.

She had just about convinced herself that she could pull off an emergency call from the bank president when the door opened. Elsie Emerson pushed through, letting out a gasp of surprise when she saw Jenny.

"Oh, I didn't know anyone was out here." She glanced around as if worried she'd be caught.

"It's just me." Jenny moved closer, gripping the door for her.

"Okay," Elsie nodded and leaned back against the door. "I needed some air."

She closed her eyes. Objectively, her friend was as put together as ever. Elsie had pinned her gray hair back in a twenties-style wave over her forehead, her dark green blouse buttoned primly.

"What's going on in there? You look terrible." Jenny asked, holding the door open.

"Frank, um, Mr. Mullins . . ." Elsie looked at her and paused taking a slow, weighted breath. Then closed her eyes again. "Goodness, people aren't supposed to die like that."

14

Frank was dead? Jenny didn't know what to say. She wanted to run and hug Nora. She wanted to bundle Lissa up and keep her safe from all the danger.

She also wanted to charge inside and prove that Frank's death had nothing to do with the confessions or hypnosis. If it was isolated then Lissa wasn't at any more risk than before.

She hated to think it after her conversation with Nora, but Frank had one of the strongest motives against Eddie and now he was gone. If Frank was the one responsible, maybe it was all over.

"Does Nora know?" Jenny asked. Her mind spun.

Elsie sniffled watching the doorway. "She does. I called her after I called the police."

"You called them?" Jenny's eyes widened. "Did you find him?"

She whimpered a yes, and Jenny could have kicked herself for being so insensitive. She closed up her box of questions, refocusing on Elsie.

"Oh, that's terrible," Jenny said, wrapping her in a hug.

"I've never seen a dead body, outside a funeral home." Elsie's chin trembled against Jenny's shoulder, and she squeezed tighter before letting Elsie go. "I should know it never happens as neatly as that... but Mr. Mullins . . . Oh." Her hand came up, hovering against her throat and over the sides of her neck. "He had burns from the rope and . . ."

Jenny put a hand on Elsie's shoulder stopping her. "He was a good man."

"He was a good man. And usually so dependable." She chuckled behind downturned lips. The memory stirred in her eyes. "That's why it's strange, I guess."

Jenny waited, breaking the silence, after Elsie stopped talking. "What's strange?"

Elsie pinched her lips tight. "For starters, Frank didn't come in until one thirty today, that's after lunch. He had a long meeting with Ms. Harris and then he came out and told me to cancel all his meetings. Me!" Elsie sounded more shocked still, but her expression had shifted to worry, her eyebrows furrowed so tightly they almost touched. "He'd been missing all morning. But here's the really strange part. He only worked till about three and when everyone else was getting ready to leave and then he told me he had one more meeting."

Jenny waited for Elsie to continue surprised to find that was the end of her story.

"If he'd missed the whole morning, is it really that strange?" Jenny asked.

"Of course, it is." Elsie made a face at Jenny, her lips puckered downward and her eyes hooded with pinched brows. "That's why it's so strange. I didn't know about any other meetings. Nothing was scheduled. And Frank never stays late."

The change really seemed to bother Elsie. Jenny patted her hand and tried to offer some comfort. "Is it possible someone called him last minute?"

"Frank didn't schedule anything without telling me or Nora. The man wouldn't remember his own name if it wasn't printed on his desk." Elsie was completely serious.

And Jenny had to work to stifle her grin. "That is odd. Maybe the police will be able to find out who it was and solve this."

The comment seemed to revive Elsie's nerves. She glanced at the open doorway.

"Do you need to get back?" Jenny asked.

Elsie sighed. "I'm sure I do. I told the officer who was with me that I needed to *powder my nose*." Elsie raised an eyebrow at Jenny as if they should have known better.

Jenny chuckled, "You're a smart woman."

"Thank you." Elsie gripped Jenny's arm tightly. She stared at the doorway and didn't move.

Jenny hesitated, worried this was a completely selfish thought but when Elsie had watched the door for almost thirty seconds Jenny prodded her.

"Do you want me to come with you?" Jenny asked. "You don't have to do this alone."

"Would you?" Elsie jumped at the idea and Jenny relaxed. "I would really appreciate it."

"Anything you need," Jenny said following the older woman into the bank.

The room smelled like flowers and furniture polish. Old leather chairs lined the walls and crime scene tape spanned an area around the bank vault. A handful of people spoke rapidly, back and forth including the police chief and Officer Wilkins.

Jenny stayed close to Elsie.

A female police officer stood near a floral couch. "Ms. Emerson? We need —" she hesitated seeing Jenny. "Do you work here?"

"Officer Morgan." Elsie addressed the woman, while firmly gripping Jenny's arm. "This is my friend Jenny. I've asked her to stay with me. Is that a problem?"

"Uh, no," Officer Morgan said looking around nervously. "No, that's fine. Can we continue?"

The officer tapped a device and looked up. "As a reminder, we're recording this. Can you please state your name?"

Elsie nodded, "I'm Elizabeth Emerson, but you can call me Elsie."

"And I'm officer Jillian Morgan assisting Officer Wilkins on this case regarding Franklin Mullins. This is the second half of your interview."

Elsie gripped Jenny's arm, like the room might engulf her in its floral scents, swallowing her entirely, if she let go. "Ms. Emerson, we left off before you returned to the bank."

"Honey," Elsie gave a short, sad laugh. "I babysat you when you were spitting up strained peas on your mama. You kept my grandson out of prison. You can call me Elsie."

The officer's mouth lifted, almost into a smile. Almost. "Thank you, Elsie," she said. "What time did you return?"

Elsie paused, "It would have been before four, maybe three forty-five? Three fifty. Ms. Harris, she's the bank manager. She let everyone off around three for the festival weekend. Well, Frank was meeting with Mr. Bolding after hours, so I tried to give him plenty of time before I came back to check on him."

"I thought Frank met with Harry yesterday?" Jenny asked. Cherry had told her that Marcy was dropping something off for Harry not that Harry had come himself. The interruption earned her a sharp look from Officer Morgan.

"Oh, he did. This was a follow up. I guess the meeting yesterday didn't go well. Something wasn't working with the loan. It's the first time I didn't stay to help Frank close up in the thirty years we worked together. But after the way Mr. Bolding treated me, I didn't even offer."

Elsie's breath shuddered and Officer Morgan waited a moment to let her relax before prodding her on. "And how long was it after you came in, before you realized Mr. Mullins had been killed?"

Elsie shot a nervous glance at Jenny, her grip twitching on Jenny's arm. "I'm not sure. I didn't notice right away. There was no one here. I went into Frank's office and pulled his schedule, then I closed up his things, and that's when I realized the vault was cracked open. That was very strange. We don't leave the vault open after close, we just don't."

"And you reported him at four?" Officer Morgan asked looking over her notes.

"Yes, well, it takes time to close out the books and I–I waited until I came back to close out the day. So, I didn't miss anything." Elsie said.

Officer Morgan gave a slow nod and wrote a few notes in her book. "Did you and Mr. Mullins get along well?"

"Oh, sure. We were friends." She paused, shooting another nervous glance at Jenny. "As much as you can be friends with someone who works over you."

Officer Morgan made some notes as Officer Wilkins walked toward them, stopping next to their couch. "Can I speak with Mrs. Doan?"

"Of course." Officer Morgan said, gesturing to Jenny.

Elsie looked nervous but Jenny patted her hand and stood. "It's alright, I'll be back."

Officer Wilkins moved them over to the wall. "What are you doing in my crime scene?"

Jenny tried to look completely innocent. "I was being emotional support for a friend."

The officer tensed his jaw and waited.

"What? I don't have another answer. Did I want to know what happened? Absolutely, but Elsie came out of the bank having a hard time and I came in with her. That's the only reason I'm here and I've been sitting there the whole time."

"You haven't interfered with her testimony?" Wilkins asked.

"No."

"When I listen back to Officer Morgan's recording, I won't hear Elsie talking to you, or answering your questions, or comments? Nothing?"

Jenny hesitated, "Well, maybe once or twice."

Wilkins crossed his arms and his brows lowered. She could feel the reprimand without a single word.

"It was helpful." She said in her own defense.

The officer didn't seem pleased. "Jenny," he said. "Stay right here. Please."

She opened her mouth to respond and then closed it. A frown tugged at her lips. "You don't want me to leave?"

"I want you to stay right here, where I can see you. Don't go running off. Don't go start your own investigation. Don't speak to anyone." He pointed at the ground. "Do you understand."

It felt like a trojan horse but she couldn't turn the gift away. "Yes."

Officer Wilkins nodded as he turned, and Jenny could have sworn she saw a grin.

Was he laughing at her, or helping her? She watched him go and looked around. Directly across from her was the vault. It stood with the door fully open. It wasn't a terribly unusual sight, it often sat completely open during the day, reminiscent of vintage banking.

The floor is what surprised her. A red spiral, every bit as large as the one on Eddie's set, was painted on the marble floor.

"Terrible isn't it?" Ms. Harris said leaning up against the wall next to Jenny. "Poor Elsie looks terrified."

Jenny hardly had to look to know it was her. The scratch of her voice was familiar. She often stood in on the drive thru window, when her employees were sick or needed time off and Jenny knew her well.

"It hasn't been too bad. I wish she could relax," Jenny said simply.

"Elsie doesn't relax." Ms. Harris scoffed, "She's as bad as I am. Don't get me wrong, it's great for an employee. But as a person, well sometimes I worry about her."

"She seemed excited about getting off early for the festival," Jenny said.

Ms. Harris' sandpapery laugh scratched across her throat. "She loves to get out early. She usually leaves at close to go see her family. I think she was expecting one of them to meet her today though. A grandson or a nephew or something."

"She didn't mention meeting anyone?" Jenny watched her friend nervously shifting in her chair. Was it a misstep or had Elsie lied. "You didn't see who she was meeting?"

"Nah, I left at three with the rest of the staff. Elsie had the keys. What a day for closing duty though." She shook her head and nodded toward an empty desk outside an office with more than a few police officers looking it over. "That's the last place I saw her. Sitting at her desk with Frank's books. It seems terribly convenient that the internet is down today. No Bluetooth, no security system . . . Oh shoot." Ms. Harris walked away before Jenny could see what she had noticed.

Chief Cox had sent several pairs of officers into Frank's neighboring offices and Ms. Harris was across the room in seconds.

Jenny glanced back at Elsie and Officer Morgan, then again at Elsie's desk. Frank's office had emptied slightly as the police moved to neighboring offices and Ms. Harris mediated the searches.

Jenny casually walked past the busy door of Mr. Mullins' office and sat at Elsie's desk. She swiveled in the chair and looked around to see if anyone was watching. No one appeared to be paying any attention. Wilkins had entered the vault and not even Elsie had seen him.

The large wooden desk was as clean and precise as Elsie's appearance. Not a thing out of place. She slid the roller chair back, looking underneath.

Jenny pulled herself back up to the desk and opened the main drawer. Sitting on top was a note. *Thomas – 3:30* Jenny snapped a picture and closed the drawer. Officer Wilkins reappeared, and Jenny swiveled in the chair. He narrowed his eyes at her and pointed to where he'd left her. Then he returned to the scene.

If that was all the trouble, she was going to be in Jenny wasn't too worried.

She got up and worked her way across the room to the vault door, peeking around the corner. Frank lay face down in the center of the spiral.

Cameras clicked and people with gloves and evidence bags knelt over his body. Neon green and yellow rope snaked from Franks neck to the corner where it twisted into a beautiful little coil.

It was so tidy.

Jenny couldn't stop looking. From his pale skin to the marks on his unbandaged hand. She knew the police had wrapped the injuries. Whoever had done this had wanted people to know that he had tried this before.

Jenny thought about the woman outside. Yelling about the killers on the loose. She almost turned to look for her. It was so strange that she would know about the confessions. Those details weren't public knowledge. Not yet anyway.

A stretcher creaked behind her and Jenny stepped away, turning toward the wall. She found herself staring at a list of bank officers as the paramedics loaded and wheeled Frank's body out. Jenny turned in time to see him go. His head was tipped and she couldn't be sure, but it looked like he also had a red bite on the lower side of his neck.

Jenny turned back to the vault even without the body, a crime scene always had more to offer and she wasn't ready to give it up yet.

"Hello, Hamilton Police Department and the venerable Chief Cox." Eddie's voice boomed through the lobby as he strode across the room. He was dressed for his television debut in a shimmering purple lamé blouse and latex slim leather pants.

Stumbling to a stop in front of the vault, Jenny

could almost see him processing. He took in the spiral on the floor for only a second before he pushed his smile back across his lips and held up his hands.

"Chief Cox, I hope you're ready, because . . ."

The room had gone silent, every ear leaned toward him waiting to hear what the showman had to say.

Eddie milked it every moment.

He did a slow turn, looking around the room before he dropped his bomb.

"I know who our culprit is."

15

"Who let this guy in here?" Chief Cox called. "Get him out! Now!"

The shout was like a clap of thunder across the bank. Officers scattered and bank employees shrunk. Jenny tried unsuccessfully to blend in.

"No! Wait." Eddie's hands dropped from ring master to beggar as he turned to face the police chief. "I know. I really do. Hear me out."

Eddie's eyes were wide as Officer Wilkins grabbed him by the collar. Officer Dunn ran up to help as Chief Cox put a hand up stopping the pair.

"What do you know?" Chief Cox leveled a hard glare on Eddie.

Chief Cox was shorter than Jenny by a solid foot, but as she'd just seen, his presence commanded the entire room.

Jenny inched closer, how could Eddie know who had killed Frank. She was still figuring out who had it out for Eddie. But since Eddie was Eddie . . . he probably already knew that.

"I'll show you," Eddie said his hands doing a mystical wave in front of him. "I'll unravel a mystery like you've never —"

"Forget it," Chief Cox said, gesturing to Dunn. "Go put this guy in holding for disrupting a police investigation."

"It was Mr. Mullins, Frank! It was Frank!" Eddie shouted pulling his hands away and trying to slip himself out of the officers' hands.

The room seemed to pause again, and then it burst into laughter.

Chief Cox looked him up and down, "You think Frank hypnotized himself and those two kids so he could then kill himself?" He laughed and walked away. "Forget it. I don't even want him in my station. He belongs in the looney bin. Wilkins, Dunn, Get him out of here."

"No. Listen to me," Eddie shouted. "I swear it makes sense. He must have made a deal with someone to hypnotize the others. So, no one would suspect him. Then he would either ruin me or kill me." Eddie paused to see if anyone was still with him.

"It doesn't fit Eddie. Why not kill you the first night. He could have even had one of the others kill you before confessing." Officer Morgan spoke up from the couch. She talked like she knew him and Jenny realized there were probably many of the officers that had grown up with him.

Eddie jumped on her question. "Because! Benji ticked off that finance guy! Frank was supposed to kill me the first night but instead, someone was already there sabotaging my tour bus. So, he couldn't do it."

Jenny considered that. Eddie might have hit on something there. Whoever vandalized that bus could have saved Eddie's life.

"That doesn't explain who killed him today," Officer Dunn said.

"Ah I'm glad you asked." Eddie smiled waving his hands in an arc and lowering them quickly when the chief glared. "Like I said, he made a deal with someone to hypnotize the others. What happens when they start looking for the guy who did this? They don't find Frank. They find the guy who did it. All you have to do is trace the drugs."

"Frank was strangled." Chief Cox complained. "This is a waste of time."

Eddie started talking faster. "Whoever did the hypnosis job was an amateur, right? They would have had to use drugs to make the victims susceptible to the mind control."

The phrasing made Jenny uncomfortable. Even Eddie had planned to use a muscle relaxer on the trio of suspects before his hypnosis session. Is this really what they needed?

"We just have to find the drug theft. Has anyone reported a robbery of narcotics or opioids?" Eddie looked around his eyes bright, even excited, until no one responded as he expected. "Not just the clinics, homes? Nursing homes? You could use memory drugs, dementia!" He got quite a few raised eyebrows but no help.

Until Dunn raised a hand. "Didn't the doctor's office report a break in? I don't know if they were narcotics, but something happened at the clinic."

"That was this morning." The chief shook his head, "too recent. Get him out of here." He paused as he caught sight of Jenny half hiding behind the vault door. "Her too. Get these civilians out of my crime scene. The place is over run."

Wilkins turned to Jenny apologetically. "I told you to stay put," he muttered and gestured toward the door. Officer Dunn and Wilkins together escorted Eddie to the door while he flailed.

"Please, wait! Don't throw me out! I'll go!" He was begging and considering his reputation Jenny could understand. It wouldn't go well to see him tossed out on his chin.

Finally, the officers released him and Eddie scrambled to an independently upright position. "Thank you." He said and turned to the door. "Think about what I said. It makes sense."

Wilkins sighed. "Who's the hypnotist?"

"Excuse me?" Eddie asked.

"You're theory. It hinges on the fact that there's an amateur hypnotist. Well, who is it? Anyone that works for you?"

Eddie flinched, "Everyone that works for me is a hypnotist, but they wouldn't do that. And none are amateur enough to use identical and common trigger words. Are you telling me there's no one in this town that knows Frank and has been curious about hypnosis?"

Wilkins and Dunn looked at each other. "Not so

far."

"Well, you're wrong," Eddie said and grabbed the door handle, letting himself out.

"He's wrong too," Jenny said as the door shut. "Benji has said multiple times that he wants what Eddie has and I'm pretty sure Krista is cheating on Eddie with Benji. The pair of them would do very well if Eddie just disappeared."

Officer Wilkins opened the door for her. "Thank you for your input. And stay out of this Jenny. I know you like to solve problems, but someone died. There is a killer out there, maybe more than one, it's not safe. Please go home and sew your quilts."

"You let me stay in there and watch five minutes ago," Jenny said acknowledging his request and not actually agreeing to anything. It was clear enough that this wasn't safe, but it wasn't safe for Lissa either and Lissa didn't get a choice.

"Which I already regret. Don't make me regret any more decisions."

The door shut between them and Jenny did a quick search of the street. Cherry's car was still there. Beside her Eddie was being ushered away behind Officer Finnegan's bulky frame.

Jenny tried to see what had happened and Eddie was moving again. He looked over his shoulder and Jenny caught the curled graying hair of Nora, Frank's wife, no . . . Frank's *widow*, as she moved behind the building with their daughter, Sarah.

The girl Eddie had once loved.

He watched her leave and probably would have kept watching except that Officer Finnegan said something and started pulling him along.

Jenny managed to cross the sea of onlookers to Cherry. She hadn't moved except to grip the steering wheel while she waited. "Where have you been?"

"Do I really need to answer that?" Jenny asked, climbing in the front seat.

Behind her a woman's voice yelled, "Where are the rest of them?" Waving her hands in the air in the center of the crowd the woman looked incensed. "They tried to kill the Great Eduardo. Police! Where are the rest of them?"

Officer Dunn appeared in the doorway and the woman yelled louder. The crowd seemed more confused by her than supportive, thank goodness.

They separated around her like a broken zipper.

"Good riddance to killers! Stop the injustice," she waved her fist tangling the rope around her arm like it was a trophy.

"Good riddance to—killers?" Cherry whispered the words in disbelief, "She's not talking about what I think she's talking about, is she?"

Jenny fumed at the woman's angry chant. "I think she means Frank, Tommy, and Lissa. But how does she know about them?"

Cherry's face fell. "Eddie."

Jenny shot her a look. "You think Eddie told her?"

Cherry pursed her lips. "Not her specifically. But he's posted about what happened on his social media. Inviting people to 'tune in' to see him heal them."

"You're kidding." Jenny's chest crackled with

frustration like her whole body was splitting it's seams. She had to keep it together. "He's going to incite a riot without even knowing."

As Eddie disappeared the woman slowed her calls. "Save Eduardo, lock them up!"

She didn't stop until Officer Dunn pulled out his handcuffs.

Then she ran.

"Cherry? Let's go home . . . that way." Jenny pointed to where the woman was climbing into a small silver vehicle.

"You want me to follow her?" Cherry asked, pulling the car up behind her.

"Yeah, I want to see where she's staying. So, keep your distance, but—" Cherry drove straight through the intersection after the woman had turned right.

"Cherry! You lost her." Jenny stammered as they drove quickly away. "I'm sorry. Maybe I shouldn't have expected you to just do what I asked, but she's obsessed with Eddie Paris. She was chanting to lock up Lissa, Tommy, and Frank. But Frank's dead."

Jenny leaned back in her seat and put a hand to her forehead. "I'm sorry, I shouldn't keep asking you to rush into danger."

Cherry hadn't said that specifically, but it was the way things had gone multiple times. Jenny knew that. She needed to go home.

She'd be able to figure out where the woman was staying later. If she needed to at all.

The car veered right. Jenny opened her eyes and looked around as they pulled to a stop and Cherry turned right again. "What are you doing? Where are we?" Jenny didn't want to assume but it felt like—

"My car's pretty recognizable. I wanted to make sure we had enough room," Cherry said, patting the shiny red ledge of the window and Jenny had to agree. "I know what her car looks like. The boring little compact up there. Silver, the same as everyone else, except for her Florida plates."

"I'm so glad you're not upset!" Jenny's eyes were glued to the little car ahead of them. "And I'm so impressed with your driving! You're the best secret spy driver I know."

Cherry chuckled, "Thank you. It was fun to fly around a few corners. Just don't tell Wilkins. And it was very fun to have you apologize . . . repeatedly."

"I can't believe you." A bout of silent laughter filled Jenny with happy bubbles of relief.

They drove in silence as they watched the woman cruise past house after house. A truck pulled in between them before she turned into a parking area.

With a grin Cherry slowed the car and winked. "You should trust me."

In reality, Cherry was the person Jenny trusted the most, outside of Ron.

Trying to suppress the endorphin high she was riding, Jenny watched to see where the woman had gone. "Did she go into the Hotel Hamilton?"

She hoped so. The property was run by her good friend, Sierra Blueford, who also ran the quilt museum with her husband Mark. The single-story building was framed in a horseshoe shape, surrounding a large event center. It was far more impressive on the inside.

"I think so." Cherry slowed the car as they passed the parking lot.

Sure enough, the little silver car sat in front of one of the numbered suites. Cherry pulled up to the far end of the building. Mostly out of sight they hid behind the outer wall.

"I have an idea," Jenny said pulling her phone out. It took her a few tries before it would ring through. By the time it was ringing the woman they'd been following had reappeared, a purse swung over her shoulder.

"We're going to lose her." Cherry hissed, watching the woman get in her car. She'd changed into the spangled outfit from the previous night.

"Jenny! How are you doing?" Sierra sounded every bit her usual cheerful self.

"I'm great! I was going to see if you had any guests in town that might like a visit. It's Birthday Bash for one more day." Jenny hoped it would be that easy. She'd come before to say hello to the Blueford's guests, and since most of them were quilters, it was always a fun time.

Sierra was more than happy to have them and Jenny gave Cherry a thumbs up. Cherry scoffed from the driver's seat and pointed down the road as the silver car drove away, with their suspect inside.

Cherry raised her eyebrows at Jenny as if to say, "now what?"

Jenny turned her attention back to the phone call, "Well, Cherry and I are outside, if this is a good time."

A curtain moved in the hotel office window.

Jenny got out of the car gesturing for Cherry to do the same.

"No, this is perfect. I'll be right out." Sierra hung up and Jenny put her phone away.

A long sidewalk ran under an awning in front of the hotel rooms. Jenny walked along as Sierra came to meet them.

Each room had outdoor access, and someone had walked along this path before them plugging hot pink business cards between the door and the frame of every room. Jenny paused outside the room the woman had gone in and checked the doorknob, just in case. Locked.

Leaning against the frame Cherry held one of the business cards. "Parisian fan support? What do you think of this?"

Varying shades of hot pink ripples were painted across the background, reminiscent of Eddie's neon styling. In bold letters across the middle of the card it read Aria Case, President, Parisian Fan Support; first chapter.

On the following line was the title that caught Jenny's attention, Hypnotist. A pink spiral spread across the back of the card. Inside the spiral there was a QR code.

"Aria the hypnotist, huh?" Jenny snapped a picture of the card and slipped it into her pocket.

"And fan support," Cherry said perkily.

"How could I forget?" Jenny chuckled. "This could be our girl."

"Holy triangle quilts!" Sierra exclaimed when she reached them. Her shock made Jenny giggle.

Sierra's positive nature was so overwhelming even her surprise was uplifting. "I can't believe you came today! What about the quilt auction? Things have got to be crazy. Do you need anything?"

"What do you mean? The quilt auction doesn't start until seven . . ." Jenny gave Cherry a questioning look. "What's wrong with the quilt auction?"

Sierra's eyes grew wide. "You haven't heard?"

16

Sierra's surprise wasn't as entertaining when Jenny didn't understand it.

"No," Jenny glanced at Cherry. "I have no idea what you're talking about."

"One of the transformers is down north of town." Sierra watched her closely. Obviously waiting for a reaction. "Half of Hamilton is off-line."

Jenny's mouth formed a silent "O" as Sierra's concern clicked into place. "And half the quilt auction is online."

That's why the bank's security system had been down. She checked her phone. There was nothing from Ron and her text to Lissa hadn't gone through. A pinprick of worry stung her heart like pins in a pincushion, and she considered hopping right back in her car and going home.

Cherry was already on a call and Jenny would bet she was getting an earful about the internet situation.

Jenny shuddered to think of the work that could be lost and orders that would be messed up, mixed up, or lost if it wasn't fixed soon. But if Jenny knew her son, Al was probably out with a crew already taking care of things. If they would let him.

Sierra's surprise had turned to sympathy. "We're far enough out that I don't think the hotel will be affected, but I'm worried about the museum."

"Do you need to go? I understand if you do. We were checking on one of your guests." Jenny explained.

"Number twelve?" Sierra asked. The question was unexpected and she must have looked confused enough that Sierra pointed to the door beside them. "Your friend? Is this her room?"

The door had a large black number twelve on it. "Her room number," Jenny laughed. "Of course, it is. Yeah, we met . . . Aria this morning. Cherry lent her an, um . . ."

"Sunglasses. I loaned her my favorite pair." Cherry made sad eyes at Sierra and looked away. "She told me we could meet here but with the wifi issues I must have missed a text because it looks like she's gone."

"Oh, that's so sweet. Do you want to wait?" Sierra asked. "She gestured to the event center. You could go visit with our quilters till she gets back."

"No," Cherry rushed to cut Sierra off. "We've got to get back too. They're changing the schedule, I think, because of the internet issues." Cherry shook her head and gave Jenny a look of intensity Jenny could not interpret. She checked behind her, there was no ghost, police officer, or giant rotary cutter coming after them.

Jenny furrowed her brow at Cherry trying to silently ask what she needed.

"Oh, that's too bad." Sierra stepped in. "Does that mean you'll be back later? You're welcome anytime." Sierra's amiable personality always looked on the bright side.

Cherry cleared her throat and gave Jenny the same intense stare. Then mouthed "Help me."

Jenny jumped into action. "Of course, we'll be back but we really need to get those . . . sunglasses. Would you be able to let us in? She said she'd have them for us and if they're not there then, we'll leave. We've got to check."

"I'm really sorry," Sierra said. "I need to get to the museum."

"Are you sure? We won't bother anything." Jenny tried to reassure her, but Sierra bit her lip looking nervously at the door.

"Yeah. Those sunglasses are pretty important to me. They're special —"

"Prescription!" Jenny corrected, dropping a hand on Cherry's shoulder.

Cherry paused and glanced at Jenny then gave a helpless shrug. "They're a special prescription," she said. "I have really bad eyesight. And I lost—"

"Broke," Jenny cut in. "She broke her other pair."

Sierra pinballed between the two, working way too hard to follow the conversation.

Cherry frowned and turned back to Sierra heaving a frustrated breath. "I broke my only other pair."

"And she borrowed your prescription sunglasses?" a pucker formed between Sierra's eyebrows as she tried to understand.

"It's weird, right? I think she may have just been a fan." Jenny leaned in lowering her voice.

Cherry kicked her lightly and Jenny scooted away.

"Oh," Sierra looked like she finally understood.

"Yeah," Jenny agreed, shaking her head. "Anyway, she really needs them back. Could you let us in? Just to look around."

Sierra shuffled her keys in her hand and looked behind her. "Okay, hold on. You'll have to be quick. I have to go help Mark."

"Of course, we won't need long. Hopefully, she has them on the nightstand or something." Jenny breathed easier as Sierra pulled a large ring of keys from her pocket.

Flipping through the keys until she found number twelve's match. She stepped between them unlocking the door.

Sierra's phone rang as she pushed the door open. "Excuse me ladies, it's Mark, um, hold on."

Sierra stepped back onto the sidewalk the phone to her ear. "Hey, Mark. Is everything alright? I'm almost on my way?"

Jenny glanced at Cherry who raised an eyebrow and gestured into the room. Piles of props were everywhere. Striped buckets, an umbrella, a small pile of spheres that looked to be smoke bombs . . . and a collection of throwing knives.

A wave of worry washed over Jenny. One of these could be the knife that cut Lissa. Were they meant to finish her off for good?

Cherry picked up a piece of rope. "This is what she had at the bank," Cherry whispered, sending a chill from Jenny's heart to her toes. "And we just let her go."

"Don't touch it," Jenny said. "We need to make sure the police see it as it is."

Cherry dropped the rope as Sierra leaned her head in the door. "Is everything alright?"

Jenny forced herself to relax and waved. "We're fine. Still looking."

"Please hurry," Sierra said, pulling the phone back to her ear.

Jenny did a scan of the room "We should call the police."

Cherry nodded and pulled out a pair of sunglasses. "Oh, look! I found them." She gestured to the door. "Let's go."

Sierra locked the door behind them and turned to hurry away.

"Oh, goodness. Sierra!" Jenny called, pulling her friend back. "I left my purse inside. I'm so sorry."

Sierra sighed giving Jenny what looked like a forced smile. "It's fine." She started sorting the keys and her phone lit up again.

"Oh, pleats and pincushions." She muttered answering the phone. "Mark, yeah. Just a second." She held the phone away and turned to Jenny. "I've really got to go help with this. My oldest should be here any minute. If you want to go in and grab it You can return the keys to her when she gets back. Will that work?"

"Of course, I'm sorry to hold you up." Jenny took

the offered keys and Sierra dashed through the parking lot getting into her truck and pulling out before Jenny had made it back into Aria's room.

"That was slick," Cherry said following Jenny back in the dark room.

Jenny shoved the keys in her pocket. "I really left it. See," the object in question was resting on the table across the room.

Cherry made a face of resigned appreciation, her lips pressed together and her brows raised. "I didn't doubt it for a second."

"Why do you think she has all of this?" Jenny asked stepping over the piles of smoke bombs.

"She really wants to be the Great Eduardo?" Cherry suggested.

"The Great Aria doesn't work as well. Unless she wants to do musical hypnosis."

Moving around the desk Cherry paused. "That has potential. Maybe we could leave her a note."

The room grew quiet as the two women looked through the room.

"Jenny?" Cherry had leaned in the bathroom. "You need to come see this."

Jenny followed her into the tiny room taking in the scene. A dirty neon rope hung over the edge of the counter. Used it didn't look nearly as enticing as the ones in Eddie's show. It lay on top of several brightly colored scarves with dark stains but it was the knives she was sure Cherry had called her for.

Blood sat in the creases of the blade. They'd obviously been wiped with the scarves but they weren't clean.

Chain Piecing a Mystery

It was Cherry that had to smack her hand away this time. "Don't touch it."

The command was becoming a mantra.

Her hand fell and she looked closer at the knives. Sharp and thin they could easily cut through the skin of someone's hand, and as Lissa had imagined, into a man's back.

"Why would she do this?" Cherry asked. "She doesn't even know them."

Jenny let out a slow breath. "This doesn't mean she did it. It's just a lot of potential evidence."

"I'm calling the police." Cherry already had her phone out when the door handle cranked and Jenny heard Aria's voice as she came into the room.

In a silent motion Jenny closed the bathroom door and leaned against the wall.

Cherry's phone rang internally but in their hiding place it sounded like a trumpet call.

Jenny waved at Cherry to shut it off at the same time Cherry was fumbling to make the sounds go away.

"What do you need next?" Aria asked leading someone through the room.

"You know what I need." It was Krista's voice. Jenny shot a look at Cherry listening intently to the women.

Aria scoffed and there was some shuffling on the other side of the door.

"This is a crazy plan you know that? We should be moving on to the next town already." That was Aria. She was moving things around and Jenny wished she'd left the door cracked open.

"You and Benji should go on together if neither of you wants to be here."

"I thought she was a fan." Cherry whispered.

Jenny shrugged as confused by the conversation as Cherry was.

"I'm not interested in being with Benji."

Krista laughed, "You're missing out."

There was a scuffle and something crashed behind the sound of someone sucking in breath.

"You don't deserve him," Aria said. There was more scuffling and Aria started a monologue Jenny didn't fully comprehend.

It got quiet on the other side of the room and Jenny's mouth slowly opened as Cherry pulled out the pink business card. "She's a hypnotist." She mouthed pointing to the title under Aria's name.

Jenny listened harder.

"When I snap my fingers, you'll forget about the murder confessions and this publicity stunt. When I snap them a second time, you'll realize you're tired of Eddie and ready to move on. You won't want to come between me and Eddie when you do. When I snap a third time you'll stand up and leave."

There was an ominous silence on the other side of the door broken by a loud snap.

Nothing happened and Jenny waited feeling Cherry beside her. There was another loud snap.

One of the women in the main room was breathing heavier now. It was so quiet.

The final snap shocked Jenny and she jumped startling Cherry.

There was finally movement on the other side of

the door as someone, Jenny assumed it was Krista, stood. Cherry gripped Jenny's hand and Jenny squeezed back. Footsteps moved to the door and paused. The quiet dissolved into laughter as Krista thoroughly enjoyed her joke.

"Well, you're no Eddie Paris." She finally said still laughing. "Just so you know, it's not actually hypnosis if it's already true."

Aria swore and threw something at the wall. "Take what you came for. Get out."

"I plan to." She paused, "Cute purse by the way. It looks like Jenny's. Uh oh. Do we need to tell Eddie that you have a new person to super fan over?" Krista's laugh died as she left.

Jenny's throat was dry. Her purse. Aria moved to the kitchen area of the room on the other side of the door.

Jenny held her breath and Cherry squirmed. The pile of rope, knives, and scarves all fell to the ground and Cherry looked up fear in her eyes.

Jenny barely had time to think before the bathroom door swung open.

Aria stood on the other side still in her silver dress a huge smile on her face. "Jenny Doan. To what do I owe the pleasure?"

17

Strapped in a chair with a watch swinging in front of her face would've been more in line with Jenny's expectations than what Aria had done.

"Sorry about the mess," Aria said picking up the bloody knives and scarves. "I didn't know they hired celebrity housekeepers here."

Jenny laughed awkwardly and held up her hands. "Surprise. We're helping Sierra out of a jam."

"It's still strange." Aria paused shifting a pile of tumbled buckets. "I thought I asked for no housekeeping."

"Sorry," Cherry responded quickly, "I must have missed that. My fault. We'll get out of your way then."

"Oh, that does make more sense." Jenny raised an eyebrow at Cherry. Not moving toward the door at all. "What happened in the bathroom? That was a lot of blood."

"That? Nothing. I was practicing an act and flipped a knife wrong. Cut right through my leg. I don't think I'll ever get the hang of the knives. Unless Eddie can hypnotize me before I use them." Aria squinted at the wall as if considering that as a good solution.

"You were practicing an act? What exactly do you do? Do you have a show?"

"Me? No." Aria laughed and looked around. "I'm in love with Eddie Paris."

Jenny didn't know how to respond to that. "Really?"

Aria smiled. "What else. He needs me and I'm here. I'll do anything to keep him in my life."

"And all this is . . . memorabilia?" Cherry asked with a heavy dose of judgment behind her words. Jenny could hardly blame her but Aria didn't appreciate it.

"No. I follow the show. I'm their supply crew. And super fan. I help people get excited."

"You're the storage shed."

"No. Sort of." Aria frowned. "It wasn't always like this. I auditioned to be Eddie's assistant first. Benji was supposed to demonstrate an act with me." She turned and displayed the puckered lines of the scar on her face. "That's how I got this."

Cherry gasped. "Benji cut you in an act?"

"It was an accident and my fault. Benji threw the knife and I got nervous. I jumped, tipped the wheel, everything moved, and the blade caught me. I'm lucky I can still see."

"You're lucky to be alive." Cherry replied.

Aria nodded touching the scar almost reverently. "Eddie saved me. He was amazing. He used hypnosis to stop the pain and got me all fixed up. Then he helped me get over the fear that caused me to jump. Unfortunately, by the time I was feeling better he'd hired Krista. Then he married Krista."

Her gaze turned dark and her jaw shifted as her past pain came front and center.

"That's a rough deal," Jenny said starting Cherry toward the door. Dark Aria didn't feel safe. "I'm so sorry we bothered you."

"It's fine I wanted to come talk to you anyway." Aria pointed to the chairs she'd pulled out earlier.

Jenny held back. She didn't want to end up tied in place as the guinea pig of an amateur hypnotist.

"Sit." She insisted.

Jenny sat followed by Cherry.

"I need you to explain why your company brought Eddie here and then allowed him to be threatened and put in danger." The tone of the conversation shifted quickly, Aria's face going stony. "Someone was killed today. What if it had been Eddie?"

"But it wasn't. He was a friend. And he's gone."

F abric and plants were the balm Jenny needed. The quiet sunlit studio harbored her personal treasures and she dropped onto the couch breathing in the familiar space.

She was alone.

It wouldn't last long. Cherry was somewhere

across town recapping the meeting she'd missed and would be back with a new schedule in soon.

Aria's interrogation had left Jenny feeling inadequate and raw. She wouldn't identify the victims of the hypnosis, for good reason, but that made it difficult to defend what they were doing. There wasn't a single thing she'd come up with that satisfied Aria's fear for Eddie's safety.

In the end, Aria had chastised them, threatened them with legal action, and thrown them out.

Jenny looked around the room. Maybe it was a little too quiet.

Jenny hopped off the couch and grabbed a stack of blocks from her desk. Spreading them out on the cutting table Jenny couldn't settle on a good layout. They were simple pinwheels, for a simple Fall quilt but she didn't feel simple. Nothing felt simple.

Cutting the finished blocks in pieces, Jenny reordered them and changed the design. Zipping the new fabric sets through her machine she began recreating the pattern. Pair after pair she stitched in a long chain of blocks.

The growing string of chain pieced blocks spoke to her as the machine hummed along. *Lissa is innocent. Someone is lying. Frank is dead.*

Every block that went through the machine ticked a new thought in her mind. She couldn't let it go. *Eddie is desperate. His team wants him gone.*

Jenny reached for another set of blocks to stitch and found she'd sewn them all.

Cutting her thread Jenny pulled the banner of blocks across the room. She loved stretching her chain piecing out to its full length. It was as long as it would ever be in that moment. And Jenny felt powerful seeing what she'd accomplished.

Working through the long string of blocks Jenny clipped seams and pressed them open. Clip, press. Clip, press. She could almost see the pattern but not quite. It never quite came together until the final step when the blocks were complete.

She repeated the process, nesting their seams and sliding them under the presser foot. Every set was the same, but when she opened them up, the quilt would be a flood of colors.

She began laying out the blocks in their new design. They fit better this time. Still, her mind wouldn't stop dancing around her thoughts and worries after Franks murder.

In heat sensitive ink Jenny wrote on the fabric.

Lissa's name went on the first block. Then grabbed a block for Tommy Webb and Frank Mullins. All three quilt blocks went on the design wall.

Moving them to the top of the wall she made one more block. Eddie, she wrote in large letters across the center.

His block went on the very top and she stood back. She stared at it thinking and shook her head. Reaching up Jenny made a single adjustment. She moved Eddie's block down below the three hypnotized victims.

Eddie wasn't the top, but the center of this mystery. Seeing him there helped focus Jenny's mind.

If she wanted to keep Lissa safe she would need to find out who wanted to kill or destroy Eddie.

Benji and Krista got their own blocks. Jenny placed them below and to the side of Eddie's. She sashed them with Fame and Cheating.

Frank's block was directly above Eddie's and even though he had been killed Jenny sashed his block with Revenge and Family.

She flipped the pen over in her hand and considered the things she'd learned over the last day and a half. She pulled a sashing strip and wrote News Story across it and hung it on the side of Krista's block.

Jenny stepped back, the blocks telling a simple story. *This is where it gets complicated*, she thought. She focused on Eddie's block, letting her mind tie them all together. All three of the victims had a tie to Eddie. Even Lissa had interacted with him before the show.

Benji and Krista. They were suspects for the hypnotizing, but the murder?

Jenny took a deep breath. She looked down at the blocks she had pieced. Slowly she took another one from the pile. Almost hesitantly writing the next name down.

Aria.

The name turned around in her mind. Aria was different than the other two. They had solid motives, but Jenny questioned if they would kill for what they wanted. With Aria, Jenny couldn't pinpoint a motive, but she defended and protected Eddie so aggressively that Jenny wouldn't have been surprised to find out she'd been behind Frank's death.

She put the quilt block on the wall. Aria could hypnotize but her motive was protection. She put that word on a sashing strip and put a border around Aria's block. But she still lacked an initiating motive. Unless she set Aria's block with Eddie's.

Jenny swapped Aria and Krista's blocks so that Aria's was directly beneath Eddie's. If Eddie had met with and hypnotized the three victims before his show it could have worked.

The matching trigger words made sense so it would look like a less experienced hypnotist. Even Eddie's social media posts fit. If he believed he would scare them and heal them there was no danger in talking about it. But then . . . Aria came along.

Publicity. She wrote on a thin sashing strip and set it between Eddie and Aria. *Publicity.* It was a cruel possibility.

She added Harry's name to a block and even Eddie's mother. The hypnosis was a problem for them but Harry's motive of money and Rachelle's anger about losing her son tied directly to Franks death.

Frank was killed hours after Jenny had told her about what had happened with Eddie.

Jenny still had a lot of questions, but it was good to see it laid out.

A door slammed in the basement and Cherry's voice floated up the stairs. "How do you like my secret entrance?"

"As your local law enforcement, I'm ashamed to say I didn't even know that door worked."

Wilkins? Jenny's eyes shot to the wall as Cherry laughed. She was flirting with him! Jenny didn't have time to be excited for Cherry. She wasn't sure how the police officer would respond to her display of murder suspects and victims.

Their footsteps hit the stairs and Jenny grabbed the first large piece of fabric she saw. She pinned it to the corner high above the blocks on one side of the design board. Jenny spread the fabric out over the blocks hiding the murder quilt.

"What are you doing with that?" Cherry asked as she emerged from the basement stairs with Wilkins on her heels.

"Just pinning up a background." Jenny smiled. "I'm considering a background fabric feature for the spring."

"Are you?" Cherry grinned, like she was laughing at some internal joke.

Jenny smiled back and finished putting her pin in the corner. "What is it?"

"That's not background fabric." Cherry covered her giggles with one hand and gave Wilkins a quick glance. "That's the top half of my old bed sheets."

Jenny looked back at the floral fabric noting the wide hem on one side. "Yes. It is, isn't it. You have very good taste. I've used sheets as quilt backs before. Are you surprised?"

"A little," Cherry admitted. "That was going to be donated."

"Well, that's convenient," Jenny said climbing

down from her stool. She caught the fabric as she came down and the lonely pins holding the fabric up came down.

Several of blocks came down with the sheet Jenny scrambled to gather them.

"So, how's the investigation going?" Wilkins asked after Jenny stood with her handfuls of fabric and stray blocks.

"I was going to ask you the same thing," Jenny said setting her blocks out.

Wilkins scanned, her blocks and grinned. "I think we're both doing pretty well."

"I'll be home soon." Jenny promised and Ron groaned a goodbye.

"How's he doing?" Cherry asked climbing into the convertible.

Jenny considered the stilted conversation and her lips pulled down in a frown, her heart stretched thin between her and her husband.

"He's getting worse." She admitted.

Cherry shot her a surprised look her sunglasses halfway to the bridge of her nose. "Really?"

Jenny nodded. "I'm calling Dr. Butler when I get home. That prescription isn't doing what it's supposed to do."

"Why don't we stop at his office on the way? You can save a little time and maybe get a replacement," Cherry said pulling into the street. She handed

Jenny a bag of food truck barbecue that smelled incredible.

"I thought you might like some dinner."

"Thank you. I was dreading having to figure out food when I got home. Gas station pizza was on my list of most likely possibilities." Jenny opened the bag and her mouth watered as the heat hit her face and the smell pulled her closer. "I'm sure Lissa will thank you."

"No problem." Cherry shifted in her seat and opened her mouth to say something twice before Jenny huffed a breath.

"What is it? Does my barbecue come with strings attached?"

"No! I knew you'd need something like that tonight. But I also didn't want you to be upset when I tell you we're doing trivia night tonight instead of the quilt auction."

"Trivia night?" Jenny's throat tightened and she looked at Cherry. "I don't have to prepare, do I?"

Cherry shook her head. "You just come and be your usual charming self."

"That I can do." Jenny teased.

It wasn't long before they pulled into the doctor's office parking lot and Jenny excused herself. "I'll be a minute."

She hurried inside. The lobby was quiet with only one person at the counter. Jenny slipped in and took a seat in the corner. The man didn't seem to notice her.

"You shouldn't have been there at all." Nancy said to the patron at the counter.

"I wouldn't have if I could help it. Nance, I'm doing this for you . . . for us. You know that, right?"

Jenny glanced up recognizing Harry's voice and then back down at her lap. If Harry and Nancy were trying to make up she did not want to interrupt.

"I would have been happy with flowers and a few dates." Nancy made a frustrated sound and lowered her voice. "I don't see how creating a city-wide internet outage helps us."

18

Nancy didn't speak softly well and criminal offenses weren't the kind of information you could choose not to listen to.

"I didn't know that was going to happen." Harry's voice was softer than Nancy's, but it was hard to disguise sounds in a quiet room.

The couple leaned closer over the counter, Nancy working on something between them.

"They paid you five thousand dollars to flip some switches. What did you think was going to happen?" Nancy's frustration rose the timbre of her voice and the man at the counter glanced over his shoulder.

He didn't really look but turned back hushing Nancy and lowering his voice further. "I'm sorry. I've got to—one more problem. – I'll be out of—"

She could only pick out pieces of the conversation now and when Harry pulled back from the counter Jenny was surprised to see that Harry had a large bandage over his forearm.

"Well, you should be grateful I know how to

handle burns," Nancy said, her voice returning to normal, plus a little smugness as she examined the wrapping.

"Thanks, Nance." Harry leaned over the counter to kiss her, but Nancy pulled back.

She'd spotted Jenny.

With a quick glance between them Nancy smiled at Harry and he adjusted kissing her cheek instead.

"I'll see you later." His whispered goodbye brought a blush to her cheeks and Jenny smiled softly.

"Jenny, I didn't know you were coming in." Nancy said looking down at her computer nervously. "Dr. Butler's not here. I was closing up. I guess I forgot to lock the door."

Jenny hurried to stop her worry. "Oh don't worry about it. Is Harry alright? How did he hurt his arm."

"Oh, just a burn. He was doing some electrical work."

"Isn't he a finance guy? I didn't know he did electrical."

"He doesn't and sometimes I wonder about those finance skills too." Nancy laughed. "Well, I'm sorry if you had an appointment. Our system is still down with the outage and Dr. Butler's already gone home."

"No, I didn't. Ron's antibiotic isn't working and Dr. Butler told me to let him know if that was the case. I just stopped by. Is the internet going to be a concern for you guys over night? I heard you had a break in today."

"No. We've got a great tech guy who set up our

system. Our security is hardwired, I guess. Our scheduling system not so much." Nancy looked confused.

"Oh, that's good. I was at the bank and heard their security was down without the internet."

"The bank? That's strange. No, our security system doesn't rely on wifi. I'm surprised the bank would have a setup like that."

"That is strange isn't it. Maybe I got the over simplified version," Jenny said trying to explain the concern away. "So did you get video of the break in here?"

"Break in?" Nancy asked.

"Yeah, I heard there was a break in this morning. I wondered if they'd caught the guy."

"You're very well-informed Mrs. Doan. I don't know if they did. But Dr. Butler already told the police who it was. We've got a young man that runs orders for us and he was supposed to be in this morning. Instead, our drug cabinet was smashed open and emptied." Nancy started clearing her desk. "I'm sure it will be settled soon. Anyway, I really need to get going. Was there anything I could do for you?"

"Would you be able to set up an appointment for Ron tomorrow morning. I'd like Dr. Butler to check on him."

"I can't set an official appointment, but I can make a note." She started scanning the desk, her brow furrowed. "I should have a dozen pens up here." She laughed anxiously and Jenny offered her one of her own pens. "What time would you like?"

"As early as possible. I'm sure it's going to be a busy day."

"Eight o'clock it is. Seven forty-five if the doctor is as early as usual and you're here." Nancy offered.

"Done," Jenny said. She turned back to the room waiting while Nancy wrote it down.

Noticing the blue fabric on the coat rack. Jenny stepped over retrieving her scarf. "Goodness, I've been missing this." Her original plans for Cherry and Dr. Butler felt a little silly now. "I must have left it here the other day."

"I'm glad you found it." Nancy said handing Jenny's pen back. "I didn't know who it belonged to."

The note lay on the counter with Harry's name above Jenny's. A large 5:30 was circled in red beside it.

"Do you have a date tomorrow?" Jenny asked. With the way Nancy had talked about Harry before Jenny was surprised, she was getting back together with him. But she hoped Nancy was finding happiness wherever it was.

She smiled warily, "No. What makes you say that?"

"Oh," Jenny's eyebrows rose and she thought quickly trying to figure out how to explain her snooping. "I saw his name on the note, but I shouldn't have been looking. Sorry."

Nancy picked up the note quickly. "No, it's not a date. I have a delivery at 5:30 tomorrow. I'm a doodler. When he came in I wrote his name down." She gave a short laugh. "Give me a pen and you never know what's going to end up on my paper."

Nancy grabbed her purse. "I'll follow you out if that's alright."

"**Y**es!" Jenny cheered as the computer screen loaded a solid page full of files.

Tech had never been Jenny's strong point. She was from the era of files and secretaries. But with a family business Jenny was invited to a lot of meetings and got updates on even more.

The file in front of her was shared by Harry Bolding, Junior Finance Analyst. It was a good title for a friend of a friend.

Jenny scanned the screen for the most recent files and then backtracked. If Harry's financials weren't adding up today, it didn't start here.

Jenny clicked a link and crossed her fingers.

She really hoped she'd find something that could tell her why Harry was in so much trouble he was threatening people and hurting himself.

There were pages of numbers, most of which only made her brain hurt. When her phone rang next to her Jenny didn't care who was calling. She answered it and clicked the screen closed disappointed that she'd spent over an hour on a mind-numbing project and learned nothing.

"Hello," she said leaving the counter and her computer and dropping onto the living room couch.

"Mrs. Doan," a young man's voice wavered on

the other end of the line. "You said to call if anything went wrong."

"Tommy? What's going on?" She'd forgotten to look at caller ID but his voice was unmistakable.

"Did you hear about Mr. Mullins?" A mix of worry and fear tangled in Tommy's voice.

Jenny sucked in a breath. She hadn't even thought about how Tommy would take the news. "I did. When did you hear? Are you okay?"

"I don't think so." His voice trembled as if that proud seventeen-year-old boy was on the verge of tears. "The police found me at work, asking all kinds of questions. They think I'm going to die, don't they?"

Jenny nodded and closed her eyes. The flood of emotions was overwhelming. She was angry with Wilkins for scaring the poor kid.

"Mrs. Doan?" he asked and she opened her eyes realizing she hadn't answered. "What about your niece? Do they know who's next?"

"Nobody knows, Tommy. Until we find out who is behind all this we can't know."

That puts you and Lissa right in the line of fire.

Tommy was quiet on the other end of the line. His breathing was backed by the sounds of wind and the occasional car. The bubble of background noise made it feel like she could see him, sitting on his porch, probably taking a break for the first time all day.

"What if someone was mad at Mr. Mullins."

Jenny adjusted the phone and tried to understand. "Like, they killed him just because? I guess so but they would have had to work pretty hard to find out about the connection to Eddie and get the right props and everything to stage it like they did."

"Oh, I didn't know all that."

Jenny flinched, she probably wasn't supposed to know all that either. "It's possible though. It would just be hard."

"Okay," Tommy said slowly. "Because I saw Mr. Mullins fighting with someone today. It was pretty bad."

"Who was he fighting with?" It was an interesting thought and slightly comforting to think that maybe Franks death hadn't been connected to Eddie.

"I want to say it was Lissa but that doesn't feel right." Tommy's voice trembled and broke on the few words.

"And Lissa was with me before Frank died." Jenny hesitated, was she? She'd actually dropped Lissa off so she could go visit Nora Mullins and Rachelle Paris. Jenny swallowed hard. "You don't sound certain about that. Who do you think it was?"

"I don't know, but I swear he had sideburns and dark hair." Tommy was so confused Jenny hurt for him.

"Like Harry?" Jenny prodded when Tommy didn't say more. "Then what happened?"

"I don't really know that either." He sounded frustrated and upset.

Jenny closed her eyes, trying to understand.

"I was visiting my Aunt Elsie at the bank. Well, she's not really my aunt but she watches out for me, and after she left I went back. I can't remember the details but I had paint on me when I woke up at home later and I know someone was really angry. Every time I try to remember my head hurts so bad. It doesn't go away. The headaches and the urge to confess. Is it like that for your niece?"

Jenny's hope died in the swirl of a red and white hypnotist's spiral. "I don't think so. Lissa's been struggling but it seems to be getting better as the day goes on. At least that's what she made it look like."

"That's pretty lucky if it's true. I thought about killing Eduardo pretty much all day."

"Maybe you need to take a break. I know you've got a couple jobs to deal with but Eddie's not performing any more right? Maybe you can get some time off?" Jenny didn't know if he'd take the advice but she worried about him.

"Eddie might not be working, but I still have the grill, and Dr. Butler. And I clean pools for a few people . . . I still have to close some of them up for the season."

"I didn't know you worked for Dr. Butler." Jenny sat up straight, hoping he would say he was a janitor or chauffeur, anything else.

"Yeah, I do med deliveries for him. He does some big money that way."

Jenny released the breath she'd been holding. "Tommy did Dr. Butler say anything to you about the break in this morning?"

It wasn't a straight up did-you-do-it question but it was blunt and she expected a blunt answer.

"I didn't know there was one," he said. "I wasn't there today?

"Are you sure?

"Yeah, I was in the police station this morning?" His breathing got faster.

"That's right. You were in there until . . . ten? Is that right?"

"Almost eleven. I was late for the grill." Tommy's frustration cleared up the truth.

Nancy or the doctor had blamed Tommy for the theft, it could have been blind prejudice and assumption but hopefully, Jenny'd get to ask some questions in the morning.

"That's right you had a busy morning didn't you. Sorry about that. You may wan to check in about deliveries too."

He growled under his breath. "Oh geez. I needed that job. I'm gonna be short again."

She knew the feeling of needing every penny. Jenny wouldn't blame him for wishing he hadn't gotten mixed up in all of this. She felt the same way.

"Mrs. Doan?"

"Yeah?" she asked, exhaustion spreading through her body. She fell back against the couch as a knock sounded at the door. Jenny checked her watch, seven o'clock. Cherry was early.

"Thanks for talking with me." Tommy was quiet on the other side. "No one else cares."

It left a bittersweet taste on Jenny's tongue. She was grateful to help, but this boy had been through too much. "I'm happy to." Something crashed outside and Jenny jumped from her seat. "I've got to go. Maybe we can talk more tomorrow. I'll be at the Tractor Pull if you want to."

Jenny hung up with Tommy and marched to the door. She refused to feel guilty when she still had a full thirty minutes to get ready for the evening activity. She couldn't see anyone through the window and Jenny hesitated with her hand on the doorknob. Something didn't feel right.

Flipping on the porch light footsteps pounded away and Jenny yanked the door open. A brightly painted knife pierced the middle of their large wooden door. Stabbed through a simple sheet of paper, the knife held a note made from a series of letters pasted across the page. Jenny's heart rate sped up with the adrenalin that coursed through her. The note wasn't signed, she couldn't even focus enough to read it yet.

She scanned the yard. In the dusky night Jenny couldn't see much beyond the brightly lit porch. A flowerpot had fallen from its stand and smashed across the porch floor. Jenny bent to pick it up and a prickle ran down her spine. Someone was watching her.

She looked toward the hedge and decided to let the pot shards stay where they were. She'd clean them in the morning.

She tore the note from the door, leaving the knife and locked herself inside.

Hypnosis can't bring you back from the dead.
Stay out of this.

19

Ron scanned the empty parking lot and turned to Jenny like he'd won the prize. "I told you it was too early."

"Trust me," Jenny said unbuckling her seat belt. "Nancy said Dr. Butler gets here by seven forty-five almost every morning."

"Even so, he won't be able to see us that early."

Ron didn't usually grumble this much, and Jenny patted his arm, biting her tongue.

The sky was darker than it had been yesterday but Jenny didn't mind. She had her favorite scarf back and she liked nippy mornings. The two of them walked into the unlocked front entrance of the doctor's office.

"They're open." Jenny whispered to Ron as Nancy saw them and stood smiling.

"I'm so sorry. He still isn't in." Nancy said gesturing to the lobby chairs. "Do you mind waiting? You can just take a seat anywhere. I'll let you know when he gets here."

Ron leaned over. "What? That's such a surprise."

He had that half grin on that she loved. "You sit," Jenny said. "I'll be right back."

Jenny walked over to the desk and leaned toward Nancy. "Thanks for working us in so early. Do you know what's holding the doctor up?"

Nancy glanced up, her mind obviously on her computer screen, and shook her head. "Sorry, I haven't heard from him yet. I've sent him a note about your appointment and I'll let you know as soon as he gets here."

"Thanks, but maybe it's a good thing. I had a question for you. You mentioned a tech guy that came and set up your security system. Do you still have his information?"

Nancy looked like she wanted Jenny to be anywhere but standing there, talking to her. She blinked her big eyes up at her and nodded. "I will try to find that before your next appointment."

Jenny clenched her teeth. "With everything that's been going on, I'd really like to get it today."

"of course." Nancy glanced down at her computer screen and stood. "Let me go check back here with the receipts."

Nancy disappeared into the little room behind the reception desk and Jenny glanced down the hallway. It was completely empty. The smashed medical cabinet would be somewhere down there.

Jenny glanced back to make sure Ron was alright and Nancy's computer caught her attention. She had apparently been looking at her e-mail and hadn't closed it down and there was a message from Harry on the screen.

—I don't even know what happened to the money, but if I don't find it, I will go to prison. If it doesn't work, I may be begging you for your grandma's inheritance.

And now Benji wants me to pay double for the show. That's almost 20 grand!

I love you, but if I don't figure this out I'm so dead.

Twenty thousand dollars, and that was just part of it. No wonder Nancy had looked so stricken. Jenny scrambled to the edge of the desk as footsteps sounded down the hall.

"Jenny?" Dr. Butler appeared behind her and paused, looking between her and Ron. "I take it you're here for the worm buffet?"

Jenny laughed awkwardly, "Always the early bird."

"So, I see." He grinned.

Nancy emerged at the sound of Dr. Butler's voice. "Patient rooms are almost ready Dr. Butler. I just have a couple things to get the computer up and running."

Nancy rushed over clicking out of Harry's email before Dr. Butler could see what was on it.

"Don't worry about that." Dr. Butler turned to Jenny and smiled. "Let me check in with Nancy and we'll get you situated." Dr. Butler beckoned Nancy to follow him, and they turned down the hall disappearing at the end, where his office was tucked away.

When he returned, Dr. Butler gathered their paperwork while Nancy walked them to the patient room.

"I'm so sorry I couldn't find that information. I'll try to find it while you're in with Dr. Butler."

"What is that you're trying to find?" Dr. Butler walked up behind them as Nancy finished.

Nancy jumped and smiled up at Dr. Butler. It wasn't as bright as it had been a couple days before But it seemed impossible that Nancy could not be charming. "Jenny is looking for contact information for the gentleman that did our security system updates."

"Oh, that's easy." Dr. Butler led them down the hall. "I was looking at it yesterday because of all the issues in town. Come with me, his cards in my office."

Ron looked anxious as they walked away from his normal spaces. "We can wait in the room if that's better."

"Nonsense," the doctor said as they turned the corner. "You'll have to excuse my mess. We had an incident with a delivery boy and some missing medications. It's quite the mystery. The police have been very responsive though."

Dr. Butler stepped past a tall white cupboard against the wall. One side of the cabinet was bent and broken. The latch assembly was twisted with one of its connecting pieces gone.

"Wow. I heard it was broken into, but I didn't realize it was so bad."

Dr. Butler gave a resigned frown. "Yes, it's sad.

Tommy had a reputation, you know, but he was always good to us"

"Here we are," the doctor said and stepped through the door into his office. "And your information, Mrs. Doan."

Dr. Butler picked up a card up off his desk and handed it to her. Bunches of Tech by Terry Bunch.

"Thank you. Do you mind if I snap a picture? I always lose the paper ones." Jenny walked into the office and set the card against a lamp snapping a picture. "Oh shoot, let me get one more. I covered it with my shadow." Jenny turned the card to the other side of the lamp and adjusted her camera to get the card and a large shot of the open doorway, including the broken medicine cabinet. "Thank you so much. I really appreciate that."

Dr. Butler nodded and walked them back down the hall to the patient room. Going through the motions Dr. Butler checked Ron over. When Jenny confirmed how much he'd been sleeping the doctor's eyebrows pulled low, darkening his already gray eyes.

"Well, Ron. You're an interesting patient. Those aren't good signs."

"I never had this problem with Dr. Carmichael." Ron harumphed sitting back in his seat.

Dr. Butler's mouth flatlined and he kept one eyebrow low as he looked at Ron. "You certainly know how to play to my competitive nature don't you?" the doctor smiled at Jenny. "Don't worry. I think I know how to handle this."

Dr. Butler finished up his notes and grabbed the

door handle stopping and turning back to Jenny. "How's Lissa doing? I was wondering if she needed some follow up. Tommy has been having continued issues and with Frank . . . I'm worried about letting her power through."

Jenny nodded. "I am completely worried. And follow up is exactly what we need. I really appreciate that you're thinking of her."

Dr. Butler grinned. "Appreciative enough that you might hang around when Dr. Carmichael gets back in town?"

Jenny laughed as Ron gave a grumpy. "No."

He glared at her and Dr. Butler's grin grew. "Competitive nature. I'm gonna getcha."

"Well, thank you. I can only do what I can do and the medical side is what's missing, and after Frank's passing, I don't know if we'll be able to do the hypnosis reversion therapy."

"Oh, that's too bad," Dr. Butler said looking relieved. He let go of the doorknob turning back to Jenny. "It sounds like the safe plan though."

"I guess so. It felt a little bit like a life line though. Something that could put her back to normal."

"I can understand that. But she will get back to normal. I'm sure and farbeit from me to indicate hypnosis could have any basis in reality but If Mr. Paris did hypnotize them or try. They probably don't want him trying to cover things up."

Jenny cringed. "That makes sense. And I just want Lissa safe."

The doctor tapped his pen against the edge of his clipboard. "Good, then I'd like to start having her come in every few days till it's resolved. Would that be a feasible situation?"

"I think so. I'll have to ask her, with insurance and whatnot."

"Don't worry about the insurance. We'll call it observation. I'll check on her and make sure she's not getting headaches or other illness. With Ron sick too, I'd hate to get any wires crossed."

"That is incredibly generous," Jenny said. "Thank you again. Dr. Carmichael is gonna have a run for his money when he gets back."

Dr. Butler's grin split wide across his face and he laughed as he left the room.

"Al, you really need to check Harry's work," Jenny said into the phone. She hated calling him out but it sounded like Harry was going to need back up before he got himself into an even bigger mess.

"I saw a stray email. That's all. I don't know the details but Harry is getting himself in trouble and the company could face some serious problems if we don't address it."

She bit her tongue as Al placated her. "Just look. If I'm wrong I'll be thrilled. Harry's a great guy. I think he's gotten himself into a tough situation."

Alan gave in and promised to look over some things with him before he hung up.

When he was gone Jenny sighed as heavily as Ron when he laid down after the doctor visit. Jenny picked up the breakfast tray she'd prepped and carried it up the stairs to check on him.

"Ron? I brought you breakfast." She finally made it down the hall and found him in bed. "Ron?"

He cracked his eyes open and smiled wanly. "I'm not hungry, Jenny. But thank you."

Jenny set the food down anyway.

An empty glass sat on the nightstand next to his bottle of antibiotics.

Jenny picked up the bottle setting it aside. He'd doubled their antibiotic dose with a standard horse pill of meds for Ron to take twice today and tsunami his immune system before letting the antibiotics clean the rest out. She figured he'd have to be home for a week or two after to rebuild the good bacteria they were destroying in an effort to keep this good man alive.

She leaned over and kissed him on the forehead. "Well, I'm going to go and chase down a few bad guys tonight, okay?"

Ron hummed his approval and Jenny frowned. She'd meant it as a joke and it worried her that he had so completely missed it.

She kissed him again, letting his clammy skin rest against her lips. "Well, that's two men that aren't listening to me tonight." She pulled the covers up around his neck. "Maybe tomorrow will be better."

"Doesn't matter," Ron mumbled. "Two men? You're one good woman. Love you."

Jenny's frown cracked, her lips turning up into a soft smile as the man she loved settle under the large quilt, eyes closed, sweet nothings on his lips.

20

Engines cranked as friends and family cheered each other on. Tractors, with wheels as tall as she was, rolled onto the field. On the other side of the field, personal lawn mower-sized vehicles spit dirt and mud as they rolled after each other.

The Penney Days festival – Tractor Pull was the slowest competition Jenny knew of and the whole town loved it. Jenny could feel the town pride as people took pictures with their favorite ractors and friendly rivalries carried more weight than a trophy.

She stood on a makeshift stage behind the high school running track with Penney High's homecoming king and queen. The girl wore a formal dress, elaborate crown, and sash, while he had on jeans and a sportscoat. The mismatched pair talked quietly, while Jenny scanned the crowd.

"The Quilt Auction is tonight now, but you've got, the Sew-lebrity Sew-a-thon, a Live filming, and a giveaway before then." Cherry had her list on her phone today and with the chance of rain in the forecast it was a smart choice.

"Jenny?" Cherry snapped her fingers. "Did you hear any of that?"

"Of course." Jenny looked back at her assistant and wished she could make the list disappear. "I'll be very busy, and you will make sure I'm everywhere I need to be."

"Or we're both fired." Cherry finished with a nod.

Jenny chuckled. "They won't fire us. But they may conveniently forget to tell us about the next publicity shoot."

"Right. The boys will take over triple play and your grandson will step in as the next Jenny." Cherry ticked something on her phone. "Perfect. I've made a note."

Cherry caught Jenny scanning the crowd again and frowned. "Seriously though, you listened, didn't you?"

"I listened. Now you need to get back down there. It's time to announce the next race." Jenny grabbed the mic and a clap of thunder rolled in the distance.

The click of high heels stamped next to Jenny. The homecoming queen shivered in her strapless gown, goosebumps rising on her arms. "Let's get this show on the road. It's gonna rain and I'm so cold."

"I hope it rains," the young man next to her said offering her his coat. "Then we'll get to see 'em pull in the mud! I love it when it gets all nasty like that."

The girl rolled her eyes and Jenny pulled her thick cardigan tighter. They seemed to share the same level of enthusiasm for the idea of the Tractor Pull turning into a mud marathon.

Jenny's part of the event was simple enough. She introduced the contests along with the homecoming king and queen then they awarded the prizes. Well, usually the girl in the crown awarded the prizes.

She hadn't seen Tommy all morning. After his call she'd thought he might want to talk again. She'd seen Harry wandering in the distance and even Benji. But Cherry was the one standing front and center in the crowd. Her mustard yellow shirt contrasted the deep turquoise drunkards path pattern running across it that made her easy to spot. Over the white slacks and chunky heels Jenny didn't know how she'd managed to even get out of her car without ruining her outfit.

A muddy child ran for the bleachers with a silver trophy in hand, almost barreling into Cherry. Her dodge was close, and as she danced out of the way she had to lean away from a waving soft pretzel on a stick. All Jenny could do was chuckle.

They'd already introduced the peewee competition with homemade tractors and go carts. Now it was the big kids on big wheels. They repeated the process for the other field where the biggest tractors hooked themselves to stacks of lumber provided by the local lumber yard and revved their engines.

The smaller tractor in the race was eeking ahead of the biggest, and the crowd was going insane with a wild mix of cheers and boos. It was every bit as enthused as the Sew-lebrity Sew-a-thon would be.

The rain had held off and Jenny started

announcing her final event when she caught a glimpse of Benji's neon pink sport coat through the slats of the bleachers next to Harry.

She couldn't hear them, but her forehead had started to ache with the intensity that she was watching their argument. She wondered if Al had talked with Harry yet. Being so zoned in on their situation, she half expected the words to jump out at her like subtitles on a screen.

"Mrs. Doan," The young woman in the crown and formal, touched her arm to get her attention. "Are you ready? I think they're waiting on us."

Jenny turned back, trying to relax. This was the Tractor Pull, a family event full of fun and — a metallic thump echoed behind her.

Jenny spun back in the direction of Benji and Harry's argument. It blended into the chaos, but Jenny could see Harry laid out on the bleachers as Benji strode away.

"Take these," she said, handing the young queen her notes. The girl's eyes were wide. "There's only one more event. You've been promoted." She gave the girl an intentionally perky smile and a pat on her shoulder.

Hurrying off the stage, the only one who noticed Jenny's departure besides the new MC was Cherry.

The two women met on the ground Cherry stopping her progress. Before she could argue about responsibilities Jenny waved in the direction of the incident.

"It's Harry! He's on the bleachers. I think he's hurt."

Cherry shot a look that direction and started running. She jogged from one patch of grass to another, surprisingly graceful as she followed Jenny's lead.

"Benji and he were arguing. Benji just walked off," Jenny said through short bursts of breath while they emerged from the crowd and Cherry dashed ahead.

Jenny followed, her curiosity over what they'd been arguing about was like a guilt-inducing fire burning beneath her feet. She had to know.

Cherry made it to the bleachers first. Climbing halfway up to where Harry lay between the rows. Cherry knelt beside him, speaking quickly. Jenny followed, but she wasn't fast or close enough yet to hear what Cherry said to him. She could only see that Harry wasn't responding.

Cherry held Harry's head in her lap gingerly touching the side of his face. A streak of red had worked through his dark hair and sideburns and when Cherry's fingers came back red the younger woman looked up to meet Jenny's gaze.

"I'm going to call the police. You've been attacked and someone is at fault," Cherry said, pulling her phone from her skirt pocket.

Harry grimaced in pain as he put out a hand to stop her. "No. Really, no police. I'm fine. I just fell."

Cherry shot Jenny a look that told her she didn't believe a word of that. Jenny slid into the row next to Cherry, getting a better look at the injury. "Did Benji do this? If he did, someone needs to talk to them. They travel the world and if he's dangerous, Eddie at the very least should know."

"How did you know I was talking to Benji?" Harry's gaze had focused on Jenny. His eyes cleared the longer he stared at her.

"I saw you. It's fine though, we don't have to call the police." Cherry scoffed in disbelief, but Jenny ignored her. "We should call the doctor, though. The spot right there that's bleeding looks like a pretty good-sized gash. Dr. Butler would take care of it quietly, I'm sure."

Harry accepted, even though it looked like he was still processing the concept. Cherry immediately had her phone out dialing.

"Hello, Dr. Butler? Yes, this is Cherry. Are you busy? We have an emergency."

Harry's brow furrowed. Cherry wandered down the bleacher, keeping the conversation private.

"She won't go off telling anyone, will she?" Harry groaned as he pushed away from the metal bench. He prodded lightly at the skin around his wound and flinched. "It's pretty bad, huh?" He looked around and finally closed his eyes, settling back into the awkward position that let him lounge between the rows, his legs dangled over the bench.

"We'll get you cleaned up. But yeah, between that and your arm, it's pretty bad."

Harry glanced at his arm the bandage that Nancy

had put on him last night peeked out from the edge of his sleeve. He tugged it down self consioucly.

"Do you think you can stand?" Jenny asked waiting to see if he wanted help or if he would attempt it on his own.

He took a deep breath and pushed up. It was a slow process, and eventually he did take Jenny's hand, putting an arm around her shoulders for added support. After only a few steps, things started to get easier. Harry gained his ground and only hung onto her for balance.

"Benji looked pretty angry," Jenny said, looking expectantly at Harry.

It was all the prodding he needed. Harry gave a breathy huff. "He was angry, all right. He accused me of knocking out the internet transformer last night. He thinks I did it to make them stay in town."

"Did you?" Jenny asked. She'd heard the conversation with Nancy and didn't know what Harry would be honest or lie about.

"Why would I do that?" Harry asked only tripping over the words a little.

Jenny didn't miss the fact that it wasn't an answer. "Did you argue with Frank before he died?"

"Did Elsie tell you that? The little snoop was supposed to be gone. We argued but I didn't kill him. When I left Frank was very much alive."

"That's good," Jenny said. "Because I heard you arguing with Benji days ago. I know finances are tricky this year. Harry, if your in trouble we can help." She hoped it sounded like she was on his side.

His step faltered and his grip tightened on her

arm. "What do you mean? I'm not in trouble. There's nothing wrong with my finances."

"I didn't say 'wrong'." Jenny backtracked. "But if you were trying to get a loan, we can try to get you more options at least. You're not alone here. I don't know if that helps or if you've gotten mixed up in something that you shouldn't but don't do anything you'll regret."

Harry's grimace was back, and she must have struck a nerve because Harry came to a full stop. "Do you think I killed Frank?"

It was a straight question to which Jenny did her best to give a straight answer.

"I don't know."

Harry looked at her and squeezed her shoulder with the arm he had around her. It hurt. "If I did, you've put yourself in a dangerous situation."

Cherry called out, "I'm going to go get the car. Dr. Butler said he could see Harry now if we can get him there."

Cherry was further back than Jenny realized and a glance at Harry's dark unwavering eyes made her wonder if he could kill someone. "Did you kill Frank Mullins?"

The question was by no means admissible in court, but nonetheless, Harry looked pleased that she'd asked.

"No," he said. His face relaxed, a ring of honesty in his voice. It was all he said.

A raindrop landed on Jenny's cheek. Harry must have felt it too, because he looked up to the sky and Jenny started moving again. "We should get going."

21

It was somewhere after two in the afternoon and Jenny was sitting in a dumpster.

She'd officially missed her first event of the day. She wasn't just late. It was over and gone.

In half an hour the Sew-lebrity Sew-a-thon would start and Jenny would still be sitting here baking in the stench of a metal box that smelled like garbage. It was the price she paid for eavesdropping on a criminal mastermind.

At least it was an empty dumpster.

She did her best not to touch the slowly heating metal of the waste blackened box. Although she would have avoided it even if it was perfectly room temperature.

It had felt like a serendipitous situation. After dropping off Harry they'd wound their way through the spitting rain and by the time they'd returned to the center of town for the giveaway, the sun was shining. And it had been shining since.

"I'll meet you at the Live filming in twenty minutes?" Cherry asked. It wasn't really a question.

The giveaway had gone without a hitch earning

Jenny a little freedom. "Perfect. I'm going to grab lunch."

Jenny had seen Aria in the alley, which was suspicious enough. and then she'd seen who she was talking to.

Krista. Neither one of them looked happy. Aria said something sharply, and Krista's expression darkened.

Jenny clung to the corner of the bakery. She couldn't walk in the alley and hide; they'd see her. She still had ten minutes before Cherry returned. Jenny hurried around the buildings and into the floral fabric shop.

By a little miracle no one had stopped her and she'd made it to the back of the building in less than four minutes. Jenny looked through the back door window and twisted the handle as casually as possible.

Each of the shops along that row had a deck out the back for trash disposal and out-of-the-way parking. If they saw her, she wanted to look like she was just checking on things.

And that's when serendipity told her to leap.

A group of tour buses drove down the alley. It was loud and distracting, and her suspects weren't looking in her direction at all.

Setting her phone down on the railing, she sat on the edge of the porch and looked into the dumpster. It was mostly empty with only a few fabric boxes in the bottom, and close enough, she could dangle her feet right in. A tour bus bumped down the road, and urgency shot through her. She had to move or she'd be caught. Shimmying to the edge of the porch Jenny dropped into the dumpster.

It wasn't so far down, and the cardboard helped muffle her landing.

When the tour buses passed, Jenny was quiet as a rock.

"You really think we can get away with that?" Krista had asked.

"I told you we could, didn't I?" Aria's confidence was enviable. And then serendipity struck again. The pair walked even closer to the dumpster. Krista threw in an apple core.

She dodged it, but something hit the metal outside. The metal of the dumpster rang in her ears.

"Are you ready for this?" Aria asked.

"I'll be there tonight."

Tonight. But where?

She didn't get to find out. The pair shuffled something around and left.

After a few minutes of silence, Jenny reached for her phone. Only it wasn't there. She looked straight up. The edge of a silver case glinted on the railing. She'd left her phone behind.

Of course. The dumpster walls were high enough, she couldn't see anything lower than forehead height, and it was mostly sky. She pushed up on her tiptoes and could see the ground but pulling herself out would be impossible. The dumpster walls were smooth, disgusting, and she wasn't strong enough.

Jenny looked around at her heavy steel prison. She was stuck.

Fifteen . . . ish minutes later Jenny shot to her feet.

Laughter had never sounded so good. It echoed off the steel walls of her cage in mirthful tones.

Two familiar police officers leaned over the porch railing, thoroughly enjoying her situation. Officer Dunn seemed to be having the most fun with it. He'd removed his glasses and wiped tears from his eyes, unable to stop the steady stream of chuckles. She should probably be embarrassed, but she didn't care.

"How did you find me?" Jenny asked, overwhelmed by the prospect of finally getting out.

Fighting to keep a straight face, Wilkins scrubbed a hand over his jaw. "We got a call about suspicious sounds coming from back here. I don't know, though. Things look pretty normal to me."

Officer Dunn guffawed, slapping the railing and almost knocking her phone down, a feat she'd tried to accomplish for the first half of the ordeal before giving up. The suspicious sounds had likely been the phase where she tried calling to random passersby. That had only made her throat raw, as nobody really wanted to see who was impersonating Jenny Doan in the dumpster.

"Can you help me? What do I need to do? I want to get out of here."

Dunn shook his head. "Not yet." When Jenny's face dropped, he was overcome with a much shorter stream of chuckles. "I have to go get something first. If I yank you out of there, it's going to hurt. So, I'm sorry, but I have to leave you in for a little longer."

"You're leaving me here?" It was shocking enough that no one had been by until now, but now they were leaving her too.

"Don't worry, Wilkins will stay with you. He's pretty worthless in these situations anyway." Dunn didn't even notice the dirty look Wilkins aimed at him. "I'll be right back." From a little distance, he called out, "I really am sorry!"

Wilkins watched his partner leave. Then turned back to Jenny. "He doesn't know anything. We could probably get you out before he gets back."

"I'm game to try anything." Jenny looked up, trying not to let hope overshadow realism. "For your information, the cardboard boxes in here do not support my weight or stack high enough to get me out."

"Noted," Wilkins said and unbuttoned his cuffs, pushing his sleeves up.

"What are we doing?" Jenny asked, a note of panic in her voice. He looked like he was getting ready to do exactly what Officer Dunn had forbidden and just yank her out. "I don't know if this is a good idea."

"Of course, it is." Wilkins squatted down, his legs wide. He clapped and rubbed his hands together, his elbows propped against the inside of his knees. He beckoned her with both hands.

Jenny snorted. "I do not have the strength to pull

myself out of here."

"You don't have to. I'll help. We'll do it together." He adjusted his position pulling at his slacks to loosen their grip, then stuck his hands out to Jenny again. "It's more like climbing than pulling."

"Here goes nothing," she said under her breath, then reached up to put her hands in his. She couldn't get worse off, right? "I think you overestimate my abilities."

Wilkins laughed, still settling his body into a fully braced pose. "Watch out for the railing. We're shooting to have you come through the opening, not into the rail. Okay."

"Yeah, good plan." She gripped his hands, wondering if she'd even be able to hold tight enough. He gripped back, much tighter, reassuring her. She put a foot on the wall to try and climb out as they pulled.

"Ready?" They pulled slightly against each other, and he started counting. "On three. One, two, three!"

He tugged and she tugged, but he was so much stronger and she just kind of . . . fell, with a mangled "aaagh" as she tried not to land against the trash blackened walls.

Wilkins climbed off his backside and Jenny brushed at an unknown substance on her shoulder. She was, luckily enough, still fine.

Above her, Wilkins was setting up again. Jenny shook her head. "Not again. I'm not strong enough. Let's wait."

"Don't talk like that. This is all about teamwork. We have to find the right balance." He adjusted into the sumo pose, hands against his knees and a look of determination on his face. "Come on, Jenny. Be my teammate."

Jenny hadn't always been older. She'd been an athlete once. She knew how to do this. Her body knew how to do this. She breathed in, nodding as she continued to repeat positive thoughts. She could do this. Jenny gripped his hands and looked up at him. "Okay."

"A team," he said. "Here we go. Three," he said, and Jenny gripped his hands tighter. "Two." She put her foot up. "One!"

Jenny pulled as the officer leaned into his grip. Her body lifted and then both of them fell toward the dumpster.

"What the—" Wilkins made a quick hand adjustment that only made the pull less stable, and Jenny slipped. Wilkins reached for her ducking to avoid the rail and grabbed Jenny's forearm, as they both tumbled into the dumpster. "Woah!" he yelled, arms spiraling as he went. His shoulder hit the metal box's lip and he crashed onto the cardboard, narrowly avoiding landing on top of Jenny.

Jenny sat up, a sing-song whine in the back of her throat. She felt so defeated. She had to remind herself that another police officer was out there, and he was definitely coming back with something to help them out.

Wilkins rolled over and groaned. He had one hand holding his shoulder and his eyes closed.

"That can't be good." Jenny inched back, trying to make space.

He pushed up on his elbow and sucked in a breath. "It's fine. Sore is all." He stretched the range of his shoulder and cringed.

"If you say so." Jenny watched him shift until he got comfortable.

Footsteps padded outside and Jenny's hope skyrocketed. She got up on her knees, but Wilkins put out his hand and shook his head. Jenny mimicked Wilkins, who was holding very still and listening. He put a finger to his lips and Jenny tried not to move.

"What?" she mouthed.

He made the tiniest gesture with his hand. She waited. She listened. The footsteps carried a strange cadence. They would shuffle quickly, then stop. Then, shuffle again, and stop.

For several minutes, they listened to the stranger. Jenny's brow furrowed. Wilkins was carefully easing his body up. The shuffling came again, and for longer. Jenny's heartbeat sped as they slowed to a stop right outside their hiding place.

Something thunked on the ground outside, and Jenny felt her heart jump. Wilkins gestured for her to move to the back of the dumpster.

Jenny hesitated, then carefully lifted up, moving a little at a time. The dumpster creaked and she froze.

Silence. Jenny looked at Wilkins apologetically.

He didn't move, just closed his eyes and listened. Whoever was out there shoved something, scraping it along the ground. It hit the dumpster and everything swayed. Wilkins straightened out, looking around the edges of the box. Jenny should have told him to stop. He was shorter than she was and wouldn't be able to see anything. Then the footsteps ran and Wilkins reached up, bad shoulder and all, and grabbed the lip of the dumpster, lifting his torso out and launched himself over the side.

"It's happening," Jenny whispered to herself as Wilkins and Dunn examined the box that had been shoved under the porch.

They had to be careful. It was obviously a drop, but they didn't know who was picking it up and only that the person that dropped them was slight and very fast. Jenny thought of Aria and how she'd run from the police officer outside of the bank.

Wilkins was banking on it being someone unimportant that was doing a job for the money. And that sounded like Tommy.

"How do you get yourself into these kinds of messes?" Cherry whispered.

Jenny let out a breath. "This might be the biggest mess I've ever been in." As far as she could tell, she didn't have a way out. "I sent Lissa to stay with Sarah. Hopefully she'll be safe out there."

Cherry looked up, her eyebrows lifted slightly. "Did you put Lissa in lockdown? I'm impressed."

A distasteful smile twisted Jenny's lips. "I hate it.

But if she's got to be somewhere Seth will keep them all safe. Then Lissa can stay put for a few days." Jenny confirmed the thought in her mind. "It's not really lockdown. She's not some rebellious teenager."

Cherry smiled sadly and put an arm up to hug Jenny then thought better of it.

"Sorry," Jenny said looking down at herself. "I think I'll have to burn these clothes."

The frown Cherry pulled was pathetic. "I bought you that shirt."

With a deep sigh Jenny looked deep into Cherry's eyes. "You can have it back if you want."

Cherry laughed and both Wilkins and Dunn shot them annoyed looks.

"Sorry!" Jenny said holding her hand up. "Sorry."

The officers turned back to their conversation. They'd found the heavy box under the deck beside the dumpster and inside it had heavy weights like the one's that had weighted the "tightrope" Jenny had been meant to use, and bucket's filled with painted knives.

Jenny was pretty sure who they'd all come from and it wasn't Tommy.

Wilkins and Dunn were having an animated conversation over the box, and although Jenny knew it was none of her business, she walked over anyway. Cherry stayed behind.

"We should track down the drop guy, trace him back to find the real criminal."

"How long will that take?" she asked.

Both officers swiveled to look at her.

She ignored the implied imposition and asked again. "To track down the person who made the drop and use them to find their contacts and whoever is looking for the weapons in there. How long will that take?"

"That depends on how willing our people are to talk. I'm thinking one, maybe two weeks."

"If we're lucky," Dunn grumbled, flicking Wilkins' shin so he moved out of the way.

"You two are like siblings." Jenny craned her neck, trying to get another peek inside the box.

"We are not," Wilkins grumbled.

Jenny didn't feed the beast. She focused instead on the plan. "I don't think we have a choice," she said as she processed all of it. "The drop is set, as long as it's not too obvious that you guys have seen it all. We just need to see who's coming. Then you can backtrack, okay?"

Jenny made a great tiebreaker.

22

It would be impossible to fully get the smell off her skin. Not for many more showers.

Still, Jenny let the steam and floral scents fill the bathroom so she could pretend she would smell that way again.

She had dried off and dressed before she noticed the text from Cherry.

— Eddie needs to see you.

Jenny ran a brush through her hair while she blow dried it. She hadn't seen Eddie since yesterday and she couldn't figure out what he might need.

— Did he say what he wanted?

Cherry answered quickly.

— He wants to meet at the trailer.'

Not what she'd meant, but at least it was

direction. And she was close.

Jenny shot back a confirmation and finished getting ready. Ron was sitting up with a late lunch already starting to feel better, as the doctor ordered. With a kiss Jenny left and went to meet Eddie.

Pulling up in front of Eddie's Jenny started laughing.

"Where is Cherry when you need her?" she mumbled the comment to the giant tractor flying the Penney Days Festival banner.

Parked directly in front of the neon motorhome. Jenny figured she would need to send them a thank you note. Apparently she wasn't the only one not appreciating the brightly colored visitor. It didn't help that the beaten corner of the vehicle was still missing and the paint badly scratched where it had been vandalized the night after the show.

It's not over. Jenny hadn't thought about the ominous message scratched in the back of Eddie's tour bus since this whole thing had started.

Standing in the shadow of the large farm vehicle created a strange sense of privacy, and she worried less about knocking on the trailer door. She stepped over the crowbar that had moved from one side of the motorhome to the other but was still laying on the ground.

She knocked. No one answered.

Her phone buzzed and another text popped up, this one from an unknown number.

— On my way. Go on in if you're there.

Jenny looked up from the text. She was alone, but it felt weird to walk in. She might have even welcomed Benji being there, if he wasn't upset.

She grabbed the door handle, intending to click the latch, but it didn't work . . . the dented and scratched door, however, swung away from the trailer at the slightest touch.

Jenny gripped her phone in case she needed to call for help. She clicked to her recent calls screen. Good, even the police station was on there.

She pulled the door all the way open and stepped inside. "Hello?"

The silence was somewhat anticlimactic.

"Well," she said to the empty room, "I guess I'll make myself at home."

She'd stepped into the little kitchen area. Like most motorhomes, it had a window over the sink. This one was looking out at the cement block wall of the building beside them. She turned in a small circle. "And that's the full tour."

She smiled to herself, sitting at the small table. She listened to the clock tick for a full minute before she stood and started wandering again. The back room was obviously Eddie and Krista's. In the trash was a hot pink business card.

The business card. She scrolled to her phone and found the image of the one she'd gotten from the hotel.

On a whim, she reached down, retrieving matching card.

Something glinted in the dim light behind the trash can. Jenny jiggled the can, and the clink of glass caught her attention. The dispenser looked as if it would normally slide into the wall to keep the limited space clear, but a heavy cardboard poster had been jammed behind it, keeping it from closing.

Jenny stuffed the card in her pocket and tugged at the heavy cardboard sign. Wedged into the hinges of the door, it took several tugs to release it.

The retracting hinges of the trash can engaged and pulled the can into the wall, the trash door smacking closed. Glass clinked like someone had dropped a box of perfume bottles. Jenny got a bad feeling and lifted the door to the trash can. The little can slid out like it was supposed to. She wiggled it and it lifted easily out of the metal frame.

The space behind the door was dark, seemingly empty, but Jenny cautiously reached in. A tumble of glass bottles was pushed against the wall. She picked one up, a slight pain cut through her skin. Pulling back, a droplet of blood rested on the tip of her finger.

"Ouch." She lifted the finger to her mouth to clean it until her instincts told her that was a bad idea. Back in the kitchen, she set the bottle on the counter and grabbed a napkin. With it wrapped tightly around her finger, she pulled her phone out and dialed.

"Hi, Nancy. I'm trying to reach Dr. Butler."

Jenny took conscious breaths, keeping her heart rate in check while Nancy explained in long form that Dr. Butler was with a patient.

"Okay, do you know what drugs were stolen from the office the other day? And how dangerous are they if they get in the bloodstream?" She glanced down at her finger. A bloom of red spotted the napkin. It wasn't that bad. If it wasn't going to poison her.

What are you doing with these Eddie? She wanted to believe he was innocent. She wanted to believe he was as honest as he seemed.

"I don't know . . . really, anything about that." Nancy's voice had risen in pitch. She was worried. "I'll ask the doctor as soon as I can. Can I call you back at this number?"

Jenny confirmed that she could and hung up the phone. The tractor outside was moving. Should she move her car?

She set the bottle on the table instead, looking at the label. Haldivan. Antipsychotic neurologic base. For professional medical use only. The warning label held the traditional side effects of drowsiness, irritability, and, well, death. Jenny raised her eyebrows at the bottle. "That's quite a range."

She pulled her phone out. No call, no text. Nancy, Eddie, Cherry, police, nobody. She blinked at the phone. "I should call the police."

Her brain lit on the thought, recognizing that it was odd that she hadn't called them yet. She looked at her finger. "Is this your fault?"

She didn't know if her oncoming exhaustion was more worrying or the fact that she was talking to herself. The exhaustion could be explained away. It had been days of constant worry, always afraid of who was out to get someone else. She hadn't been threatened, but Lissa was practically in hiding. She regularly talked to herself, though –

Someone banged on the door and Jenny sat straight up. "Eddie?" Let it be Eddie. Then she glanced at the bottle of psycho drugs. Maybe she didn't want to be trapped in here . . . with a man . . . who now appeared to have stolen a supply of test drugs . . . that had likely been used to convince people that they were killers.

She forced herself up and flattened herself against the wall, though she still looked out the window at the same time. She couldn't see anyone. The door was closed tight enough that no light could get through, except by the handle. In the dim light, it looked like the handle was bent.

Jenny went down a couple of steps. She used her uninjured fingers to pull on the gap in the door, and it didn't budge. She pushed on the full door. The entire thing was bent, a seam puckered through the middle of the panel. Fear washed over her like she'd been out in a downpour without an umbrella. Chills raced through her body, raising goosebumps across her skin. Panic gripped her as hard as she gripped the handle. She shook it without any change. The edge of the crowbar showed through the frame.

They'd pinned her inside.

Jenny flew back up the steps, grabbing her phone off the counter. The recent calls were still open. She clicked the police's number.

"Hello? Hamilton police."

"This is Jenny Doan. I'm on Main Street, locked in the trailer of Eddie Paris. Aaah!" She screamed as the trailer lurched. She gripped the wall and the counter. "Please, something's wrong." The trailer lurched again as if it had been hit. Metal crunched, and Jenny couldn't help her screams.

Cars honked, and Jenny tried to understand what was happening. She was moving, that much was now clear. No one was driving the trailer, but it was moving forward. Jenny went completely numb. Metal screeched against concrete. The trailer itself twisted. Glass exploded in the front cabin. Maybe they'd hit the building. The windshield shattered. Why didn't they stop?

Jenny stumbled forward till she stood in the doorway to the back cabin. Glass was everywhere. Only half the windshield was still intact, and it leaned forward like they were driving at an angle toward the pavement. The other corner of the vehicle was crunched in like they'd been shoved in a trash compactor. The sounds of the tractor engine rolled steadily from behind her. Someone had used the tractor to ram the trailer. It was pushing her into the road.

The front of the motorhome lurched as its front end dropped off the raised parking lot and into the street. She gripped the door frame. Cars honked and swerved to avoid her. Jenny held tight, then backed up. She couldn't watch this. But there was no way to stop it either.

"Hey!" Someone yelled from the sidewalk. "What are you doing?"

Jenny wanted to scream at them. Why couldn't anybody help instead of shrieking at her?

In the main part of the motorhome, Jenny was

lost. She could only stand there and try not to die. She pushed herself back as a vehicle hit them from the front. A white car was crunched against the driver's side. She forced herself forward to the driver's seat, feeling for the brake below. It dropped to the floor with no resistance. Cut. Not that it would have done anything anyway, but knowing it was cut was worse.

Jenny yanked the wheel to the side. She half-expected it to throw the vehicle on its side, but the slow turn of the nose as the tractor pushed her dropped her heart through her stomach. A scream tore from her throat, she gripped the wheel. She stopped.

The sound of the tractor engine died, and people's voices clamored around the damage. Jenny stood there, fingers numb around the steering wheel. A cheer rose up at the side of the vehicle. She did not feel like cheering.

Jenny craned her neck and caught sight of a handful of people circled around a young man in a cowboy hat. Bryan Cobb stood near the back of the motorhome, the motionless tractor at his back. Bryan Cobb had saved her.

Jenny turned around and stumbled to the door of the trailer. It was still wedged shut. She pulled herself back to the front of the trailer and cautiously leaned out the window. "Help me! Please?" Her voice quavered. "The door is locked. Can someone help me?"

Several people heard her shallow, worn cry and looked up from the chaos. She pointed to the door and went back in, their voices fast and strained, and after what sounded like someone throwing a brick at the door, the end of the crowbar disappeared. The door cracked open and faded light flooded the vehicle.

23

Jenny climbed out of the trailer like she was emerging from a tomb. Her whole body was pulsing. The quiet ringing in her ears, felt like a lie. The ground lurched under her and she stopped, her hand out to grab a wall or cupboard, but there was nothing there. She was on solid ground. It felt like an earthquake, but it couldn't be. Her knees shuddered under her.

"I need a minute." The words were raw against her aching throat. Her whole body hurt.

The young people around her said something she didn't hear, and then disappeared around the tractor.

As her heart rate came down her muscles relaxed, and the tension felt like she'd come from a three day boot camp.

That was terrifying, but she was still alive.

Her brain slowly ticked pieces into place. The fog that had filled her head before she'd been locked in and driven onto a busy road was gone. Her adrenaline had probably burned off any tiny amount of substance that would have affected her.

Jenny leaned against the wheel of the tractor. The festival banner fluttered over her head and someone walked around from the front. "Oh my gosh, Jenny, oh gosh. I didn't know you were in there. Are you okay?"

It was Cherry's voice. Jenny nodded her head without looking up. "I'm okay. Just catching my breath."

Cherry came and put her arms around Jenny. Both tried not to cry.

"It's okay. Everything's going to be okay."

Jenny nodded again. After a couple minutes like that Cherry squeezed her shoulders and Jenny finally looked up. Cherry's eyes were the first thing she saw, muted green eyes that were swimming with compassion.

It was too much. Tears brimmed Jenny's eyes, and she squeezed them shut. "I thought I was going to die.

Cherry wrapped her arms around Jenny and held her close. "You cannot die, Jenny Doan. You have things to do! Nobody's going to hurt you on my watch."

Jenny looked up at her friend. Gratitude and doubt tangled inside her. Her lip trembled when she spoke. "You don't know that."

"Watch them try and stop me." Cherry pulled her back into a hug and Jenny squeezed her.

They were so different, and yet not at all. Decades apart in age, but Jenny would have sworn they were born sisters. As Cherry hugged her, Jenny's heart opened a little more.

"Okay, can you walk?" Cherry wrapped an arm around Jenny's waist. She got on her feet, and the ground was much more solid than before.

"What's going on over there?" Jenny asked.

The crowd of a half dozen people she'd seen when Bryan had stopped the tractor had swollen to a chaotic mash of dozens of bodies.

"Someone was hurt, I think. Do we need to go see?" Cherry paused, "I can probably sneak you home from here."

Jenny considered. It was better to know.

They made their way around the back of the tractor, sirens blaring as police arrived on the scene. When she came out from behind the remains of the vehicles, she had prepared herself to be mobbed by worried people, but Jenny quickly realized she was not the big story.

The crowd was surrounding the little white car that had hit Eddie's trailer. She couldn't see around them, but as the officer's pushed people back, a perimeter developed and Jenny could tell enough. A body hung between the front and back seats. They couldn't have been wearing a seatbelt.

"Do you know who it is?" Jenny asked quietly. The paramedics and police officers worked together to get inside.

Cherry shook her head, straining to be taller without looking morbidly curious. "Do you think they'll be okay?"

Jenny hesitated to answer. She stood with the rest of the crowd and waited, unable to tear their eyes away from what was happening. While Jenny could understand the need to know, gratitude echoed in her heart for her safety, and guilt gathered behind it that someone else would never get to go home.

The sun had fallen behind clouds again and the gray, misty sky felt more than appropriate for the scene.

Once the paramedics pulled the body out the noise of the crowd rose. Jenny's eyes grew wide. The body was wrapped in neon cords.

"Lissa?" Jenny's calm was replaced with panic as she strained to get past the group of curious onlookers. That body could be one of three people. Eddie, Tommy, or Lissa. "Tell me that's not Lissa." Jenny begged.

The first responders laid the body on a stretcher and as it wheeled by she finally caught a glimpse.

Tommy Webb lay on the white sheets burns corroding his body.

She wasn't glad it was him. She wasn't, but her lungs belayed that truth. She felt like they'd been basted to her rib cage and as soon as she'd seen Tommy's face the basting had broken free. She could breathe again and tears streamed down Jenny's cheeks.

As Tommy was wheeled away. Paramedics covered him with a sheet and Cherry wrapped her arms around her.

"It's not her," Jenny sobbed. "It's not Lissa." Jenny reached for her phone, "I need to call her. I need to know that she's safe."

"Let's do that." Cherry agreed. She hesitantly let go of Jenny. "Where's your phone?"

Jenny dialed the number and held it to her ear. She answered immediately when her voice answered. "Lissa?"

"Hi! I'm not available right now. Leave a message."

"Lissa's fine," Cherry reminded Jenny. "Sarah said she was watching a movie with her kids."

Cherry said the words and Jenny heard them but she couldn't get over the feeling in her gut that Lissa needed to come home.

"She's fine," Jenny repeated.

If that was true Lissa was the only thing that was fine. When Cherry'd gotten Jenny home, they'd found Ron sick again and still insisting he'd get over it soon.

The cold, gray evening had given way to a drizzly night. Cherry had driven Jenny home and stayed. It started with dinner and Cherry turned their quiet empty house into a warm and welcoming haven. The bubbling scents of fall veggies, nutmeg, and cream filled the air.

When breadsticks came out of the oven, Jenny found herself hovering at the table, dumbfounded that she hadn't imagined the scents of baking bread. "When did you make those?"

"A chef never reveals her secrets." Cherry giggled stacking the fragrant treats on a plate.

"I thought that was a magician," Jenny teased.

She'd half expected to hear Cherry had gotten them from a can, but Cherry didn't cook like that.

"Is it?" Cherry asked, ladling creamy, sweet potato stew into bowls.

Jenny took a deep breath and narrowed her eyes. "Hmm, maybe it's both."

Jenny carried a bowl up to Ron and the two women sat in the living room soaking up warm soup and not talking about what they'd seen that evening.

A knock at the door interrupted the chatter, and Jenny shot a glance at Cherry.

"Are you expecting someone?" Cherry asked pushing away from the table as her spoon sank into her bowl.

Jenny waved her breadstick at Cherry. "Sit, sit. You've done your work tonight magician." Jenny took a bite of bread. "You don't need to answer the door."

The rain fell lightly outside the porch light. An umbrella was all that was visible through the high window on Jenny's front door.

"Officer Wilkins? What can I do for you?" She kept her voice cheerful while she spoke, refusing to let reminders of the day drag her back. She was okay. Tommy was gone, but it wasn't her fault.

"Can I come in? I have some questions for you." He had closed the umbrella before Jenny could invite him in.

"Of course." She held the door for him. We're finishing dinner. Have you eaten? Cherry made soup."

"Cherry?" Officer Wilkins sounded confused

until his eyes lit on the woman sitting at the table. The firelight lit the grin on the officer's face like the Cheshire cat.

"You had some questions," Jenny said picking up a breadstick and dunking the end in her soup. She still had half a bowl and wanted to enjoy it.

"Can you tell me what happened today? Starting with why you were alone in Eddie Paris' motorhome." Wilkins looked like he wanted to chastise her, but thankfully, he just put his pen to his paper and waited.

"Well, I wasn't snooping, or not at first." She glanced at Cherry. "Cherry messaged me that Eddie wanted me to come by."

"Wait, wait, wait. I did no such thing. When did this happen?" Cherry leaned forward, set her food down, and retrieved her phone. "No, look." She held up her message thread with Jenny.

Jenny dug into her own phone. "But you did." She pulled up the screen and showed it to both of them.

Jenny watched him make his notes and waited till he looked up. "Do you still think it was Eddie?"

"You found experimental drugs in his trailer. It's strengthening my cause."

"I know. I just don't think it's him. He wouldn't have destroyed his own tour bus." Jenny couldn't imagine him doing that.

"He lured you to his trailer, locked you in, and tried to kill you. Are you really defending him?"

"No, but what about Benji? He attacked Harry this morning? And what about the murder weapon drop? Did anyone pick it up?

"Not yet. I think they saw that we had found it."
The officer sounded a little frustrated at the failure.

He stood, taking a breadstick from the tray in the center of the room. "As for Benji, he was at the bar. We have video surveillance."

"Well, what about Aria?"

24

Officer Wilkins looked at Jenny, "I'm sorry, who?"

"The woman from the alley, Aria Case." Jenny prodded and recognition dawned on the officer's face. "I told you about meeting her yesterday, didn't I?"

"Yeah, you did but why should I be worried about her?" Wilkins gave a thoughtful nod, lips pursed.

"Well, she has a room full of props. So, she could have used or planted any of the evidence. And she's been threatening the hypnosis victims because she thinks they're out to get Eddie."

Jenny tried to remember if there was anything else he should know, but when she tried to picture the events, it all crashed down on her with the windshield busting and the white car slamming into the trailer.

"What about the car?" Jenny asked. "Tommy was all tied up, and I saw his face. He was dead long before he was put in that car."

Wilkins put his pen in a coat pocket and stashed

his notebook away. "The car belonged to a neighbor. Someone put him in there and stuck a brick on the pedal."

Jenny remembered his story. He believed that he'd burned his hand in pool chemicals while drowning Eddie Paris. Now, he was the one gone.

Officer Wilkins apologized again for interrupting their dinner. And when Cherry handed him a fistful of fat breadsticks, Jenny was only a little jealous.

He gave a smile and a nod to Cherry before he left. When the door closed, Jenny turned to her friend. "I saw that."

"What?" Cherry asked from the couch in the living room where she was gathering empty bowls.

Jenny raised an eyebrow and took the stack of bowls from her. "Don't try and deny it. Every time that officer shows up, he's giving you special smiles and gentlemanly nods. Now you're giving him our breadsticks?"

Cherry stalked into the kitchen. "We had plenty of 'em. Who makes him bread on a stormy night?"

Jenny winked at Cherry. "You're right. It was a very generous gift." The doorbell rang, and she raised an eyebrow at Cherry. "Why don't you get the door this time?"

Cherry walked away, "I have no problem with that."

Jenny grinned. "He's like a puppy. Feed him once, and he keeps coming back. Feed him twice, he'll never leave."

"You're terrible!" Cherry shouted on her way to the door.

Chain Piecing a Mystery

Jenny held her hands up and followed her. "I'm just giving you fair warning."

She opened the door, certain Wilkins had forgotten something, but no one was there. "Hello? Officer Wilkins?"

Who else would show up at her house on a dark rainy night? Jenny was about to close the door when she saw the package. Next to the door, on her porch bench, sat a small grocery sack wrapped in twine. It was obviously not an accident. Jenny picked it up and shut the door.

The sound of Cherry's voice carried through the main level of the house, but Jenny had stopped listening. Jenny and Cherry took their soup and the package upstairs.

"Jenny?" Ron had fallen asleep in his chair at some point and Jenny leaned over and kissed him. His eye popped open and he grinned. Kissing her cheek Ron pulled himself out of his chair. "I'm going to bed. Love you, Jenny."

She smiled up at him and kissed him. Helping him to his room and returning before she opened the bag.

Cherry sighed a deep sigh after Ron left. "I want what you have. Jenny, how am I ever going to find a Ron for my life?"

"He's pretty special." Jenny agreed without looking up. She reached out, pulling the twine off. She needed to know what was inside. "Someone left a package for me."

Cherry didn't look excited, and after her day, she was trying not to think too grimly. She'd been warned once today. She wasn't sure she could handle it if something else went wrong.

She opened the bag with the flap facing away from her. Nothing happened. She looked inside.

"Well," she said, reaching into the bag and pulling out a blank DVD case. "What's a slumber party without movies?"

Half an hour into watching the strange DVD, Cherry grumbled, "This is the most boring slumber party movie I've ever seen."

She wasn't wrong. It was a surveillance video showing short clips of Dr. Butler's waiting room, file room, and office. It was scratchy and only played white noise.

When she'd opened the DVD case, a note had fallen out. "You need to see this."

It was written in black ink on white paper. There was the tiniest spot of red in the corner. Slightly sheer, like lipstick, the color was bold red.

Not many people could pull off that color but Nancy did. And she knew Jenny was curious about the surveillance. Would she have sent Jenny these tapes?

Who had given it to her, though, and why? Nothing happened.

It started Wednesday before Eddie's show when Nancy closed up shop. Then Dr. Butler returned. He invites the tech guy in. The guy fixes things, stops to look at the antiques like Jenny had, and then leaves. After that, it's a very long video of Dr. Butler working late and falling asleep in the lobby before it fuzzes out and ends.

The sudden noise woke Cherry, who looked up

groggily. "Did you learn something amazing?"

"No!" Jenny was exhausted. She tossed the note in the grocery sack and shut off the TV. "That was an eternal waste of time."

Cherry chuckled in half-dazed sleep. "So glad we could do this," she said, giving Jenny a thumbs up.

Jenny ignored her. "I should have gone to the bar. Benji would have been more interesting."

Cherry opened one eye to look at Jenny and said, "Those are words I never thought I'd hear you say."

She laughed out loud and stopped herself, afraid she'd wake up Ron. "That is so true." Jenny didn't drink and going to the bar had never been on her list of things to do for fun unless there was dancing, but that had been a long time ago too.

"We could go hang out with the Eddie Paris Fanclub," Cherry offered helpfully, with a sleepy smile on her face.

"We'd have to make sparkly outfits and pink business cards." Jenny teased. The Eddie Paris fan club. She'd forgotten about the business cards. She instinctually checked her pockets before remembering she had changed clothes.

Cherry rolled back, squinting up at Jenny. "How do you feel about fake eyelashes?" Her commitment to the idea only lasted about fifteen seconds, and she laid back down, yawning. "Can we fangirl in the morning? I'm tired."

"I'll be right back." She whispered to her incoherent friend before she walked as quietly as her old house would let her down the hallway.

She almost didn't hear Cherry respond, "Bring

me back a tiny umbrella, okay?"

Jenny refused to laugh. She closed the distance to her room and quietly found the black pants she'd been wearing earlier hung over a chair drying. She was pretty sure she'd dropped them on the floor. Even when sick, Ron took care of her. She blew him a kiss and felt in her pockets. Retrieving the business card, she put her pants back on and escaped down the hall to the brightly lit family room.

Jenny finally sat, examining the card she'd fished from Eddie's trash can. Aria Case. There was nothing special about the front, and Jenny was a little disappointed that it really was just a business card. She flipped it over, finding a note on the back. *Out of ashes, we rise.*

The little message was written in shimmery purple ink and signed with her name at the bottom. The message was personal, even if cryptic. Seeing her with Krista that afternoon in private conversation brought new possibilities to Aria & Krista's role in Eddie's fate.

She turned the little card over in her hands a couple of times. Aria was a wild card. She didn't fit the profile. She adored Eddie, and yet she was a part of every bad thing that happened. At every crime scene. She needed to know more about her. Jenny didn't have a clue where she was, but she knew where she was staying.

Looking over at Cherry, her face had softened, and she was sleeping deeply. Jenny had almost woken her. Turning off the light, Jenny grabbed her coat and went downstairs. Her keys were in the kitchen. She grabbed her umbrella and hurried out to the car.

Jenny loved a good stakeout. She was parked in the parking lot of the Hamilton Hotel directly across from Aria's room, her car hiding comfortably in plain sight.

She hadn't thought to bring snacks, but she was a sucker for games and she was patient. Jenny watched as quilters finished their projects and turned in for the night. Aria's light never came on, and Jenny didn't see the silver car she'd been driving. She contemplated knocking on the door but didn't want to give herself away. So, she waited.

Jenny pulled out one of Aria's business cards from her pocket. Eddie Paris fan club, President, Parisian-level 1. She wondered if actual Parisians would take offense to that nickname. Jenny decided it was a good thing Eddie's super fans were a small group. Quite possibly only one.

At least at her level.

Jenny used her phone to click the QR code on the back of the card and found Aria's Eddie Paris' fanclub website. It was pink, cheap, and everything Jenny had expected.

The main page was essentially a digital tribute to her favorite hypnotist. As Jenny clicked through the pages, she found links for hypnotist conferences and classes, information on the Great Eduardo himself, and even a page of selfies featuring Aria's face and Eddie Paris in the background.

Jenny sat forward, her skin crawling. This wasn't just a tribute. She had pics of Eddie signing autographs or performing at public events, but others featured him coming out of the grocery store, driving the motorhome, and even him and his wife.

As she scrolled through page after page of pictures, she found the latest ones. She showed herself in Hamilton with Eddie in the background talking to Lissa, and her face was X'd through ominously.

It got worse. She had pictures of Lissa, Frank, and Tommy, and most recently, a picture of Aria posing with puckered lips and one of Eddie's throwing knives laying against the scars on her face at Hamilton's four-way stop.

Those were the knives Lissa had believed she'd used. That was how she was supposed to die.

The picture had to have been taken that day because Lissa was behind her in Jenny's dark green coat, the one she'd borrowed that morning.

The image was captioned, "Missed you this morning. See you tonight."

Jenny tried to see if there was any other explanation before panicking and calling the police. She couldn't come up with anything. She flipped to her contacts and dialed Officer Wilkins. Sometimes panic is exactly the right response.

Jenny had the phone on speaker, still scrolling through images. When a voice spoke through the phone, "Hamilton Police Dep—"

"Wilkins? Hello?"

—artment. Our local station is closed. If this is an emergency, please call nine-one-one or stay on the line and you will be redirected to emergency services."

Jenny hung up the phone. She'd hit the wrong button. She knew the police station would be closed and didn't want to get transferred to the county seat and have her call shuffled around until someone could come. She needed Wilkins. She found his contact again, this time clicking his personal cell number.

"Jenny? Do you know what time it is?"

"Yes, I do." She said, checking her watch. It was after midnight. "I'm at the Hamilton Hotel. You need to get here, now. Aria's going to kill Lissa. Tonight."

"I'm on my way." The phone went silent, and Jenny stared at the door ahead of her.

She called Lissa, but she didn't pick up. Jenny took a deep breath. It was after midnight, and it was normal for people to be sleeping if they didn't expect to be murdered. It was fine. Wilkins was on his way. They'd find Aria.

Jenny looked at the dark hotel room. What if she was too late and Aria had already gone. She could easily have followed Lissa out to Sarah's that morning.

Jenny called Sarah. "Sarah? Where's Lissa? Have you seen anyone around your place?"

"Mom?" Sarah had been sleeping, and Jenny tried to be patient as her daughter found consciousness.

"What's going on? Seth? Do you know if anyone's been hanging around out here?"

Sarah was Jenny's second daughter and lived outside of town. It had felt like a safe place when they had made plans for Lissa to stay there.

But it was late, Seth was sleeping, and the fear that Aria knew where Lissa was had taken life in Jenny's mind.

"I think we're good, mom. Did something happen?" her voice still held the scratch of sleep, and Jenny wanted to shake her.

"Can you go check on her?"

"Who?" Sarah asked, not feeling Jenny's urgency at all.

"Lissa! She's not picking up."

"Well, it's midnight. No, it's closer to one at this point. What is going on?" Sarah's confusion was maddening. A light flashed through the parking lot as a car pulled in. Wilkins, she thought.

"Never mind." Jenny snapped the phone off and practically fell out of the car as she dashed across the lot to Aria's door.

Jenny banged on the panel and grabbed the door handle. It opened, and Jenny lunged through the doorway and was met with a scream.

25

Candlelight flickered across the floor, one of the flames growing. Jenny couldn't see who was screaming, but someone scrambled away and hit the light.

Several of half a dozen small pillar candles had been knocked over, rolling against an arrangement of photos and memorabilia.

Several of the photos had caught fire and the display was quickly becoming kindling.

"My tribute!" Aria gasped staring at the flames.

Jenny pointed to the small sink against the wall. "Get that towel wet!"

Aria made it to her feet and dashed to the sink. Water splashed into the bowl, and she plunged the nearest towel under the stream of water and turned toward the growing flames.

"Watch out!" Someone yelled, shoving past Jenny and scattering the little pile of flaming pictures and neon items.

Wilkins reached up and grabbed the sopping towel, smothering the remaining flames.

Then it was over.

Only a few of the pictures remained uncharred. A blanket hanging over the curtain rod at the window had hidden the light well. Open flames weren't allowed in the rooms, but Jenny was the one who'd flown in and caused the damage.

"Put those out." Officer Wilkins ordered, pointing at the still flickering candles.

"What's the matter with you?" Aria shouted.

"Me? What about you?" Jenny flung her hands out at the flaming candles.

"Somebody better explain what's going on here because I'd really rather be sleeping right now," Officer Wilkins growled, as he reholstered his gun in the shoulder harness he wore over a t-shirt and plaid pajama bottoms.

"I was meditating when she came in and attacked me." Aria started blowing out candles, picking them up and shooting Jenny with painful stares.

"Meditating?" Wilkins asked glaring at Jenny.

"I thought you were gone." Jenny tried to explain, her embarrassment turning the corner to awkwardness en route of humiliation.

"And if I was? Why is that a problem?" Aria finished removing the hot candles from the floor and picked up one of the remaining pictures. "These are rare, signed photos. You destroyed them."

Jenny looked down, chagrined. She was pretty sure Eddie would happily sign more publicity photos for her. But she had dramatically misjudged the situation.

"We're going to leave now." The officer put a

hand at Jenny's elbow, "If there's any damage to the room, I'm sure Jenny will take care of it. Sorry for . . . this."

Jenny did a quick check to make sure there wasn't any other damage in the room and let Wilkins usher her out.

Wilkins walked with her to her car. He probably wanted an explanation. But she didn't really have one. She'd panicked.

"Well," Wilkins prodded. "What made you so sure we had to go in there? She didn't look like she was getting ready to kill someone."

Wilkins had propped one foot on top of the other. Standing barefoot on the gravel wasn't a favorite experience.

"I know," Jenny said one hand rubbing her temple. She still didn't understand what she'd missed. "She posted it. She had the knife and pictures of Lissa . . . and she worships Eddie."

"So, I saw," Wilkins said matter-of-factly. "But there's a big jump between stalker and killer."

Jenny let out a breath the cold night air turning it white. It had felt so plain. "You're right. I was so certain. She knows how to hypnotize people. All she had to do was convince Eddie he was in danger and then one by one she makes him safe again. What better way to get noticed than saving his life? With all of that and the post saying 'see you tonight.' Then Lissa wouldn't pick up. I lost it."

Wilkins watched her, considering. "You can never lose it, Jenny. You can't. Not in this line of work."

"Yeah, if I don't keep a level head while I'm quilting, it does not go well." She shouldn't be snarky right now, but sass was in her nature, and Wilkins was there.

He raised an eyebrow at her. "That's not what I meant." He glanced at Aria's room. "Your breed of quilting is a lot more dangerous than most. You have to think about how everything comes together before it happens, cause if you don't ..."

"My quilts could kill people?" Jenny questioned him and Wilkins gave a shrug.

"You never know. At the very least you don't get what you planned on. You end up with a Triangle quilt when you wanted a Churn Sash." He tapped the top of the car and opened the door for her.

"Churn Dash." Jenny gave a short laugh. "And you're not wrong. There's no point in cutting the full yardage if I never checked the measurements."

Wilkins' face twisted in concentration, lines creasing his forehead. It looked like he'd reached the end of his quilt metaphors.

Jenny slid into the car and let him off the hook. "I'll try to think before I act and not jump to conclusions."

"That would be appreciated." He held the door open, having a silent battle with himself. Finally, he let go, folding his arms. "I'm not going to be able to keep you out of this, am I?"

Jenny shrugged, feeling a little guilty. "Quilting is kind of a passion. It helps people, and helping people is important to me."

He let a breath out through his nose, his tension

adding to his tough guy look. "That's what I thought. I've said it before, but I need you to be careful. Keep your cool, look for *facts*, don't get yourself in dangerous situations."

Jenny nodded, "Got it. Follow the pattern and don't make killer quilts."

"Be careful, okay? And call me first . . . before you decide to go take down the bad guys."

"It's not like I'm running around looking for trouble." Jenny frowned.

"And still, you find it. So, let me know what's going on, and maybe I'll be able to keep you safe." He shut the door and walked back to his car.

Jenny sighed. "That wasn't what was supposed to happen."

Her phone lit up in the console next to her. She had a string of missed texts from Lissa.

— He's here. what do I do? He tried to get me but I'm hiding

— He's got a knife.

— I'm in the shop across from the brewery. What do I do?

— Help!

Jenny read the whole thing in seconds. Wilkins was pulling out of the driveway, and Jenny tried not to panic. She slammed her palm into the horn and jumped out of the car. She'd probably woken half the building. Wilkins climbed out of his car and walked toward her. She couldn't see his expression in the dark, but his body language was stiff, and she knew he couldn't be happy with her.

"Wilkins. It's not over." The phrase flashed in her mind as the carved threat on the back of Eddie's tour bus. She couldn't think about that. For Lissa the danger was now and this was definitely not over.

Wilkins glanced at Aria's window. The blanket was pulled back, and she could see the woman watching the exchange.

Jenny shook her head. "Not Aria. We need to go to the brewery. He came after Lissa. She's hiding." She hoped she was still hiding. "She needs help."

"You're sure?" Wilkins asked, his head tipped and his eyebrow raised.

Jenny held out her phone. He took it and read quickly. With a nod of his head, he gestured for her to follow him. "Come with me. I'll be faster."

26

The old shop was dark and empty. Jenny wasn't even sure if it had electricity. The giant sliding door stood open on what was essentially a shed, full of wood working projects old tools and older projects.

"Lissa?" Jenny found the girl hiding behind a worktable and pulled her out.

"Where is he?" Lissa asked. Her eyes were wild, and she couldn't focus on Jenny. "Did you find Eddie?"

"Eddie was here?" Jenny asked trying to get her attention. "Is that who was after you?"

Wilkins stood nearby, as soon as Lissa nodded he jogged off, searching the area.

"He had a knife. I was getting into my car, and he grabbed me. But I bit him, and he let go. I just ran." Lissa kept looking around. She was understandably shaken, but she looked safe.

"We already did a search. We didn't find anyone here. I think it's safe." Jenny kept her voice calm and stroked Lissa's hair back. She nodded as Jenny spoke, gradually letting go of her search of the darkness and letting Jenny soothe her.

"That was terrible." Lissa's breathing slowed as Jenny turned them toward the door, walking her out to the car.

Wilkins jogged back to the group. "Nobody's seen him. Are you sure it was Eddie?"

Lissa nodded. "When I ran away, I didn't know where to go. I hid between the cars at the brewery. He started walking around and calling for me. I think he could tell that I hadn't left the parking area." She paused, her gaze drifting to the cars.

Jenny held her eye contact, trying to keep her attention focused. "Don't think about it. Tell us what happened. How did you know it was him?"

Lissa's brow furrowed as if reliving it. "He kept calling me. His voice was weird, and he'd say, 'it's me, Eddie.' He called me by name. Lissa let's have more fun. He never said the whole thing though. More fun, more . . . you know. I guess he was a little worried. But that's when I texted you."

Wilkins took some notes on his phone. It was weird to see him without his yellow notepad and weirder to see him doing police work in pajamas.

"Where are your shoes?" Lissa asked noticing his bare feet. He'd propped one up on the frame of the car.

He lifted his toes and shrugged. "I heard you were in trouble, and I couldn't find them. I'm not officially on duty yet so, I came without them."

Lissa nodded and relaxed, sitting against the hood of the car.

"Why don't you girls stay here? I've got to call this in." Wilkins walked several paces away before making the call.

Voices and music filled the night. It mingled with laughter and conversation spilling from the brewery doors. They were closed tight during the day, but spilled light across the street in the dark. "I thought you were at Sarah's."

"I was. I got bored. I messaged Nancy, and she suggested we meet out here. It was fun until then." Lissa leaned into Jenny. "Nancy went home first. She had some kind of last-minute thing to take care of for Dr. Butler. And so Benji and I hung out. I know it was dumb but there were so many people there. It felt safe. And he was being really sweet. I'm sorry."

"It's okay. You're safe now." Jenny tried to piece together the puzzle. To examine the pieces of the quilt, so to speak, before she put together the pattern. "Was Benji there the whole time?"

"He came later. And Harry was there, Nancy still likes him, I think. So, she was showing off, and once Benji showed up, she was gone." Lissa shook her head, "I want to go home."

Jenny apologized and squeezed Lissa's hand. "It will just be a little longer until Officer Wilkins can take us. He may have to check some things out here before we go home."

Lissa didn't say anything. "I keep feeling his stubble against my cheek. When he first grabbed me, he put his face right next to mine, and it rubbed against me while he spoke." She shivered, and

Jenny wished there was another way.

Tapping Wilkins on the shoulder Jenny whispered. "Do you care if I call someone to come take us home? Do you need a statement or anything?"

Wilkins looked over Jenny's shoulder at Lissa. "Just a second," he said into the phone and lifted the speaker away. "I need to ask a few more questions. Can I come by tomorrow?"

"Of course," Jenny replied.

"Good. Thank you. That'll let me go in and talk with the staff here. See if anyone's seen anything. Keep her talking, okay? She's been traumatized and could be in shock. And it will help her remember."

Jenny could do that. "What about Eddie? If he's not here, where is he?"

"We don't know. We've got people checking his parents' house, and the patrol officer is looking for him." He looked over Jenny's shoulder at Lissa. "We'll find him."

He hung up, crossed the street, and went into the brewery. Jenny sent Ron a text and joined Lissa at the car.

"I'm trying to get Ron to come grab us. It'll be a minute, though. It's nice that you and Nancy have gotten along. Did you say she had work to do still? That's so crazy. I thought she was the office manager. Does she do other stuff there?"

Jenny couldn't imagine what after-hours things a local doctor's office had to do in the middle of the night.

"Yeah, I think she was surprised too," Lissa said.

Ron hadn't replied, and considering the time of night, she sent him another one, and one to Cherry, just in case.

"I'm so sorry about tonight. I was more worried about Benji than Eddie."

Lissa's lips turned up slightly. "I wasn't worried about either of them." Lights flashed down the road, and Lissa sat up, craning her neck. "What's that?"

"I don't know." She said as Wilkins burst out of the brewery, running full tilt toward the lights. "Come on."

They weren't far away. Only a block or two over, but Lissa lagged behind Jenny as they walked quickly down the block. She stopped outside the radius of the lights, the two women trying to see what had happened without getting in the way.

Officer Wilkins was kneeling over someone as Officer Morgan cuffed them. Jenny's heart pounded in her ears. Had they found him already?

"Oh, this is a small town," Lissa whispered as she watched them lift the man from the ground. Eddie Paris was standing there, dressed up like he was going to a party with his hair done and a clean shave. He walked with Officer Morgan while her partner questioned a man standing on his porch. "I didn't do anything. I didn't touch her. I didn't do anything to that girl."

Officer Wilkins spotted them and jogged over. "You shouldn't be here. I thought you guys were getting a ride home."

"I'm trying. I think all my people are asleep, though."

Wilkins nodded and watched as Officer Morgan helped Eddie into the police cruiser.

Cherry's convertible pulled up alongside the three of them. The top was up, but there was no mistaking her little speedster. "I thought I'd find you here."

Jenny looked at her phone. Cherry replied a few minutes ago. Ron never had. He must be sleeping hard. He was usually the one she relied on to hear the middle-of-the-night calls and messages.

"Is this your fault?" Cherry asked Wilkins.

He leaned down, looking through the open window. "Cherry Carmine, do I need to warn you about loitering? It's the middle of the night, and you're holding up traffic."

Cherry gasped and looked behind her, "I'm so sorry, Officer PJ's. I guess I better get on my way. Come on, girls. I'm holding up traffic."

Wilkins grinned like he'd been given a free pass to the ice cream store. Jenny pulled the door open for Lissa and climbed in with her.

Wilkins gave a little finger wave as they started to roll away. Cherry missed it, watching the other side of the car.

"I wonder what he was doing tonight?" Cherry asked.

"I don't want to talk about it," Lissa mumbled, looking at her hands. She was pointedly ignoring the man.

"Okay," Cherry let the car roll while she watched the exchange of the police officers. "That baby face, though. Must think he's handsome or something. I like my guys with a little scruff on them."

Cherry grinned obviously not thinking about Eddie.

Lissa giggled, "Like Wilkins?"

Cherry laughed, "He is nice to look at. But that poor boy. He wouldn't know how to flirt if Cupid came down and kissed him."

"Why do you need to flirt if you go straight to kissing?" Lissa leaned forward, obviously grateful to have something else to talk about.

Cherry looked at Lissa in the rearview mirror and her smile dimmed. "You don't, I guess. Nah, he's handsome, but he's not for me." Cherry was quiet before making a loud, *mmm*, "He does have a nice profile though. Doesn't he?"

"Yeah," Jenny mumbled while the other two enjoyed the joke. Something had been bothering her. "I don't think it was Eddie."

Jenny sure knew how to kill a vibe.

The laughter died as Lissa stared off, and Cherry tried to figure out what she meant.

"Of course, it was Eddie," Cherry said. "We all saw him." She forced a laugh, but it obviously didn't make sense to her.

"I know that was Eddie." Jenny looked behind them. "But Lissa, the guy who attacked you tonight. I don't think it was him."

"You were attacked?" Cherry yelled at them.

Lissa stared at her. "I heard him. He said his name. It was him."

"That's not helpful." Cherry burst out, torn between her obligation as the driver and her desire to learn what had happened, she kept glancing back and forth. "Somebody better tell me what happened, or I'm pulling this car over right now."

"I don't . . . I can't—" Lissa tried and failed to get the words out.

"Lissa was attacked as she was leaving the brewery tonight." Jenny answered for her.

"Like a creepy guy in town hitting on you or someone beating you up?" Cherry pulled into the driveway and shut the car off. Then she turned in her seat to face Jenny's niece.

Lissa looked between the two older women. "Neither. Someone I thought was Eddie threatened me with a knife, which is supposedly my planned demise, but Aunt Jenny apparently doesn't think so . . . so?"

Jenny frowned, "Well, you said he put his cheek so close you could feel the stubble when he spoke."

"But Baby Face Eddie doesn't have stubble," Cherry said looking at Lissa.

"Exactly," Jenny said as understanding dawned on Lissa.

"So, who wanted to kill me?" Lissa's confusion carried a heavy pain. It was a question she should never have had to ask.

Jenny undid her seat belt wishing she knew the answer. "I don't know. I feel like we're back at square one."

"Except in square one, I haven't been attacked and threatened at knifepoint."

"Whoever it is, he won't get away with it." Cherry's accent cradled the words in Southern determination.

Lissa clicked her seat belt. "Can you let me out?"

"Oh, right." Jenny climbed out and leaned the seat back forward so Lissa could get out.

She did and quickly went inside.

Cherry shut the car door, and Jenny did the same, joining her as they walked to the porch.

"I hate that in a few words he made her believe him," Jenny said softly.

"She trusts people. That's not a bad thing." Cherry nudged Jenny and followed her into the house.

Jenny almost regretted saying anything. She didn't want Lissa's lessons from her to include how not to trust people. But trust was a double-edged sword not made for the gullible. And Lissa had the faith of a saint.

27

Jenny turned on the DVD that she'd found on the porch. Cherry had fallen asleep like it was her white noise machine, and Ron had finally gone back to bed.

Lissa sat next to her, flipping the note over in her fingers. "I swear, I'm fine. I basically took a nap."

"If you say so." Jenny was only in the first hour of the recording, and she already felt like she needed a shot of adrenalin. "So, what do you think about the note?"

"It looks like Nancy's handwriting to me." Lissa set the paper down, and Jenny picked it up.

"That's what I figured. It was the lipstick spot that made me think so." She looked at the note, annoyed that they knew who had written it, what it was for, but not what they were supposed to find on it. It made Jenny second guess Nancy's role in all of this. If she was in on the hypnosis or killings, why would she want Jenny to figure it out? If was trying to throw Jenny off she was going to be upset.

She'd liked Nancy.

Jenny pouted at the screen as it cycled through sixty-second blips of each office-type room. Nancy had taken the doctor's arm and walked off the screen in the previous hour. Jenny hit fast forward, a luxury she hadn't allowed herself the last time she'd watched it. How would she find what she needed to find if she fast-forwarded?

She watched the leaves dance on the trees and the coats shift on the rack when the heat and air came on.

It was an empty office.

Lissa started snoring. Jenny looked over, wondering if she should keep Lissa awake because of shock. Looking at the film they were watching she didn't know if she'd be able to keep her up anyway. She put the film on triple speed and watched everyone dance across the screen.

When Dr. Butler came back, Jenny laughed. He zipped through the office, working in tiny, quick motions that an elf would have admired. And that was about it. The trees danced, and the coats shifted.

Wait.

Jenny hit play, and the film slowed to standard speed. Something had changed. The coat rack was different. She paused the video and looked at the film. She hit rewind and let it zoom even faster, jumping over whole chunks of the video, and then paused.

Yes! There it was.

Jenny's scarf was hanging from the coat rack. The bright blue scarf was a deep gray in the black and white flick. And then, she zoomed the video ahead to the evening, after everyone but Dr. Butler was gone. After the tech guy left, it disappeared.

Something had been altered. She watched it again, more slowly, to figure out exactly when it happened.

"There!" she shouted, jumping from her seat. Lissa screamed on the couch next to her.

"I found something!" Jenny was absolutely giddy.

Lissa rubbed her eyes and pushed herself up. "What is it?"

Jenny rewound the video. The tech guy was walking around the room before the break.

"Woah," Lissa said. Jenny was about to tease her with a fake "haha," but Lissa got off the couch and walked closer to the screen. "What is he doing in there?"

Jenny gave a quiet "ha," as she watched Lissa, still half expecting her to break her composure and yell, "Got you!" It's what her kids would have done. It's what she would have done in the right situation.

Lissa didn't, and she glanced over her shoulder. "Is that it?" she asked. "What's Harry doing on there?"

A familiar lump returned to Jenny's throat. It had taken half the day to get rid of it after being compacted inside a tin can and shoved into the road. "How did I not see that?"

Lissa stopped herself before she could agree. "It's totally Harry. Does it ever show him and Nancy together?"

Jenny shook her head and watched him circle the room more closely. He stopped at the bookcase like he had earlier. He pulled out one of the books and opened it, then put it back and walked away. Nothing special. She pushed the video back again. She'd almost missed it. He stuck something in the book—a business card.

She played it again but couldn't read the business card. She didn't know if it was his but Jenny pulled out her phone and found the picture she'd snapped of the tech guy . . . Harry's business card.

The video played while Jenny read over the card. Terry Bunch, IT , Tech, Security Systems. It wasn't Harry's name but he was definitely the guy.

Harry was in the Dr.'s office now and he circled the room. Harry paused in front of a photo for a long time, even picking it up to look at it closer. Maybe she could get into Dr. Butler's office tomorrow and see what was so interesting.

I ce cream and peach cobbler in the middle of the night were completely inappropriate.

And that's why she had Cherry.

"Let's go." Cherry dragged Jenny from the couch.

Jenny pulled away, laughing. "Cobbler, after midnight, is not a healthy decision for me."

It took a bit more convincing but Cherry eventually got her out the door and into the car. "Nope. We're going to my house where there is always peach cobbler and ice cream." They pulled onto the road and Cherry gave her a smile. "You are going through so much. It's okay to take a break. I don't care if you eat this cobbler and laugh or cry but you need a moment to not be Lissa's protector, and not be Ron's champion, and not be the town's problem solver. Just come be my friend tonight, okay?"

Jenny's chest tightened and her eyes welled with tears. "That is not an easy thing Cherry. I'm not sure I know how to let go if I have to turn around and put myself together in the morning."

"You don't have to. I'll do it for you."

Jenny grabbed Cherry's arm. "I'd hug you if you weren't driving, but then I'd really cry so this is probably for the best."

Cherry laughed and Jenny inhaled deeply, muffling the confused half cry, half laugh, that tried to come out.

In the darkness they turned the corner past the doctor's office. A lone car sat in the parking lot.

"That's a late night for Nancy at the doctor's office." Cherry teased.

Jenny glanced up, but it wasn't the car that caught her attention. A light flashed in one of the windows. "Is she still there?"

"I'm sure not." Cherry paused at the empty four way stop and Jenny saw the light again.

"We should go back," Jenny said.

"Do you really think so?" Cherry slowed but didn't turn back. "It's probably broken down. Or she got a ride with someone."

Jenny bit her lip. Her nerves were stippled across her chest, roiling lines of quilted chaos.

"I don't know." Jenny looked over her shoulder. "I thought I saw a light in the window."

Giving her a funny look Cherry offered a suggestion almost like it was a test. "If you think something's wrong, we should call the police."

"Okay. That's a good idea," Jenny said as the light passed into another room.

"It is?" Cherry asked in disbelief. "You're really okay calling the police on this?"

"Is that surprising?" Jenny asked unbuckling as they pulled into the parking lot. She already had her phone out.

Cherry laughed softly. "Uh, yeah. You hate it when Wilkins gets information before you."

Jenny slipped out of the car and asked the officer to come out one more time. When she hung up Cherry was peeking in the windows of Nancy's little coupe.

"Come look at this." Cherry beckoned Jenny closer. "Do you see that?"

A duffel bag full of long and short knives with neon handles lay in her back seat.

"I think that's a little suspicious," Jenny said glancing at her Cherry. "Don't you?"

Cherry narrowed her eyes at Jenny. "How close is Officer Wilkins?"

"He'll be here soon." Jenny walked slowly around the car. A feeling of dread built inside her.

"I can't believe Nancy is behind all this. She was so sweet." Cherry's lament felt a little premature.

"I'm not sure that's it. Lissa said Nancy got called away on work and it's almost morning." Jenny watched the road. "Maybe it's my nerves but something isn't right here."

"It's not right that she's got a bag of pointy death weapons in her back seat," Cherry said taking a long look at the duffel.

"There's been plenty of time for those to be planted." Jenny was more interested to know how they were here and not in police custody if someone actually did go pick up the drop the police were supposed to be watching.

Cherry didn't respond and then, as another car approached, she asked, "Why is the door open?"

Jenny followed Cherry's line of sight. She hadn't noticed before but the back door was cracked open a thread of light showing at the side. "I don't know."

"Should we go close it?" Cherry whispered.

"Maybe we should go in." Jenny glanced back to the black car that had shut it's headlights off.

Officer Wilkins stepped out of his car and Cherry sucked in a heavy breath of relief. "He's here."

"And he's got shoes this time." Jenny teased.

"Well, ladies, have we begun this week's Grand Theft Auto?"

Neither woman laughed and Wilkins' expression sobered.

"This is Nancy Adams' car," Jenny said. "I got some strange surveillance videos from her earlier. And we were driving by, it seemed odd that she'd still be out. But look in the back seat."

Wilkins put his hand up against the light so he could see. He smacked a fist against the window. "No!"

He pulled out a radio immediately calling the officers who were watching the drop site.

After a few minutes of questions he glanced at Jenny and Cherry and closed the line. "It's them. They didn't believe me but when they checked, the entire box is empty." His nostrils flared as he growled the words. "It has to be Eddie."

"Isn't Eddie in jail?" Jenny asked.

Wilkins shot her a dark look. "He never made it. Someone caught them at the gas station and stole him out of the car."

"You're kidding." Cherry muttered. "This shouldn't be so hard."

Wilkins glared at her and he looked back to Jenny. "Thanks for calling me. I'll get the station to send some guys."

"That's not it," Jenny said stopping him. "We need to go inside. Someone's been walking around in there. Lights coming on and off and occasionally a flashlight. It's strange."

"Okay. I'll be right back. If she's in there, she's got some questions to answer."

"Fair enough," Jenny said.

Wilkins started toward the building. "You ladies stay here."

Jenny's jaw dropped. She looked at Cherry and shook her head. Cherry shrugged, her eyes wide. Jenny quietly followed behind Wilkins.

He circled to the side of the building, shooting the two of them a warning glance.

"Don't follow me." He hissed.

Jenny paused, and he disappeared around the

corner. Nancy would have gone through the open door. Her heart rate picked up and without another option, Jenny headed straight for the door.

She held a finger to her lips to prep Cherry as she reached the door. It opened smoothly except for the jingle of keys hanging from the inside. She stopped. *Please, whoever's in here… Please don't notice.*

Something crunched inside the building, a smack against metal, and silence. Jenny hoped it wasn't Wilkins. If it was she really had to go in. She glanced at Cherry who nodded and the two of them slipped through the door.

Keeping to the walls, the two women peeked in door after door. Every room was empty, until the last patient's room. Lying across the table was a pale, motionless woman. She could have been a mannequin, except for the golden curls that spilled around her face and deep red lips.

"Nancy," Jenny breathed.

"I thought —" Cherry began. Her confusion a stumbling block to her words. "Didn't you say she was the killer?"

"She will be," a familiar voice spoke up, followed by the shrill whine of a drill.

28

Cherry screamed. Her vivid fear shocked Jenny's system. She clapped a hand over Cherry's mouth, twisting them into the hall. The drill stopped as Jenny and Cherry dashed down the hall and around the corner. Jenny slammed into the broken drug cabinet. The door crunched further, a pile of glass bottles and bandages tumbled onto the floor.

Jenny grabbed one of the few metal tools in the pile. They looked almost like tongs but longer and thinner. Dr. Butler's office was in front of them, the door wide open.

Jenny shoved the two of them in, shutting the door behind them. She released Cherry and pushed a chair under the doorknob and turned the lock.

He would find them, there was no question. But as Jenny scanned the room her only goal was to make it harder to get to them.

Scattering the contents of the desk, Jenny searched feverishly to find something more dangerous than tongs to defend herself.

"Knock, knock!" he called. Rattling the door. A

lock clicked and Jenny sucked in a breath.

She knew that voice. *Who was it?* She couldn't make her brain work to even think through her suspect list.

A letter opener was tucked into a box of mail beside the doctor's photos and memorabilia. Jenny clawed into the box grabbing it. The photo beside the box was a picture of Dr. Butler standing next to Eddie Paris in a white doctor's coat. She snatched the photo up, her mind racing.

"He knows Eddie?" Jenny flashed through the possibilities and Jenny recognized his voice.

"I know Eddie." Their attacker sneered the words into mockery.

Only a sliver of Dr. Butler's face appeared as he glared into the room. "I know Eddie Paris. People always wondered why I didn't feel honored by that. No one says I know Greg Butler."

Searching through the narrow gap, Dr. Butler pushed and scraped as the door inched open revealing his face. When it had moved far enough, he reached in, removing the chair from the other side.

The door flew open and Dr. Butler stood calmly, watching them, like mice in a cage.

Grabbing a thin stool resting near the corner of the desk. She held it between them. Cherry backed away and Jenny followed until Cherry stumbled and cried out.

Jenny barricaded herself between Cherry and the doctor, turning to him in shock. "What is going on?"

"I'm getting ready to perform a little craniotomy.

It's a centuries old practice." He strolled into the room clapping his hands together. "You're going to love it."

Cherry pressed against the desk, her face flushed in horror.

Jenny held her stool up, and launched it at him. The doctor leaned easily to the side, avoiding the hurtling piece of furniture.

"Come now, are we barbarians?" he asked looking from the fallen stool to Jenny. It was like he had taken on the persona of the Victorian Dr. Jekyll and all his antique medical apparatuses in the lobby fit him perfectly.

A figure moved in the hall behind him. Officer Wilkins appeared and hurtled through the door as Jenny grabbed Cherry and slid them both out of the way. Officer Wilkins slammed against the doctor, launching them both to the back of the room.

The two struggled with each other, wrestling to get the upper hand. While they weren't looking. Jenny and Cherry bolted past and into the hall. From their vantage point, Nancy's hair and the old wooden drill from the bookcase showed through the doorway.

Jenny dashed into the room and started tugging at he. She was tied to the table.

"What are you doing?" Cherry hissed looking from Jenny to the hall.

"We can't leave her." Jenny responded trying to untie her wrists and failing. She started patting the girl's cheeks. "Nancy. Nancy? Wake up." She looked between the door and the woman. "This wasn't supposed to happen."

"Was any of it?" Cherry asked in disbelief.

Jenny didn't answer. She couldn't. The men were still fighting down the hall, but it stopped with a scream. Cherry flew out of the room toward the sound.

In the hallway to the doctor's office Wilkins was caught in the metal door of the broken medical cabinet. While a rolling bookcase barreled its way from Dr. Butler's office towards him.

"No!" Cherry launched herself forward, alongside the creak and crunch of the metal cupboard.

Dr. Butler shoved the bookcase into the cabinet, taking Cherry with it. She crumpled to the floor. Wilkins pounding on the bookcase he shoved it back but Dr. Jekyll had already moved on.

He looked at Jenny, the force of his gaze pushing her several steps backward.

"Why are you doing this?" Jenny asked, as she continued moving backward down the hall.

The doctor smiled without responding. "How is Ron, by the way? Those antibiotics I gave him should be tearing up his insides about now."

Jenny stumbled catching herself against the wall. "No." If she'd done any checking or had any idea. "How could you?"

"I had to do something. He was keeping your nosy self, preoccupied and you were a pain in the neck."

Jenny glowered, turning the corner into the lobby. "You're sick."

Jenny couldn't believe everything he'd put them

through. The bookcase full of tools was to the right and Jenny inched that way as the doctor let her take the lead.

"So, did you actually hypnotize them or was it just the drugs?"

His chest puffed and he strode a little smoother. He liked this conversation. "What do you think?"

"I think you hate hypnosis."

"It's so subjective," he complained. "The only way to effectively use the science is to manipulate the brain function before, so people's will power doesn't factor." His smile shifted into a sneer. "A little brain surgery to prime them for the information. I always liked neuroscience."

Intentional, amateur brain surgery on three innocent people? He was crazy.

"You know, this has been fun, but I have a patient waiting for me." He sighed and glanced at the bookcase.

"Nancy?" She asked feeling behind her for whatever she could reach.

He lunged out grabbing her as she gripped a tube. She slashed her arm around hitting him with an empty syringe. There wasn't even a needle on it but he let go. She threw it at his head and ran.

"Get back here." Dr. Jekyll called.

She hit the exit door, her body slamming against it but she was too slow.

The doctor was right behind her. His hand hit the doorframe as she twisted the doorknob. He knocked her to the side and she stumbled away.

She could barely move. She limped backward

watching him grow with confidence. If she was going to die she at least wanted to know why. "Why did you do it? So many innocent people."

"There was only ever supposed to be one." His eyes sparked with intention and Jenny found she'd backed herself into a corner.

He smiled and grabbed her arm roughly. "Come on. Hypnosis doesn't hurt anyone."

"Crazy does." She spat as he jerked her down the hall.

"Shut up!" he yelled, pulling her inches from his face. "Eddie deserved to die. It was only supposed to be him." He walked her past Nancy and shoved her into a chair and grabbed a rope.

The quiet echoed around them as Dr. Butler tied the rope around her wrists. "Eddie never believed I was any good. I had a business plan and he stole my clients. Then he felt guilty. Told the authorities I was selling prescriptions under the table. And guess what I lost my license. But Eddie? Nope. He got off scot-free. And then? He quit anyway!"

Jenny groaned and her mind spun. Her wrists hurt, the neon rope wrapped tightly around them. But there were fibers in her hand and textiles were her business.

Now she had to figure out how to use them.

"Why do you care if he quit? It doesn't sound like you wanted him to keep going."

"It was a slap in the face." He shouted the words like they would leave a mark. Reaching over he grabbed her hair, yanking her head back. Jenny screamed as he turned her around in the chair and he leaned close the stubble of his beard scratching her neck and cheek.

"You're not running the show anymore, Jenny. I'm the doctor. You have to listen to me."

She inhaled through her mouth trying not to let herself get too close to him. Her breath shuddered as she spoke. "Sure, add another innocent to your death toll."

"You brough the innocents." He scoffed and shoved her chair up against the counter, pointing down the hall. "You put those people in danger. You'll pay for your crimes. But, first you're going to confess to killing the Great Eduardo for me. You will beg for them to arrest you. And then you'll kill yourself."

"He's here, isn't he?" Jenny began worrying the ends of the rope. The nylon fibers fraying easily at the ends.

"Why do you say that?" The doctor's eyes shot to the lobby uncertainly. That didn't seem right.

"Because he never made it to prison and you're tired of this game."

Dr. Butler smiled a self-satisfied grin. "I don't know what you're talking about." He said, the smile never leaving his face.

He walked to the other side of the room and started prepping his medical tools.

"It's more than that isn't it?" Jenny watched him while inch by inch her fingers unwound the threads that held her. "You're jealous."

Dr. Butler scoffed and shot another glance to the lobby. "I've never been jealous of Eddie."

"Right. All this time and effort you put into killing him and he's getting all the fame."

"He's not even getting blamed!" the doctor shouted slamming a fist on the counter. "I told them about the break in. That I thought Tommy had stolen the meds for Eddie. You found the entire stash of them in the tour bus! And he tried to kill you! Still they couldn't figure it out."

"So where is he? Did you lose him?" Jenny laughed and instantly regretted it.

The doctor smacked a syringe on the counter. "Here. Okay? I didn't lose him. He's right here. Now shut up, or I'm going to gag you." He exhaled furiously. "Or find the chloroform. Do you have a preference?" He mumbled to himself, "I don't need another job tonight."

Jenny closed her mouth. She needed to get out of here. Her body grew steadily colder, fighting to regulate her speeding heart. She was out of time.

She stretched the threads in her fingers measuring several inches at a time as she went. They were about twelve inches long.

Dr. Butler set down another syringe and scowled. He looked at Jenny and smiled. "Don't move. I'll be right back."

She held her breath, trying not to let hope spring up on her face. Shifting her chair, Jenny slid to one of the drawers pulling it open with her knee.

"Middle drawer." Came a rough mumble from the table. Nancy's eye were flickering but she watched Jenny with drugged awareness.

Jenny shifted again, stretched against the rope and

usted her knee to open the drawer.

It was full of surgeons cutting implements. "Thank you." She whispered to Nancy. She'd have to thank her better when they were free.

With her hands behind her back, she reached in, praying she'd pick up the right end of the sharp tools. Scissors. Jackpot.

They were too long. They were meant for internal surgeries, not cutting ropes on your own wrists.

Footsteps echoed toward them. Nancy moaned and Jenny shushed her, pushing the drawer shut and putting on her innocent act.

He bought it. A narcissist was easy that way. They believed what they wanted to believe.

Jenny moved the scissors in her hand. Every time they got low enough to cut the rope, she couldn't squeeze them closed.

The doctor picked up his syringe and moved to Nancy. Instead of injecting her he set it down and pulled something out of the cupboard.

Jenny flipped the scissors over while Dr. Butler twisted open whatever he'd gone looking for.

She threaded a section of the long string through the loop at the end of the scissors, tying it in a knot. "When all this comes out, what will happen to you? Aren't you worried you'll lose your license?"

A slow smile spread across his face. He chuckled. It curdled her stomach and edged her to work faster. She threaded the other handle, tied it, and flipped the scissors.

"They can only do that to a man once. Besides, who's going to know?" He checked something on the syringe and closed the bottle. "Nobody suspects me. I've been so helpful. Whatever the police want, I take care of it."

The scissors now floated in Jenny's hands, and she manipulated the blades safely under the rope while he gloated. He disgusted her more with every word.

"I was going to have Nancy confess to killing Eddie, but using you works so much better. I'll drug you and Nancy both. Hypnotize you as Eddie's killer, and Nancy will never remember anything . . . possibly at all."

Nancy jerked her head. Jenny tightened the scissors as much as she could with her fingers, getting them to bite the threads though she still couldn't squeeze them from that angle.

"Short term is tricky when you do these kinds of procedures," he continued, "but don't worry. I'll keep Nancy on. I'm a nice guy like that. Your friends, on the other hand…" He gave a sad sigh and looked at her. Jenny let the scissors hold in place and carefully picked up the threads tied to each scissor handle, then swapped them. Holding the handle in place with a precariously balanced finger, she gripped the threads and tugged. Butler shook his head, 'tsking' at her. "They won't be so lucky."

The scissors bit together as she pulled, and the silky threads gave way. Her bindings fell to the ground. "You're a terrible person."

"And yet everyone is going to think it's you." He turned toward her. "Nobody will know about me."

"I do." Jenny didn't waste a single second. She

jumped out of her seat and ran for the door. She scurried around the corner and slammed into Wilkins. "Eddie's in the file room, I think," she said breathlessly. "He kept looking to the lobby when I asked."

Wilkins disappeared, and the doctor grabbed her. He held up a syringe like it was a butcher knife. "Are you ready to be on the cutting edge of science?"

Jenny tightened her lips, tugging away from him.

"I prefer... more fun."

Jenny hadn't said the words. And Dr. Butler gasped as a fist connected solidly with his jaw.

He slumped to the ground and Eddie Paris stepped forward massaging his knuckles. "And more surprises."

29

"No, it was Nancy that picked me up from the station. I guess Greg told the officers he was supposed to do some kind of medical examination. It was perfect really." Eddie ran a hand through his hair and rubbed his jaw. "I walked in, he chloroformed me, and I woke up in the file room at the clinic." Eddie's statement had been more than enlightening now that they knew who was behind the hypnosis and chaos of the recent events.

"And you didn't know that Dr. Greg Butler was your old classmate, Greg Carter?" Officer Dunn asked with eyebrows raised.

"No, I didn't. It blows my mind. I recognized him as soon as I saw him though."

"How long have you known him?" Dunn always clipped his sentences when he wanted to sound more professional.

Eddie shrugged. "We met in class a few years ago. We'd both recently graduated and were starting residencies, but our college recommended some specialties. He and I happened to pick the same one."

Jenny shook her head. "I can't imagine Dr. Butler–er, Carter–ever choosing hypnosis."

Dunn ignored her, but Eddie laughed. "You should have seen him the first day. He raised his hand for everything, answered every question." Eddie shifted his position, looking across to where they'd booked the con man. "Until practical applications started. I tutored him cause he was so terrible at it. Then we became friends and I found out about some things he was doing that I wasn't okay with. They pulled his medical license."

Dunn cleared his throat and moved forward. "Are you able to stay in town or provide contact information while we take care of details here?"

"Absolutely." Eddie agreed and Dunn shook his hand, leaving Jenny and Eddie sitting outside the clinic.

The sun was coming up and Jenny honestly didn't know how she was still awake.

"You must be anxious to get moving on to the next place," Jenny said, feeling more than a touch of relief that it was finally over.

"I don't know. I kind of feel like I need a change. Or rather less change." Eddie leaned back on the bench he and Jenny occupied.

"What will you do?" Jenny asked watching his face light with the rising sun.

He took a slow peaceful breath. "I hear there could be room for a local family practitioner in town." He turned his casual glance on Jenny, probably curious how she'd react.

"Is that something you'd want?"

Eddie grinned at the sky. "You know, when those three came out of nowhere saying they'd killed me, I knew something was wrong. And the only thing I wanted was to help them.

"I've spent so much time lately helping myself, I forgot how nice it is to care about other people. And I mean really care– invest in the town."

"Krista won't like that," Jenny mumbled into her cup, unsure if Eddie would want to hear that comment or not.

He laughed again. It was a nice laugh and comforting for Jenny to be around someone who was so free with their joy.

Eddie took a breath, really thinking about things, and seemed to settle. "No, she will not. But I've been fighting to keep her in my trust almost since I married her. I like her. But I don't think she likes me."

"Like?" Jenny said, surprised at such a mild sentiment from the passionate young man.

"Oh yeah, we've never addressed the love bridge. We got married in Vegas, and I'm the kinda guy that thought he could stick it out." He took a drink, swallowed, and let out a long breath. "Turns out, it takes two."

It was a difficult conclusion to accept, Jenny could imagine. She changed the subject. "Eddie, I don't know why we didn't know you better when you were growing up here, but I am so glad you think you'll stay."

"Me too. I'm diggin the small-town vibe here. I missed it more than I'd thought I would."

"It grows on you," Jenny said with a fond smile. Hamilton had done the same to her when she first moved there with Ron and their family.

Officer Wilkins walked past with his arm around Cherry and Eddie gestured to the couple with an eyebrow raised. "I heard that was an impressive story."

Cherry's arm was temporarily immobilized after it was broken when she jumped between Wilkins and the bookcase.

"Miraculous." Jenny waved to Cherry when she caught her eye. "Truly, though, they were both heroes tonight. I'm glad we have them here."

Wilkins ushered Cherry to his car, and they both knew he wouldn't be stopping for anything till he was sure Cherry was safe.

Nancy walked over hesitantly "I wanted to thank you for saving me tonight. There's a very real possibility that if you hadn't my life wouldn't be my own today." She fiddled with her hands. "I don't know how you repay something like that."

"I could say the same thing." Jenny squeezed the young woman in a hug, her smile warming Jenny. "Thank you for not giving up. And that's exactly what you've got to keep doing. Don't give up, keep going, and don't give anyone a reason to doubt who you are." Jenny winked at her and Harry, who had his arm around her. "And hang around with people who can help you remember."

Nancy offered a smile to Harry before leaving

Jenny alone. Eddie had been caught for an autograph and Jenny was alone for the first time all night.

She picked up her phone and called Ron. He didn't answer. Jenny smiled a sad smile, wishing she could hear his voice. He was surely sound asleep though..

The cops had managed to get a confession from Greg about Ron's treatment, and Eddie had reassured her that though the doctor's treatment was cruel, it likely had no permanent effects.

It would wear off just fine.

Jenny wandered back to her car. It was time to go home and help Ron start getting better. She ached, knowing he'd been used as her personal torture device and that he'd suffered so much of it alone.

That wouldn't happen again, she resolved. She had been excused and after blankets and tea and time, she finally felt like she could drive home. And home was the only place she wanted to be.

Food had no right to be so healing. Jenny yawned as she took a bite of the blueberry cream cheese pincushion rolls. There was enough sugar in them that she'd likely be awake till Tuesday.

After staying up through sunrise that morning, it was a necessary precaution.

Cherry sat next to Jenny with her list of events in hand but before she could start Jenny held out a simple white bag labeled with one word. Peach.

Cherry nearly jumped back out of her seat. "You got me pie!"

She wrapped her arms around Jenny and opened the bag breathing in the sugary heaven.

"I'd say you're lucky except he was already saving them for you." Jenny checked to be sure her bags of strawberry and blueberry pies that she was taking home to Ron were still safe in her basket.

"No!" Cherry looked back to where the Amish hand pie booth was starting to run low on inventory. "He's amazing."

"He's forgiving. All I had to do was tell him it was for the Southern red head who adores his peach pies and he knew exactly who you were."

"Alright, you're free for the afternoon. Anything you want." Cherry's eyes rolled back as she took her first bite of pie. "You are divine. Sorry Jenny, not you. You." She said to her pie.

Jenny laughed and Cherry groaned happily.

"How's Ron this morning?" Cherry asked after settling herself at the table.

Jenny clasped her hands grateful to finally have something positive to report. "Much better. Now that he's off those ridiculous antibiotics he's getting his color back and he's sitting up."

"Can I sit here?" Brooke Webb asked.

"Of course." Jenny looked up smiling. "Brooke! It's been a while. Oh, please sit. How are you feeling?" Brooke moved to sit, her smile sad and distant. She carried a basket of french fries in her hand. It was an interesting breakfast choice. Jenny shifted to make room. "I'm sorry. I can let you eat, but I wanted you know. I got to visit with Tommy several times last month. And I thought you'd like to know what a great kid he was."

Brooke's hand paused over her fries and Jenny caught the smile forming there. Good. Brooke deserved to be proud of Tommy.

"People didn't know him," Brooke said. "He always took care of me, though."

Cherry offered a smile as well. "It must be hard without him."

She nodded, "He worked right over there." She made eye contact with Jenny for the briefest second. "He made great fries."

That explained her breakfast choice and Jenny couldn't blame her. When her grandma had passed she'd wanted Swedish meatballs for a month straight.

"I bet he did."

She looked up again, this time giving Jenny a heart-opening smile. "He'd started working there before he passed. I think he liked bringing home the leftovers."

"That's adorable." Jenny could still clearly visualize the chemical burns on Tommy's hands and face. It was nice to think of him in happier ways.

"He always wanted to take care of me." Brooke repeated the sentiment from earlier and Jenny suspected that would play a big part in her life.

"It's been hard having him gone. I never wanted him to take care of me . . . but now I'm having to remember how to do it myself, and, well, it's a challenge."

"Have you been able to get a job?" Jenny asked. Brooke's hair was brushed, and her clothes were clean, which was a little out of the ordinary for Brooke.

Brooke smiled and pointed a french fry at Jenny, as if she'd pinned her. "I did! I'm working at the grill." The pride in her expression made Jenny's heart ache, and she added, "I think Tommy would be glad."

"I think so, too. He loved you so much. This will be great for you." Tommy's death might actually be saving his mother's life. Jenny could easily imagine him on the other side, still prodding her and doing more now than he'd been able to when he was alive.

Jenny visited with Brooke and Cherry a while longer before excusing herself to see Ron.

She walked in the house and paused. Something was making noise in the kitchen and Jenny hurried around the corner finding Ron there, wearing his Quilter's are HOT apron and stirring a pan of hashbrowns.

Jenny caught a little sob in her throat. "You're up?" Jenny leaned over and kissed him. "Is everything okay? Can I get you anything?"

Ron gave a tired smile. "No. I just got hungry. Would you like some? I'm making breakfast a la Ron."

"That's my favorite kind." Jenny promised setting her pies on the counter for later. "I've missed you this week."

"Mmm, I've missed you too. How was Birthday

Bash? Did I miss everything?"

Jenny gave a short laugh, "You missed a little bit. I can't wait to tell you all about it. But first I really need a nap."

"Ooo," Ron said bringing Jenny a forkful of hasbrowns with bacon to try. "That sounds right up my alley."

Jenny tested the breakfast creation for him and happily tested a second bite as well before Ron fixed them both plates.

"Here you go Mrs. Doan. And when we're done, would you do me the honor of a nap together?"

"I thought you'd never ask," Jenny said.

Acknowledgments

Hey guys! This has been a crazy roller coaster! I hope you've loved this story as much as I do. I snuck in family references and locations that are near and dear to my heart. I may have taken out a family reference or two that shared a bit too much truth for a fictional cozy mystery, but I love that I get to share all this with you.

Such as my adoration of the Amish hand pies that they sell in Hamilton. If you're ever there on a day they're set up and still selling. Buy one, or four. You'll thank me!

My fabulous editors betas and team have a special place in my heart and should have the same in yours! Thank you to Germancreative and Ujala Shahid who once again designed the beautiful cover and artwork of Chain Piecing a Mystery.

Thank you to all of you who gave me the confidence and drive to keep writing Jenny sotries!

— Hillary

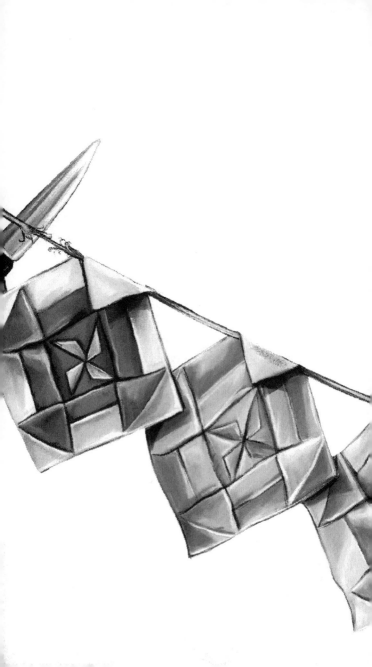

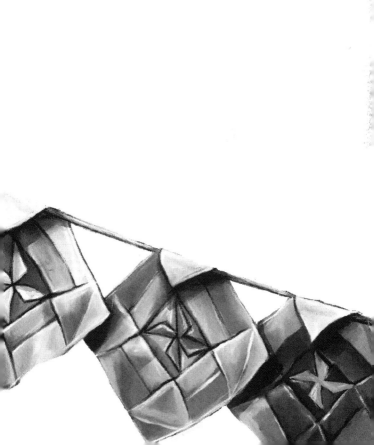

My name is Hillary Doan Sperry. I'm a quilter and a writer among many other things that make up me. I love steak, feta and cheesecake and the glorious smell of walking through a fabric store!

My favorite color combo is turquoise and a soft coral. And I absolutely adore dreaming up strange new things for Cherry to wear when she's hanging out with Jenny in the Missouri Star Mystery books!

If you want to read more of my books check out your favorite library or online through my website hillarysperry.com; on the MSQC website or your favorite online retailer! Thanks for reading with me!

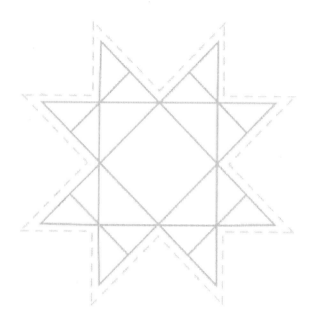

www.hillarysperry.com